MW00572853

THE C*CK DOWN THE BLOCK

THE COCKY KINGMANS
BOOK ONE

AMY AWARD

Copyright © 2023 by Amy Award

All rights reserved.

No part of this book may be reproduced in any form or by any electronic or mechanical means, including information storage and retrieval systems, without written permission from the author, except for the use of brief quotations in a book review.

Cover Design: Leni Kaufmann

COCK DOWN THE BLOCK

Always the nerdy girl, never the girlfriend~

Until her cocky best friend and his *ahem* rooster take charge.

Look, I've had it bad for the girl next door with all the curves forever. She turned me down in high school and since I'm not a total douchecanoe, I lusted after her all by myself in my shower, and we stayed just friends for years.

Now she's the adorkable librarian next door and I'm the star quarterback of the best pro football team in the league.

So when she asks me to be her fake date to her all-girls school reunion, I am totally down to show her off to the mean girls who bullied her back then so they can see just how incredible she is.

I'll be the best boyfriend they've ever seen. The best fake boyfriend that is.

Until I find out from her slightly-stalkery classmates that she still has her v-card. I don't see how that is even possible. Not with how sexy and sweet she is. Could it be because she knows she belongs with me?

This curvy girl and football quarterback sports romance has a baddie plus-size woman who knows her own worth and a Bridgertons-meets-American-Football family you'll wish you were a part of.

CONTENT NOTE

This is a book of fluff. (Fluff that I worked really hard on and am extremely proud of.) It's meant for escapism and laughs. We need fluff; it's the insulation from the harsh world around us.

I think it's important to have fat representation in the media, and I do that by showing fat women getting happy ever afters without ever having to lose weight.

However, that doesn't mean there won't be any conflict or angst.

While it was really important to me to write a story with a confident plus-size - fat - curvy heroine whose inner strength and love for herself doesn't waver, I will always put pieces of myself into every one of my curvy girl FMCs, and I'm still working on my own journey of self love - aren't we all?

That means that the heroine does face some external fatphobia in this book. It's not the main storyline, but it is an important part of the conflict. If you still want to read the book, but skip that particular part, don't read chapter twenty-six.

(but if you've got the mental space for it, try it out and see.)

There is also talk about loss of a parent in the past. Our Cocky Kingmans were raised by a single father.

What I can promise you though is that my books will always hold a space that is free of violence against women including sexual assault. That just doesn't exist in the world I create in my mind.

And finally, I love to write about funny animals and pets. No pets will ever be harmed or die in any of my books.

I like to cry at touching Super Bowl commercials and Broadway musicals about witches who defy gravity, not in my romances.

wink

For all the woman who have done, or are doing the work to love yourself from the inside out.
You're allowed to take up space.

For my mom who taught me to love myself and football.
Go Big Red

A rooster crows only when it sees the light. Put him in the dark and he'll never crow. I have seen the light and I'm crowing.

— MUHAMMAD ALI

CRASH INTO ME

CHRIS

I have never been a morning person. The butt crack of dawn can suck it as far as I'm concerned. I wouldn't even be awake at this ungodly hour, getting in some cardio, if it wasn't for Luke Skycocker, the god damned noisiest rooster, who lives next door.

I'd have already thrown him into my morning protein smoothie, feathers and all, if it wasn't for Red Pooper One's owner. Trixie would murder me with a jar of pickled eggs if I strangled her favorite chicken. Dumb fucking rooster.

I may want her to squeeze some parts of my anatomy, but not my throat. Well... maybe. No. We didn't have that kind of relationship. What we did have was a long-standing friend zone situation that meant I got to stare at her plump ass as long as I didn't say how good it looked.

Like right now, when she's bent over in the middle of the damn street to pick up Luke Skycocker, who is doing his best to terrorize all of our neighbors into waking up. Every time she got close, he trotted away, flapping his wings and sounding his annoying alarm clock crow to the rising sun.

"Luke, if you weren't so adorable, I'd cook you for dinner. Come here you little rat." Trixie crept up on him again, arms outstretched, ready to snag him, and my heart beat harder than my morning run dictated.

Probably because she was wearing one of those floofy fifties-style dresses she liked, and every time she bent over, I got a glimpse of the back of her thick thighs and her sexy as fuck polka dot panties she kept flashing me. At this point, I was rooting for Luke just so I could stare my fill of... something I'd never have. Fuck.

Time to quit being a dick being controlled by my actual dick and help.

We're just pals and have been since high school when she friend zoned me so hard, I still haven't recovered. Doesn't mean I don't still jerk off in the shower thinking about her. But my mamma didn't raise no jackasses, and my father ground into all seven of us boys to be gentlemen.

She said no, and I would never push that boundary. She wanted to be friends, so we're friends. Doesn't mean I don't look. Every chance I get.

If I wasn't lost in a very dirty fantasy of having her bent over my couch, I might have seen old Mrs. Bohacek barreling down the road at eleven miles an hour. She wasn't tall enough to see over the steering wheel of her pristine, vintage, one-owner only 1974 Oldsmobile Toronado which normally wouldn't matter, but Luke Skycocker was headed straight toward the front grill, with Trixie trailing behind.

"Trixie, look out for Mrs. Bo in her boat." I jogged toward her but picked up speed when Luke took flight. He was headed straight for the windshield.

"Luke," Trixie shouted, "use the force you dumb rooster, use the force."

The stupid chicken was going to smash into the car, probably splat all over the window, and scare the shit out of Mrs. B in the process. No way I was letting Luke kamikaze the Olds. Trixie would be devastated if her rooster went to the big chicken coop in the sky.

I hated when she cried. My agent, coach, and offensive line would kill me if they knew I was about to dash into oncoming traffic. Yet off I went to jeopardize my career by jumping in front of a car to save a stupid rooster.

Should be easy peasy.

Except seeing a giant rainbow-colored rooster flying straight at you would scare even the coolest and most calm drivers. That was not Mrs. Bo on a good day. She swerved one way, then the other, like she was three sheets to the wind. I still could have darted into the street and back to get her and the bird, if Mrs. Bo hadn't freaked out and stepped on the gas. She was up to at least fourteen miles an hour and climbing.

"Fast feet, Beatrix, hustle, hustle." She was already trying to anticipate Mrs. Bo's swerving, but nobody here had a good escape route.

The familiar adrenaline of being on the field coursed

through me. My vision went crystal clear and I lasered in on the car, the rooster, and my girl, quickly calculating the route I could take to make this play and avoid being sacked by the Olds.

I bounced on my feet and took off at a dead run. In a Super Bowl worthy move, I jumped onto the hood of the car, extending my reach out as far as I could, and grabbed Luke Skycocker by the long and danglies of his tail, pulling him down and tucking him under my arm like a football.

Then I pushed off the hood, snagged Trixie around the waist, and tucked and rolled off the side of the car, my hip jarring against the polished metal as Mrs. Bo swerved again. I took the brunt of the fall, protecting the rooster and Trix from the hard ground.

We skidded across the grassy curb between the street and the sidewalk in front of my house. Mrs. Bo skidded to a halt. The three of us laid there for a minute, my chest heaving, sucking in deep breaths, pushing the air and adrenaline back out of my system.

Trixie's breath was rapid and ragged too. She lifted her head from my chest where she'd landed and pushed her glasses back up her face. "Why, Mr. Kingman. Is that a rooster in your pocket or are you just happy to see me?"

Even if I hadn't already been half-hard fantasizing about Trixie's ass, adrenaline does things to the anatomy. I'd had plenty of stiffies during intense football games. But combine the two, and this hard-on wasn't going anywhere without some help.

Which I wasn't getting from the woman sprawled across my body at the moment. Luckily, Luke Skycocker chose that moment to stick his head up between the two of us and peck me on the arm, twice.

He jumped out of my hold and sauntered across the yard and up onto Trixie's front porch as if nothing in the world bothered him. The little shit.

Trixie shook her head and gave a little snort. "I think that's his way of saying thanks for saving us."

No it wasn't. That rooster pecked anyone who wasn't Trixie, especially guys. He loved her, and I'm pretty damn sure he thought she was his true love and fated mate.

"Yeah, what's your way?" Son of a bitch. That just slipped out, all flirty and filled with innuendo. I knew better than to say shit like that out loud.

She stared at me for an entirely too awkward minute. That was weirder than I could deal with at seven o'clock in the morning. I sat up and carefully moved her well off my lap and subsequent hard-on, then stood and held out my hand to help her to her feet.

She took it and it was far too difficult to not haul her into my arms when I pulled her up. She dropped my hand before I was ready and dusted off her skirt with a few slaps to her hips and butt. I had to bite my fist to keep from helping her or saying anything.

There was a long, icy cold shower in my immediate future.

"Hey, you kids stay out of the street. Don't make me call your parents to tell them you were fooling around in traffic," Mrs. Bo hollered at us, like we were still eight years old and running through the neighborhood on a Saturday morning.

"Sorry, Mrs. Bo. We'll be more careful." Trixie gave our

elderly neighbor a wave. That placated her and she harrumphed but continued down the street at an even more leisurely pace, like she owned the place.

In fact, I did.

"Come over tonight and I'll make you a roast chicken dinner to say thanks." She glared at Luke Skycocker contently roosting in the flowerpot next to her front door. She loved that stupid chicken and he loved her. No way we were ever getting to eat him.

"Can't. I promised Johnston I'd make an appearance at Manniway's fancy-ass grand opening tonight." I'd had big shoes to fill when the Mustangs drafted me to be the backup quarterback to the most beloved player in franchise history. Manniway had immediately taken me under his wing and told me he'd make sure I won more Super Bowl rings than he had. He was genuinely a good man, and I would always go out of my way to do anything for him. Not like drinks and dinner at his bougie new restaurant in Cherry Creek was a hardship. "Come and be my date."

She wrinkled up her nose in that cute way she had. "Umm, no. I am not Manniway's Steak House material. You need a cheerleader or, oh, I know, ask the new anchor woman from 9NEWS. She's all polish and sophistication. You could be Denver's new power couple. We'll give you a cute couple name like Chrisangela or Angtopher."

Yeah, no. I'm sure Angie Cruz was a lovely person, and probably as boring out on a date as watching golf. "I don't think she's my type. Come on. It will be fun, and Johnston's wife made sure they actually have a whole ass vegan menu, so you don't have to order a baked potato at a steak place. They even have that weirdo fake meat you pretend is beef."

Trix spun in a cute little circle and sang her favorite FlipFlopper's theme, "Cause I'm a filthy vegan."

"So you'll go? You owe me one for saving Luke Skycocker's life." It's not like this was a real date or anything. My cock didn't appear to know that though.

"It's tempting. I do enjoy ogling football player butts." She tapped her finger on her lips, thinking. "Who else will be there?"

I wasn't jealous that she wanted to stare at other men's butts. Nope. Not me. I was also talking to the team trainers about adding in an extra glute workout to my rotation.

"Deck, Everett, Hayes," my three brothers who also played for the Mustangs, "and my dad."

Coach Kingman was football royalty in his own right. Seven national championships for the DSU Dragons was no small feat. Neither was raising eight kids as a single father for the last seventeen years, four of whom played professionally, three more currently playing competitively in college who would likely all go in the first few rounds of the draft when it was their turn, and one stroppy teenaged girl that we all loved.

There wasn't a single event in the Denver Metro area that involved sports that my father wasn't invited to. Retired now or not, he was a busy man.

"There won't be room for anyone else in the restaurant with the Kingmans holding court, and those are not the butts I want to ogle." Trixie side-eyed me. "Who else you got?"

Not jealous. Not jealous. "Some other guys from the team, and of course Johnston and Marie. But you know that's not why you want to go. You'll come for the gossip."

Trixie shrugged and gave me a big shit-eating grin. "I suppose I can find something to stare at all night, and you're the one who knows all the good dirt on the Rocky Mountain celeb scene, not me."

Aha. Got her. "Which is why you'll come with me. So I can point out who all is being recruited to host the Great Mile High Bake Off."

"No. Shut the front door." She shoved me and I pretended she was strong enough to move me by taking a step to the side. "They're coming here? How did you not lead with that? Fine. I'm in."

Trixie was eternally addicted to competition shows. Her streaming subscriptions were a monster of their own. I'd know. She made me watch them with her every damn week. If anyone found out that I even knew who Paul Hollywood, Mary Berry, and Prue Leith were, I'd never live it down.

"I'll pick you up at seven." I'd trained myself not to sound too excited when she said yes to our pseudo-dates. "See you tonight."

She jogged up her front porch stairs, pulled open her front door, shooed Luke Skycocker inside, and waved me off as if going out with me tonight was seriously no big deal. It wasn't. I dragged her to all kinds of events when my agent didn't have some kind of PR date lined up for me. He rarely set me up anyway because he knew I'd say no most of the time.

No. Big. Deal. Because we were friends. Neighbors. Nothing more.

I needed another long run and then twelve cold showers before tonight.

AND ALL I GOT WAS THIS VIBRATOR

TRIXIE

*O*ne thing I will never get used to is finding a vibrator in my mailbox.

No, wait. That's not entirely true. I passionately believed every woman should have a lovely selection of sex toys at her disposal and am a fan of online shopping with discreet packaging. I'm happy to receive my own choice of vibrator or what have you in the mail. I have a fine collection of my own, thank you very much.

What has me shaking my head, once again, is that this particular delivery is from my mother.

Yes, my mother, the former BBW porn star turned Volvo driving soccer mom turned sex educator and sex positive and body positive influencer, sends me, umm, pleasure aids, in the mail, regularly. On her many adventures around the world, instead of sending me a t-shirt that says, "My parents went to Thailand and all I got was this dumb t-shirt," she sends me the most exotic of sex toys.

An orgasm a day keeps the blues away, she always says. Like, it's literally her tagline on her Instagram account. Not that I don't love her for trying to make an impact on the world, but it's still weird in so many ways.

I begrudgingly opened the box and pulled out an intricately carved penis with an incredibly happy, smiling face on the... head. Of course, the moment I got it out, it started vibrating and swirling, and there did not seem to be an off button. I couldn't even figure out where in the world the batteries went so I could rip them out and throw them in the trash. I rolled my eyes and tossed the thing on the couch.

Luke crowed at it, flew up onto the cushions and pecked at it like the biggest, yummiest of worms. Oh, gawd. Well, as long as he didn't go wandering off with it, I guess he could have it. Maybe he'd kill the damn possessed thing, and then I could chuck it into the spare laundry hamper in my closet, along with all the other ones. At this point, I could start a sex toy donation center for women who can't afford dildos from around the world. If anyone ever discovered my strange hoard... well, not like that is going to happen.

Thank goodness I hadn't already grabbed my mail when Luke Skycocker had escaped, or Chris would have tackled me, my rooster, and my vibrating cock on the sidewalk. I'm sure he'd seen his fair share of sex toys in his many sexcapades, but even he didn't know about my dirty secret stash in the closet. I really did need to figure out how to dispose of all of them.

I reached into the box again and pulled out a bag of penis shaped lollipops and an envelope with kanji and cherry blossoms with penis shaped stamens decorating the surface. Ah, they were in Japan. I did remember her saying something about having gone to a penis festival in Kawasaki.

She must have had a blast and of course had fun shopping for this present for me there. My mother also wrote me notes about the adventures she and my dad were having, the sights they were seeing, the food they were trying, and where they were headed to next. That part, I was interested in. I looked forward to her letters.

The old fashioned-ness of getting letters that I could sit down and read with a cup of tea was something I relished. It was the gifts that came along with them I could do without.

I'd message her later to check what time zone they were currently in and see about Facetiming with her and my dad to tell her I'd gotten the box. I learned a long time ago that even if I was shocked and weirded out by the things she sent, I still had to say thank you for thinking of me.

"Hey, Luke, you kill that horrible thing yet? I gotta get to work and you are not allowed to take it out to the coop with you."

Luke flapped his way to the top of the couch and looked at me like I was crazy. I glanced down, and yep, the toy was still vibrating and dancing away on the cushion, although looking a little worse for the wear of being attacked by my rooster. "Well, good try buddy. You can have another hack at it tonight after I get home from work."

Hopefully, if I left it alone and running all day long, the mysterious hidden batteries would wear out. I picked Luke up and carried him through the kitchen and out into the back yard. He squirmed his way out of my arms and did his very cocky walk toward the coop where his girls were waiting for him. Princess Laya, Chew-bock-bock, and Kylo Hen came running over to welcome home their man candy.

Those girls followed him all over the place, my newest hen, Kylo, especially. Sadly, Luke didn't give any of them the time of day. I gave the girls some cuddles. I'd started my little flock with the two pretty silkies, Laya and Chewie. Then splurged later on Luke and Kylo. I wanted a couple more and had my eye on a barnvelder and a Wyandotte. Even had names picked out for them. But would need to upgrade the coop and their open space to do that. "Sorry, my sweet girls. He's only got eyes for me."

I'd been warned when I added Luke to our flock that I'd have to be sure to gather the eggs every day so we didn't get a bunch of fertilized eggs, but, while he was fiercely protective of the girls, as far as I could tell, he was still a virgin chicken.

He didn't question my decision not to have sex, so I wasn't going to question his.

Once everyone was fed, their water refilled, and a quick check done for eggs, I promised them some grubs later if they were good. After a quick wash up, a fresh cup of coffee in my Guess What, Chicken Butt travel mug, because the teens at the library thought it was funny, and I was on the way to work.

I had an evaluation today with the branch manager, creepy Karter. I rolled my eyes at myself. He wasn't that bad. He just always looked at me like I was a piece of pie. I also think I intimidated the hell out of him, so my evals were usually all glowing and not actually useful for being a better and more productive librarian.

Lulu, my ride or die friend from kindergarten to now, was who I went to for that. We went to library school together too, and she worked in programming for the Thornminster library system. She was the only person who would always tell me exactly like it was, and then help me figure out how to fix it so I was better. The best. That was always the goal. Be the best.

It was half of why Chris and I were such good friends. He had a super-achiever streak a mile high and wide. Couldn't be the quarterback for the Mustangs if he didn't work his ass off to be the best. He wasn't bothered by my own perfectionistic tendencies. I loved him for it.

His whole family was highly competitive. They worked hard and they played hard. I'd had more than a crush on all three of the eldest brothers at one point or another. Those football butts. Mmm.

Chris and Everett were the whole reason I had a chicken hobby farm in my back yard in the first place. They said I worked hard but didn't play enough. Kingman family game nights didn't count since I couldn't make it every month.

I needed a hobby or a pet or something. With Laya and Chewie, I got both in one go. I hadn't been sure my landlord would allow such a thing, but Chris had convinced me there was no risk without reward and pushed me to ask. When the leasing company said yes, half the Kingman clan had come over and helped me build the coop.

Why in the world Chris wanted me to go with him to the opening of Manniway's was beyond me. It gave me funny flutters in my tummy. I hated the spotlight. There had better not be a bunch of press there. Ugh. Now I had to think about what in the world I was going to wear.

One of my cutesy dresses and cardigans that I wore to work wouldn't be fancy enough. In my mind, women at events like this wore sparkly, tight dresses and sipped champagne out of long flutes with lipstick on the rim and laughed at jokes about being rich.

I'd definitely watched too many Dynasty re-runs as a kid. But I didn't own sparkly shit. I owned cute shit, a lot of comfy clothes, and four signed Denver Mustang jerseys, a dozen more Denver State Dragon jerseys, one for each of the Kingman boys on the team. It was a steak-house, right? Maybe I could wear jeans and a jersey? Yeah, no.

Well, at least I had something to distract me from creepy Karter and his evaluation while I was at work today. I was on the desk for most of the afternoon so that I was available to the teens that hung out there after school. Maybe I could ask Jules, the youngest and only girl in the Kingman clan, to consult on the wardrobe choice. She came to the library almost every day, getting hours in on our summer volunteer program. Although I think she was there just to get out of her testosterone-filled house for a while.

"Hey, Trixie." Creepy Karter held the door open for me for way too long. I had barely parked and gotten out of my car when he swung it open. Had he been watching for me? See. Creepy.

"Hi, Karter. You don't have to hold the door, but thanks." Now I had to hurry-walk up the sidewalk.

"It's no problem." He shrugged and smiled, and on anyone else, it would be endearing. "I forwarded you some emails from parents I got this morning. Thought you might like to be warned."

I frowned and straightened my spine. "Bad emails? Complaints?"

We got the occasional angry parent and our fair share of repressed parents who wanted books banned from the library, specifically the teen section, but I'd never had a complaint about anything I did. My mind raced to come up with what I could have done wrong.

The only thing I could even think of was the new program to help the older teens with their college applications. Perhaps some parent wanted to control that part of their child's life and resented the library for interfering? Stranger things had happened.

"Oh." He chuckled and looked down at his shoes. "Of course not. They're requests for one-on-one help from some overachiever kid's helicopter mom."

This is why I was the teen librarian and Karter was not. He didn't like teens or their parents. "No worries. I can take care of them. Thanks for warning me."

I slipped into the building and didn't miss the way he stood in the doorway just enough in the way so that my hips brushed against his as I went by. Blech.

Thankfully, my desk wasn't in eyesight of Karter's office, and I didn't have to feel his eyes on me as I got settled and started in on my to-do list for the day. The parent's request was the first thing, and it wasn't even what Karter had said it was. They just wanted to know if they could come and ask some questions about volunteer opportunities at our next scheduled program time.

Just a few minutes before the library was about to open, two emails pinged my inbox. The first was a notification of a reschedule of my evaluation with Karter. Good. Fine. But the second one had me a little off kilter. It was a message forwarded from Lulu.

I read it twice, tried to take swig from my empty coffee mug, and read it again.

"We are pleased to announce that the following librarians have been nominated for Young Adult Romance Writers Association Librarian of the Year."

Me? Librarian of the Year? Out of the whole country?

No.

What?

No.

"Trixie, you coming to round-up?" One of the other librarians passed my desk on her way upstairs to the main desk. We all met for a quick ten-minute round up just before the library opened to check in with the day's programming and any news or info that everyone might need to know.

"Uh, yeah. Coming."

I stared at the email for one more minute, locked my computer, and walked up the stairs just in time to catch Karter start the meeting. I had no idea what he said until he excused us all to go open the doors. I walked to the teen section and sat down behind the desk, staring at the stacks of books for a full three minutes before I realized I'd left all my stuff to work on downstairs.

Crap. Since we were rarely swamped on a Friday morning, I hurried down, got my books, clipboard, and binder full of college essay samples to add to, and rushed back up to my desk. Whew. That was my workout and steps for the day.

Sitting on my desk, right where the pages placed it every morning, was a copy of the Denver Post. And of course, staring up at me from the big picture on the front page, was Johnston Manniway, standing in front of his new steak house.

I turned the paper over. I didn't have the brain capacity at the moment to think about the opening tonight and still be in shock and awe over the nomination. I could only freak out about one or the other.

I flipped the paper back over. Manniway's grand opening tonight was the lesser of two evils. It was just one night, and Chris would be there to protect me from any reporters or weirdos. Plus, I was looking forward to the celebrity gossip. Half the fun of being dragged to these events was standing at the bar with him as he pointed out who was who and who was doing who.

Okay. Okay, I could concentrate on figuring out what to wear tonight and think about the nomination tomorrow. I went over to the periodicals and pulled a bunch of fashion magazines. I was definitely making Jules go through them with me later.

Although it's not like I was going shopping later or

something. My librarian's salary covered gas, rent, chicken food, my fancy flavored creamer addiction, with just enough left over to put a little into savings like a good girl should.

Crappity crap crap. My fingers couldn't dial Lulu's number fast enough. She had ESP, because she answered before the phone even rang. "You got my email and you're freaking out, aren't you?"

"Yes. No. Yes. Gah." That anxiety attack was for later. "I have to freak out about that tomorrow. I have an entirely different crisis, and you have to help me."

"Bring it on. I got you." Her tone went from teasing to serious in an instant. "Do you have cancer, does your mom? Did your dad get thrown in jail for being in the red-light district in Thailand? Is Luke Skycocker okay? He didn't get hit by a car or something did he?"

"Lu, stop." She could go on like this for an hour without letting me get in a word edgewise. "D. None of the above. I have to go to Manniway's Steakhouse's opening tonight."

The line went completely silent. This was worse than I thought. Lulu hadn't been silent for this long in her entire life. "Why the hell did you scare me like that then? Rude."

"First of all, you're the worst-case scenario girl, and secondly," I gulped, "I don't have anything to wear."

"Oh. Shit." The actual seriousness of this situation finally hit her.

"I know." I slid the fashion magazines to the side and waited for her sage advice. Lulu always knew what to do.

"Wait. Why are you going to Manniway's? You don't eat meat." Not helpful. I already knew that.

"Chris asked me." No big deal. He asked me to do lots of stuff with him and the family. I was practically a Kingman. Like a cousin or something.

"Chris? As in Chris Kingman, quarterback of the Denver Mustangs, Denver Post's most eligible bachelor, your ultra hot next door neighbor Chris, asked you out on a date?" The sound on her end went muffled like she was covering the receiver, and she might have squealed. "Finally. Thank the sweet baby Jesus you said yes. It's about damn time."

Lulu had been shipping me and Chris since high school. It was never going to happen. He wasn't interested in me. Not like that. We were friends. Had been for a long time. I liked it that way. He was nice, safe, and an all-around good friend. "It's not a date. It's just Chris."

"You been sniffing the children's librarian's glue supply?"

"Come on. I need real help here. I don't want to look dumb." That gave me mental flashbacks to high school, and the Queen Bees' sing-songy cheerleader voice whirred in my head. I'd been teased for a lot of things back then, but it had helped me build up some good shame-proof body positive armor early in life thanks to my mother.

I knew my true worth wasn't in what I looked like, and I needed to remember that right now. It would be fine. Whatever I chose to wear would be good enough. It wasn't like this was... an awards show.

A gaggle of teenage girls walked up the stairs, startling me out of my brain freeze. "Gotta go, Lu. A bunch of teens are here."

Jules Kingman led the pack over to my desk. I pulled out the snack box I kept in my desk for them. "Got the new Dragons Love Curves book in yet?"

"I heard this one is about the mysterious purple dragon." I pushed the stack of newly added to the catalog books across the desk, and they were snatched up instantly. The girls headed over to the silent reading area and its mass of bean bags. I waved Jules over to me before she got far. "Hey, you know how the boys are all going to Manniway's tonight?"

"Sure. Not that I get to go. Twenty-one and up only." She sighed, rolled her eyes, and crossed her arms as only a put-upon teen could do.

"Uh, sorry if that's a sore spot. But Chris asked me to go too, and I have no idea what to wear. Any ideas?"

She went from sullen teen to sparkling in a hot second, then back to cool and apathetic like she'd been caught being excited about something she didn't want anyone to know about. "Oh, uh, yeah. Like, anything navy and cream. Wear that navy blue high-low maxi you had on for the college application thing we did right at the end of the school year. That was classy. But not with a sweater. Just some jewelry."

Huh. Yeah. That would work. I didn't know why I hadn't thought of it. I did look good in that dress, and it wasn't fancy, but it wasn't casual either. Without a cardigan to cover up the top, it showed off my girls a bit more than was appropriate for the library but would be perfect for a fancy restaurant opening. It was exactly right for tonight. "It's not too, you know, librarian-ish?"

"It is, but hot, sexy librarian. Chris will go all ga-ga for it." She made a face and walked away before I could say that's not what I was going for.

"Don't ship me and your brother," I half shouted after her.

"Too late," she yelled back over her shoulder.

Teenagers and their over romanticized hormones. I knew better.

JUST FRIENDS

CHRIS

*Y*ou would think I'd never been on a date before in my entire fucking life. My hands were sweating so much I couldn't even hold onto my thinking football. I tossed it around when I needed to occupy my body and let my mind just do its thing. The ball just bounced off the couch and knocked over a lamp, and all I'd done was pick it up off the floor for the third time.

This wasn't even a real date. It wasn't exactly a fake one either. I was dressed in my game day suit and tie, ready for this grand opening thing, and I had a hard-on and a half imagining what Trixie would wear.

I'd dragged her to a family events before, but nothing like this. Most of what I invited her to was casual. Jeans and jerseys, burgers and fries. Not suits and ties, definitely not dresses and heels.

This felt like a fucking date.

It wasn't and my mind and body needed to calm the fuck down.

Should I have gotten her flowers?

"What the hell is up with you?" Everett leaned against my fridge, drinking a Fat Tire. There were only a couple left in my summer stash anyway. He might as well drink them. With training camp starting in a few weeks, my alcohol consumption would go from one or two drinks a week to none.

Everett could use and abuse his body and still play ball just as well the next day. I couldn't, and he knew it.

"Not a damn thing." I tossed the ball onto the couch and shoved my hands into my pockets. I never lied to my brothers because anytime I tried, they called me out on my shit. It was the only reason Everett already knew exactly how I felt about Trixie.

But I was the oldest, and even if Declan and Everett both outweighed me and had since high school, I could still kick their asses. Partly because they knew better than to do anything other than protect the health and livelihood of their quarterback.

"Good try, dude. Spill. I'm not hanging out with a stressed out QB all night." He wrinkled his nose at me like I stank. "It repels the women."

"I don't repel women." I had thousands of adoring fans who were ready and willing to flash their tits or throw their panties at me like I was some kind of rock star. Women weren't my problem. One woman was.

He raised his eyebrow at me and took a long slow slug

of the beer while he gave me a side eye. "You're the worst. What's the last date you went on?"

I didn't have to answer that. He was my god damned baby brother. I used to scare him by flushing the toilet and telling him there was a lion in the bathroom.

"Mmm-hmm." He took another swig as if this was a conversation about when the last time I ate a greasy cheeseburger was and not my heart. "That's what I thought. You need to get laid, man."

Okay, so not a conversation about my heart. About my dick. That I could handle. "I get laid fine."

Declan crashed through the front door like it was the San Francisco offensive line. "Who's getting laid?"

Everett pointed at me with the mouth of the beer bottle. "I live across the street from you, and you're bad at hiding shit. So no, you don't. You never bring women home."

That, he was right about. I didn't bring women or anyone not inside my inner circle to my home. I didn't even allow people I didn't know and trust to rent or buy in our entire neighborhood. It even irked me that Everett brought so many women here. He didn't have the same circle of trust that I did. "Just because I don't have twelve different women in my bed every night, doesn't mean I don't get laid."

Because I wanted to actually care about the person I slept with.

"Are we getting laid tonight?" Hayes sauntered in, looking like he'd barely remembered how to put on a tie. He rubbed his hands together. "Then let's get this show on the road."

"We're waiting for Trixie." The moment I let her name roll off my tongue, I knew I'd made a mistake. Shit. I should have told these yahoos to go downtown without me. The fuck had I been thinking?

The four of us almost always went to team stuff together, and being the oldest, and the one who hated to be late, I drove. Standard operating procedure. But tonight was not a standard event.

And I invited Trixie.

As if I'd opened my mouth and crowed like Luke Skycocker, each of their faces turned toward me and stared. Hayes's mouth hung open like he was waiting to catch flies in it.

"Shut up, the lot of you." I brought out my best impression of dad and glared at them all. "It's not like I don't invite Trixie to do stuff with us. She comes to game night all the time. She's my friend and I thought she'd like to come along tonight. That's it."

Declan grabbed the beer from Everett and gulped down the second half. He opened his mouth like he was going to say something, but I wasn't having it.

"Shut. Up."

Hayes gave me a look that said he thought I was a complete dumbass, Deck glared like I'd stolen his lucky underpants, but Everett, he knew. The fucker was too intuitive for his own good. That's why he was a stellar football player and was even better with the ladies. If he wasn't my little brother, I might have already gone to him for advice.

Nope. No. I didn't need advice when it came to Trix. I wasn't lying. She was my friend. Probably my best friend.

I wasn't subjecting Trixie to the Kingman inquisition they were about to dive into. With three taps on my phone, I had an Uber Black XL ordered for them, and once she was ready, I'd get a second one for the two of us. We'd arrive later, which was fine. Didn't make my eye twitch at all. Fashionably late. I was a sports star, I could get to the party whenever I wanted to. Twitch.

"Your ride will be here in ten minutes. Julio will pick you up in a black Escalade with license plates that start with ILV. Now get out of my house before Trixie gets here." I pointed to the front door.

Hayes wasn't fazed. He never was. "I call shotgun."

He and Declan headed out to the front porch, but Everett didn't move a muscle.

I glared at him. "Git."

He pushed off from the counter but as he walked by me, he did the two fingers to his eyes and then pointed to mine. What the hell did he think he needed to watch me for? Asshat.

Once they were all out the door, I called Trixie. "Hey, you almost ready? I'm calling us an Uber."

"Umm. Maybe. Let me check."

Check with who?

"Jules? Do I fit the patriarchal male gaze look we were going for yet? Do I need more mascara?"

Trixie was doing her makeup with my sister? And why the fuck did the seventeen-year-old baby girl of the family know what the male gaze was? She'd been training to take down the patriarchy since she was two, but the male gaze? Nope. No. I did not like that.

"Let me just add this highlighter... and yes. You're officially man-killer ready." My little sister's voice went up a couple decibels. "You better keep your arm around her all night, big brother, or some manwhore will steal Trixie away from you."

Who talks like that?

Jules Kingman, youngest of eight, only girl, and the apple of all our eyes, of course. Later tonight, I was telling dad to ground her until she was thirty.

"Whore is a social construct, Jules." Trixie was missing the point all together.

"I'll come over there to pick you up. Don't let Jules talk you into—"

"Bye, big brother."

The phone went dead. Jules fucking hung up on me. My grounding recommendation just went up to age forty-two. And a half.

I went out the back door, slipped through the gate on the side into Trixie's yard to avoid my brothers, which didn't help my cause because Luke Skycocker came at me like a rooster-bat out of hell. If I didn't have finely honed quarterback skills, my outfit would be toast.

I sprinted across the yard. "Luke, I swear to god, you're going to be Sunday dinner if you peck a hole in my pants or shit on my shoes."

Wouldn't be the first time he'd done either.

I rushed the fence, used the coop as a launch pad, and leapt into the back yard of my childhood home unscathed. A pecking sound came from the other side of the fence, and a disgruntled squawking. "You underestimate the power of the dark side, Luke."

Through the French doors that opened out to the

back yard, I could see Jules and my dad in the kitchen. But when Trixie walked by, my heart skipped a beat and then pounded against my chest. I raised my hand up to make sure it wasn't popping out the front of my shirt.

My career was over. It would be irresponsible of me to play a professional sport with a heart that didn't work right. Game over.

Trixie was fucking gorgeous. A dark blue dress that showed off every god damned curve, a pretty blush to her cheeks, and shiny heels with red soles that I caught a glimpse of when she walked.

I was dead. Dead meat.

Or I thought I was until she turned and caught me standing in the back yard like a dumb, slobbering zombie. Because she smiled, and holy fuck. The curve of her lips... that was my favorite curve of all.

I forgot how to speak, how to move, how to think.

She waved and opened the door, and I woke the fuck up and stepped behind the lawn furniture so she didn't see the tent in the front of my pants.

"Hey," she said as if we'd just bumped into each other while grabbing the mail.

"Hey." Sweet baby Jesus, I was so screwed.

"Ready?" She tipped her head and looked at me with slightly narrowed eyes.

Was I ever. "Uh, lemme just order the car."

I turned my back on her and gave my cock a good stern talking to, thought of baseball, the King of England, and losing the Super Bowl, not that I ever had. A few deep breaths later and our car was on the way, and my dick was only at half-mast instead of a heat seeking missile with Trixie as the target.

"You look great." I sounded like a dumbass.

She did a little flounce and twirl. "Thanks, Jules helped me put the look together. You look nice too. I always did like you in a suit."

This was it. If ever I was going to legitimately flirt with Trix, now was my chance. I could say something about how she liked looking at my butt in a uniform even more. "Yeah, this suit is... expensive."

Yes, I did just fumble the fuck out of that ball. I choked. Because Trixie didn't want me to flirt with her, and as much as I wanted to show her we could be so damn good together, I couldn't cross that line in the sand she'd drawn so long ago.

It was better to be a monk who enjoyed little more than the company of my own spit and hand than lose her friendship for a roll in the hay. Except it wouldn't be just sex for me.

Trixie gave me the side eye and a weird frown. She didn't care about my money. Even if I was one of the highest paid players in league history.

She strolled over to me and reached up to adjust my tie. This was the part where I should kiss her. Instead, I stood there like a mascot getting beaned with jeers from the visiting team. "I suppose a famous guy like you should wear an expensive suit to a shindig like this."

"We don't have to go if you don't want to. We could watch reruns of Bake Off and throw popcorn at Luke." Once again my mouth was doing things my brain had not authorized. I had to go to the restaurant opening. No way

I'd let a friend and mentor down by ditching his grand opening. Not even for a girl.

Well, maybe for Trixie.

"Oh no. You're not getting out of this now. I got dressed up and I want that hot goss on all your celebrity friends."

She really didn't have a clue. I was over here fighting for my life not to bend her over the picnic table, and she was being the good girl. "They aren't my friends, Trix. You are."

What I got for my sincerity was a smack on the chest. "Quit being so adorable and sweet. Now feed me and tell me I'm pretty."

She turned and walked toward the gate leading out to the front of the house. I let my head fall back and stared up at the sky with a sigh. She wanted to be friends, so we were friends. I put on a voice like her request was the hardest request on the face of the earth, just to give her a tiny tease. "Fine. If I have to."

I didn't follow her right away, because once again, I was taking the time to watch her hips and her round ass sway as she walked away. I would have enjoyed that sight a whole lot longer too, if I hadn't caught Jules, arms folded and an evil grin on her face, watching me through the back door.

FRIES BEFORE GUYS

TRIXIE

The Uber pulled up to the grand opening of Manniway's and the front entrance was a freaking war zone of paparazzi. This looked more like we'd accidentally stumbled onto the set of a Hollywood blockbuster premier, one with a budget that made small countries weep. Flashes popped like rabid fireflies and the red carpet stretched out longer than the road to Mordor.

One look out the window, and my insides were doing stomach flips like that time Kylo Hen got into the coffee grounds and had a caffeine buzz for three hours. But Chris, ever the pro, just flashed his signature grin. It wasn't that I minded getting my picture taken. But this wasn't a few pictures. This was an attack on the senses.

What my mouth did in reply was not even close to a smile. More like the face one might make when you bite into a moldy lemon. "You did not say we were going to be walking a red carpet."

He shrugged and gave me that look. The one he'd been giving me whenever he knew he screwed up and was sorry-not-sorry that he'd gotten me into this mess and couldn't I just forgive him this one time. The puppy-eyed look that worked on me every single time. "I honestly didn't know it was this big of a deal. We'll be inside in no time, and I promise lots of hot gossip for you. Just stay close to me. It'll be fine."

I snorted. My heart rate was already nearing game day levels. "Easy for you to say, Kingman. You probably use media scrums as morning calisthenics."

His laughter was a welcome distraction as he led me onto the red carpet. I'd been expecting chaos, but this was like being thrown into a whirlwind of sharks who had all majored in journalism and minored in shouting.

We navigated the kaleidoscopic carpet much slower than promised. A photographer stepped into our path and shouted something about 'who's your new girlfriend?' I nearly choked on my own spit. Us? A couple? Of course they would think that. No one here knew our history.

I tried to say something about being just friends, but Chris murmured in my ear to smile and slid his arm around my waist in a move so smooth I suspected he'd used it as often as he threw a football. With a swift pivot that would've made his coach proud, he maneuvered us toward the next set of photographers and ten feet closer to the restaurant entrance.

We paused again, I pasted on a smile so I didn't look

like a deer in the headlights in every single photo, and pinched Chris on the leg so he was inflicted with similar torture to me.

He chuckled and leaned down to press his lips to my ear again, which was the only way to hear over everyone shouting. His breath ruffled my hair and gave me goose-bumps. Because of all the excitement. That's why I had goosebumps on a sweltering summer night. "Remember, Trix, they're not after you. They're here for the spectacle. Think of them like seagulls. Loud, annoying, but mostly harmless, unless you've got french fries."

Seagulls, yeah. That's exactly what they were like. Squawking seagulls I could handle. But Chris was defi-nitely their fried food of choice. It took us ten more minutes to move another ten feet.

The energy of the crowd, which I finally realized was also good old Mustang football fans too, rolled over me, intoxicating, disorienting, and made me yearn for a quiet evening at home with a good book and my chickens. Chris may have been comfortable in this world of glitz and glamour, but me? I was a chubby bunny that had accidentally stumbled onto a fashion runway full of foxes.

Apparently the runway liked bunnies. The cameras could not get enough of us. Clutching his arm was my only lifeline, and I continued to fake smile and followed him through the swirling chaos, hoping to survive the rest of the red carpet without accidentally stumbling over nothing and becoming a meme.

A thousand and eleven-hundred pictures later, and we finally made it within a yard of the restaurant. I looked at Chris and shouted, "Fries before guys," and bolted inside the restaurant.

He was by my side with the door shut behind him in less time than it took me to blow out a long, pent-up breath. "Fries before guys?"

"I don't know. I panicked." I was frazzled and he was fine. "If you don't either ply me with sugar or alcohol or both, I'm going to die in the next twelve seconds."

And by die I meant burst into tears or throw up. Either seemed equally likely at this point. It wasn't that I was upset, but the pure adrenaline of that gauntlet of eyes and attention was more than had ever hit my bloodstream in my entire life combined.

This was why I was a librarian. The most public-facing excitement I could handle was being in charge of the seniors' book club when the ladies chose a very spicy romance novel for their summer reading and the gents wanted action adventure. I'd given them werewolf smut, and that satisfied both camps.

Chris lifted my chin and tilted my head up to look at him. "You were fucking spectacular out there. I'm sorry it was such a paparazzi shit show, and I swear I'll make it up to you for the rest of the night."

I wasn't going to say no to that. Especially when he was giving me the sparkly-eyed puppy dog look again. "Thank you. But I still want that drink and you better reveal somebody's deepest darkest secret life creating cakes that look like octopuses or something equally as crazy, or this night will be a total dud."

Everett sidled up next to us with a drink in each hand. "What's that about octo-pussies?"

"We aren't talking about your sex life, buddy." I patted Everett on the shoulder as if in sympathy. If anyone had ever had a menage-a-oct or dallied in tentacle sex, it would be Kingman brother number three. He exuded sex appeal. Add to that he was a genuinely nice guy, and he had to beat women away with a stick.

"What else would we talk about? This event is boring as shit, and I haven't found any single women to ply my charms upon. Wanna go home with me tonight, Trix?" He waggled one eyebrow at me just like he had at every event I'd ever been to with the Kingmans since middle school. The whole lot of them were flirting machines.

Chris literally took a swing at his younger brother. Everett ducked and then winked at me.

"You're an insufferable flirt, and no. I'm here for the food and the gossip. But give it a few more minutes. There are still some french fries stuck out on the red carpet." Everett looked toward the front entrance and back at me like I was speaking another language.

Hayes, brother number six, the adorable youngin' that he was, popped into our small circle. "There're french fries? I haven't seen anything but these weird veggie appetizers. Oops, sorry, Trixie, vegan extraordinaire."

I grabbed Hayes by the unbuttoned collar and gave him a little shake. "You get me some of those filthy vegan treats and I won't tell your father."

Hayes's eyes went big and darted around. He lowered his voice, but it still had a squeak of fear. "Tell him what?"

"Everything." I gave him my best demonic older sister crazy eyes. I didn't have any siblings, but I'd grown up

THE C*CK DOWN THE BLOCK

with these boys and could tease any of them as a well-practiced skill.

"Shit." Hayes stood back up to his full monstrous height, almost taking my fake nails with him. "Veggie snacks coming right up."

The vegan snacks and bubbly were doing their job. I'd just polished off an avocado roll when a presence that could only be described as a mountain of pure charisma and gridiron history descended upon us.

"Mr. Kingman." Even though I'd known this man most of my life, and he'd been like a second father to me, I still always felt like I should curtsy or something. He just had such a, well, kingly presence. His stern eyes twinkled with a hint of humor, and even I could admit his graying hair just added to his rugged, formidable silver fox attractive-ness. I wasn't the only one who was surprised Bridger Kingman had never remarried.

"Call me Coach, Beatrix," he grumbled, because we had this conversation every single time I saw him. "It's good to see you here."

"It's a wonderful place, Mr. Kingman. Johnston and Marie did a fantastic job," I replied, motioning around at the swanky restaurant that was filling with more bodies.

"We all know it was mostly Marie. The only thing Johnston knows how to make is a touchdown. If it wasn't for his wife, he'd probably have starved to death before winning a ring."

"Oh, I've heard the horror stories of his attempts to grill, and how he kept the Blizzards supplied with steak hockey pucks." In fact, I had noticed none of our cup champion hockey players were in attendance so far tonight.

"I see my number one is keeping you company. He keeping his hands to himself?" Mr. Kingman asked, his eyes twinkling with mischief. It felt like being simultaneously hugged and threatened by a bear.

"Always, sir." Chris saluted his dad, the picture of innocence. I had to stifle a snort.

"Good." Mr. Kingman nodded and placed a meaty hand on my shoulder. "But I wouldn't mind if he didn't."

Chris nearly choked on his drink while I blushed a shade that rivaled pink dragon fruit. Mr. Kingman laughed heartily and clapped Chris on his back before sauntering away, leaving us in an awkward silence.

After a moment, Chris cleared his throat. "Sorry about my dad, Trix."

"Your dad's awesome," I managed to choke out, trying to regain my composure. He was terrifying and comforting at the same time, like a freight train wearing a teddy bear costume.

A moment later the ding ding ding of a glass sounded, and Johnston and Marie Manniway stepped up onto a small platform at the side of the room. "Welcome, everyone, to the grand opening of the best steakhouse in Denver. I'm not great at speeches, so I'll just say thanks for coming and dinner is served."

Marie smiled up at his every word and he gave her a sweet kiss. I felt the tiniest pang in my heart at seeing how intensely in love the two of them were. I wanted that someday.

Ooph. That wasn't something I'd ever say out loud.

The doors to the dining room opened and Chris extended his arm. "I happen to know there's a staircase that leads up to a balcony with only a few tables. We can get a little peace and spy on the celebs and gossip all we want up there."

"Ooh, I love a man with the inside scoop."

Chris gave me a funny look, but only for a second, and then guided me to the stairs and up to a balcony with a perfect view of the room. The waitstaff were ready for us and two other couples, but the tables were separated by tufted dividers, so it felt almost private. We ordered and sipped our drinks, and finally I relaxed a little.

Chris finally dropped the first bombshell. "Okay, don't look now, but reality baking show contestant number one is in passing range now."

"What? How am I supposed to not look, and also look where?" I asked, my eyebrows almost disappearing into my hairline.

Chris leaned in closer. "You're never gonna guess who's been invited to the celebrity edition."

"Wait, celeb edition? That means it's not necessarily someone who can bake. Who? Tell me, tell me." I was dying to know. Chris always had the best gossip.

"Johnston," he whispered, looking like he'd won the lottery.

"No way," I squealed, barely suppressing my laughter. "He can't even toast bread without setting his kitchen on fire. This is going to be a disaster. A beautiful, must-watch disaster."

Chris laughed. "Exactly. Can't wait to see him trying to

bake a cake while singing and juggling. The show's ratings are about to go through the roof."

We dissolved into laughter, letting the night unfold around us, a whirl of glitz and glamour, star athletes and celebs. I had way too much fun.

Which is why I woke up the next morning with a hangover and my ears ringing. No wait, that was my phone. "Lo?"

"Somebody had too much fun last night." Lulu was definitely laughing at me.

I did not have a proper response for that. "Nergh."

"And I'm going to say that's why you're late." She didn't sound quite as jokey now.

I pulled the blanket up over my head to block the light. "I don't work today."

"No, but you did say you'd be my wingman for the reunion planning committee."

Oh no. I had promised Lulu, or rather been coerced into agreeing to help, with our ten-year reunion. I hadn't spoken to anyone else we went to high school with pretty much since graduation. I wasn't sad to leave the mean girls behind.

But Lu had convinced me that this reunion was just as much ours as it was theirs. Plus, there was the charity fundraiser each class did every summer. I was hoping to help the school restock the library with some material newer than 1955. Being late for the first meeting wasn't going to help my cause.

Especially if Rachel was on the committee too, and unless she'd moved to Inner Mongolia, she would be.

I stumbled into the meeting, still half asleep and

completely unprepared for the icy reception that awaited me. It wasn't like the girls from my high school days had exactly been warm and welcoming, but I wasn't expecting them to go full Mean Girls 2.0 either.

"Ah, there's our late celebrity," Amanda, captain of the golf team and perpetual thorn in my side ten years ago, cooed from her spot next to Rachel at the head of the table. Rachel just stared at me with one eyebrow raised.

The two of them hadn't changed a bit. Their platinum blonde hairdos were perfectly styled, Rachel's in soft waves that would make a mermaid jealous and Amanda in that same ponytail she'd worn ten years ago.

And dammit, if they didn't still wear those smug smiles that were just as irritating as ever. A chorus of snickers echoed around the room as I took the empty chair beside Lulu.

"Sorry, I'm late," I mumbled, trying to ignore the new pulse of my headache.

Interestingly, Queen Bee number three wasn't here. Maybe Lacey had committed some heinous crime like being nice to someone and had been told she couldn't sit with the cool girls anymore.

"We're going over the budget. We want to make sure our class has the greatest fundraiser St. Ambrose has ever seen," Rachel replied with an exaggerated sweetness that gave me a sour taste in the back of my mouth. She'd picked on me enough in high school that I recognized that tone. She was about to say or do something downright mean.

Great. This was why I didn't want to do this. I was a full-grown adult now. I didn't care what Rachel, Amanda, or anyone else I went to high school with thought about me anymore. I was good, great, with who I'd become.

This was precisely the type of petty high school drama I had hoped to avoid. But it was too late to back out now. I'd promised Lulu I'd be here, and I was determined not to let the queen bees rattle me.

If some of my classmates hadn't grown, that wasn't my problem. Now that I had that mental armor on, I could handle whatever she was about to throw at me.

"You're our secret weapon, Bea," Rachel continued, her lips curling into a smirk. "We've been inspired to have a bachelor auction for our fundraiser, and it's all thanks to you."

Before I could respond, Amanda reached into her bag and produced a copy of the morning newspaper. With a triumphant flourish, she slapped it onto the table. There, on the front page, was a picture of Chris and me on the red carpet from last night, looking entirely too cozy for just friends.

"That's how you ended up with Denver's most eligible bachelor at the event of the season last night, isn't it? You won him or... something?" Rachel's gaze locked onto mine, her smile predatory. She was not just implying I'd paid for a night out with Chris. "I'm sure you can give me his contact info, unless he dined and dashed away from your little date."

The other girls snickered, and I felt Lu at my side, tensing up and ready to throw down.

I gripped her hand to hold her back and found myself replying, "Well, maybe he'd be willing to help out for a worthy cause. But I won't be putting my boyfriend, Chris Kingman, up for auction."

The room fell silent, and all eyes were on me. I could hardly believe the words as they left my mouth, but there was no taking them back now.

THE LOVE GURU

CHRIS

J pulled my phone out of the arm band I wore when working out, and dialed up the one other person who would take my eternal crush on Trixie seriously and help me the fuck out.

After last night, I was done fucking around. I was head over heels in love with her and I no longer wanted to be her friend. I knew full well the risk involved. I could lose her forever. She could tell me to fuck off just like she had the last time I asked her out. But we were adults now and the consequences would be a hell of a lot more serious.

It was going to kill me to ask my little brother for help, but this was what desperation looked like.

Everett was the family's one and only love guru. He always had women eating out of the palm of his hand. When he didn't answer the fourth phone call like a normal human being would, I slowly jogged in the direction of his house. It was only a block, but it was always good to check before coming over in case he was entertaining female company. Which was most nights.

Trixie and I left Manniway's last night before any of the other Kingmans, so I had to assume he had, in fact, found a single lady to woo.

I dialed again and texted in all caps that he needed to answer, or I was entering the premises with the key I knew he had hidden in the green gnome on his porch. He couldn't say no. I owned the house, he was leasing it through my company, as were most of the people that lived in the Mustang Plains neighborhood.

"What?" I'd definitely woken him up. "Why are you calling me? I hate it when you call me. Just text like a normal person."

Kids these days. "I did. You didn't reply."

"Because it's seven in the morning. Training camp doesn't start for two more weeks. Let me sleep, you dickbag." How in the hell he partied all night and was still a top-notch professional athlete defied the laws of physics. And made me feel old.

"I'm not coming over to make you run with me, and I'm already here so come open your damn door."

There was a little white sports car parked in his driveway. Everett didn't fit into little sports cars. He was as big as they were. We all were. There was a long silent pause where I was definitely on mute. "Gimme a minute and go 'round back."

Yeah, that was definitely code for I've got a girl here, and he didn't want her to walk out, panties in her pocket, in front of me. I didn't care where people got their jollies and there was no shame in it. But fine, I'd give them their privacy.

I hopped the fence and went to sit in one of his outdoor recliners by the barbecue grill. I sat for all of three seconds and then started pacing back and forth under the pergola, sat again, paced again, did my best not to press my face against the glass door to see if he and his girl had come downstairs yet, and sat one more time.

A thousand and two hours later, Everett plopped down into the chair next to me, only an open bathrobe wrapped around his shoulders, otherwise naked as the dawn, with a cup of coffee in his hand. "This better be good. I was about to get my dick wet. Again."

"Your dick gets any wetter and it's going to shrivel up like wrinkly fingers in the bathtub." He had enough sex for the entire defensive and offensive lines of the Mustangs.

He lifted his coffee cup, toasting me, and nodded. "Here's to wrinkly dicks."

"Mine is certainly not." Shit. I didn't mean to say that. Kingman rule number one—never let them see your weaknesses.

He squinted at the morning light and took a sip of his coffee. "Wet or wrinkly?"

"Neither." Fuck. I needed to tape my mouth shut.

"If that's why you're here, I can fix it. I've got at least five girls in my phone right now that will suck you off and say thank you very much."

Sigh. "You're disgusting."

"Disgustingly well laid. Unlike you." He tipped his cup

at me and then took another sip like this wasn't the most important conversation of my life.

I didn't say anything, and that got Everett's attention more than I would have liked. He sat straight up in his chair and focused in on me like he was waiting for me to pass him the ball. "You don't want me to get you any girl though, do you?"

I got up, walked towards the gate, stopped three steps away, and turned back. Being a wiener wasn't going to get me what I wanted. And after last night, I was more sure than ever I wanted Trixie. Not just in my bed, even though I had no doubt that would fucking blow my mind, I wanted her in my heart. More precisely, I wanted into hers.

That meant asking for help. Because what I've been doing for the last ten years hadn't gotten me out of the fucking friend zone.

"Well, fuck me. You're finally going to do it. You're finally gonna tell Trixie you love her."

I was a hair's breadth away from denying it. That's what I'd been doing for a long time. But Everett and I spent a lot of time on and off the field paying close attention to what the other one was thinking. It was why we had the highest passing success rate in the league. He knew what I was thinking half the time before I did. I'd come to him for his help, and he was going to give me a game plan or I was going to flush his face in the toilet. "You are a jackass. I'm not just going to blurt out that I love her. I need to win her heart and that requires good game strategy."

He stared at me for a long time, and I wasn't sure if he

was thinking or if his hangover and my admitting I had feelings for Trixie had broken his brain. He took a slow sip of his coffee, set it down on the side table, and rubbed his hands together. "You've come to the right place, brother. You are going to sweep that girl off her feet and right into your bed, uh, I mean heart."

Oh god, what had I gotten myself into?

Everett leaned forward in his chair. "I've been waiting for you to ask me this since she moved in next door when we were kids."

Trixie's family bought the house next to ours when I was ten. "Don't get all over dramatic."

"Don't lie to yourself." He made a you're-a-dumbass face at me that I was intimately familiar with. "You were in love with her the second she beat you at mud puddle golf. Everyone knew it. Even Mom."

That hit me harder than Seattle's defensive line trying to maintain their most sacs in a season record. I sat down on the nearest lawn chair so hard the metal squeaked. I wasn't prepared to bring my memories of Mom into this.

"The fact that Trixie beat me at mud puddle golf means nothing. It was one time." I knew how to deflect conversations about Mom like a champ.

"Sure, bro. Keep telling yourself that." Everett leaned back, a smirk playing on his lips, but there was that same flash of pain behind his smile too. He was the one who fucking brought her up.

"Fine. But asking her if she wants to go play in the mud with me isn't going to help me win her heart." Not that I wouldn't like to do some naked mud wrestling with Trixie.

"It could. If you do exactly what I tell you to." He grinned at me and took a sip of his coffee so long, there was no way he even had that much liquid left in his cup. He was enjoying this way too much.

But I thrived on doing the hard stuff. If I couldn't push my way through pain, I wouldn't be a top tier professional athlete. I wouldn't be a multi-millionaire. I definitely wouldn't have been able to hold it together and help my father raise my younger brothers and sister at the age of twelve.

And Everett was definitely going to make this whole thing painful, just for funsies.

I gritted my teeth through my agreement. "Fine."

He set his mug down with a flourish. "Now, why the fuck haven't you ever asked her out?"

"I have." Which I hadn't ever admitted to anyone before. "She basically told me to fuck off."

"Whoa, whoa, whoa. What? When?" He narrowed his eyes at me. "Enthusiastic consent, man."

When we each turned ten, our dad would sit us down and give us the sex talk. I have no doubt he was coached by Mrs. Moore, because this was no weird and uncomfortable, 'keep it in your pants or keep it wrapped up' with a slug on the shoulder and we're done chat.

He had fucking diagrams, and he tried really hard to help us understand that, with him, there was no shame around the subject. But his main sticking point had been exactly what Everett was trying to remind me of—enthusiastic consent. No did not mean keep pushing until she said yes. It didn't mean not right now. It meant no.

I'd battled with that a lot when I even thought about

wooing Trixie. Had I been in love with her all these years? Yep. But I didn't want to be that creep that was the nice guy and her friend just trying to get into her pants. I genuinely enjoyed her. She was funny as shit, even when she didn't mean to be. She was kind, without letting people walk all over her. Even in high school, when she had a tough time because of the mean girls, she still had this inherent confidence in her own self-worth.

What wasn't to love? None of that had anything to do with romance or sex. I sure as shit hoped that if I did ask her out again, that if she said no, again, it wouldn't make everything awkward between us. I valued her friendship more than I could say. But it might.

She meant enough to me to take the risk.

Because I wanted the woman I spent the rest of my life with to be my best friend, not just some arm candy, or a ball bunny looking for the spotlight.

Now my little brother was judging the shit out of me, thinking I was just trying to wear Trixie down or manipulate her into being with me. "Why the fuck do you think I've waited ten god damn years to try asking her out again, asshole? She's my friend, outside of the family, she's probably my best friend."

"Wait. You asked her out ten years ago and she told you no?" He shook his head at me. See? Judgy asshole. "This is one fucking long game you're playing."

"I'm not playing a game just to get my rocks off. Do I want to fuck her brains out? Absolutely. But I'm in love with her, the real her. The one who loves her weird chickens and reality TV and children's literature, who is a genuinely nice person who cares about making the world a good place to live. But we've grown up a lot since we were eighteen and graduating high school. If she tells me no again now, I'm not destroying our friendship over it. I'll just have to fucking move on."

"Good. I was going to have to kill you if you'd fallen off the big brother who we all look up to because he's a fucking good guy pedestal."

I threw a cushion at his face. "Are you going to help me or not?"

"Yeah, I am. There's one single thing you need to do."

I doubted there was one magic silver bullet here. "Just one thing?"

"Yup. Quit pretending all you want is friendship from her. Let her see you as more than a friend. You act like she's made of glass and if you touch her, she'll break. You've been friends since you were ten. She still sees you as a kid. Show her you're a man and you want her as a woman."

I didn't do that, did I? I was maintaining a respectful distance from her. Except I hadn't last night when we were on the red carpet. I'd had to touch her to guide her through that minefield. It was necessary to press my lips to her ear so she could hear me over the crowd. She definitely hadn't broken. She felt perfect in my arms then.

Okay, so maybe my little brother had a point. Not that I'd let him know that. "How do you expect me to behave around her? I can't just walk up to her and strip her clothes off, throw her over my shoulder, and carry her up to my bed."

"Christ, Chris. First of all, that was a little too specific to not be something you've literally fantasized about doing. I'll bet you a fucking house that Trixie would love for you to throw her over your shoulder and carry her off to bed."

Seeing as I owned the house he was living in, this wasn't just a friendly bet.

"If you can actually help me win Trixie's heart and not just give me some amorphous advice, I will give you this entire house, free and clear." It wasn't like he couldn't afford to buy the house, but I wasn't willing to sell my properties to just anyone.

He stuck his hand out to shake on it. "You got yourself a deal."

I shook his hand, squeezed a little too hard just because I could, and asked, "Where do I start? Roses, jewelry, a puppy? No, wait, a new chicken?"

"Don't be cliche, dude. Invite her to family game night. Hard to act fake in front of the whole family without getting called out on it."

Shit, was it really the first Sunday of the month already? First Sunday of any month during the off season was Kingman family game night. Mom started the tradition when Everett, Declan, and I were kids, and we upheld it to this day. It always got loud and obnoxious because we were the most competitive family on the face of the Earth, even with each other.

Trix had come to game night with us before, but only a few times. Probably because more than one Kingman boy walked out of the house after them with a black eye. All in good fun, mind you.

"No. Absolutely not. You said I had to show her I wasn't a little kid anymore, and game night is not the way to do that." It's not like I would ever lose a game on purpose. Not even checkers with my little sister.

"Nothing sexier to a woman than a winner, brother."

Did he...? Did my little brother just compliment me by telling me I was a winner? Sus. "What, like, you're going to let me win?"

"Not a fucking chance." He laughed and pointed that game day challenge finger at me. "In fact, I'm going to try even harder to beat your ass than normal."

This was the worst dating advice I'd ever gotten in my life. He'd better be fucking right. But I'd never known Everett to be wrong. Not when it came to women.

If I lost even a single round of a game tonight, I was going to flush him down the toilet with the lions.

Like a rookie with shaking hands, I sent Trixie a text.

> Hey, Trix. Kingman family game night tonight. Wanna join in?

I added a smiling emoji and then deleted it, because I wasn't a kid. Kiss emoji? No. Too much. I hit send before I could talk myself out of it. I waited, staring at the phone as if willing it to buzz with her reply.

And then my phone lit up with a notification. Trixie.

> Game night? Sounds fun. What should I bring?

I blew out a long breath and gave Everett a nod to confirm she was coming. Step one, done. Now on to step two, making her see me as more than just a friend. Which I had no idea how to accomplish.

Nothing. Just bring yourself. See you at 7.

I pointed my phone at Everett. "We've got about ten hours for you to teach me the moves that are going to make me look good to Trixie, so you'd better put some clothes on, dickhead."

KINGMAN FAMILY GAME NIGHT

TRIXIE

*K*ingman family game night was legendary in our neighborhood. I pulled out two extra ice packs from the first aid kit in the kitchen and put them in the freezer for later. From past experience, we'd probably need them.

The Kingman residence was already raucous when I arrived, sounding more like a touchdown celebration at an away game than board game antics. Chris's family had always been loud, an enthusiastic entourage of football fanatics who loved to make everything from grades to playing in the mud competitive. But this was game night, so everything was amplified.

Chris swung the door open before I had the chance to knock, a wide grin on his face.

I held up my welcome offering of a six-pack of micro-brew beer, and another of root beer for the non-drinkers.

Chris wasn't a big drinker even in the off season, but not at all once training started, and the two youngest Kingmans weren't old enough to drink yet. And if anyone were rule followers, it was the Kingman clan.

That had me even more nervous about tonight. Not that I was a cheaterpants or anything. I didn't care about winning games. But I was about to ask Chris to break some rules for me. "Behind every successful quarterback is a beer-loving bestie."

Yes, yes, I did blurt out awkward things when I was nervous. I didn't even like beer that much.

He gave me a weird look and took the bottles from me. "Come on in. We're picking teams."

Even though I knew my way around the Kingman house about as well as I did my own, he put his hand on the small of my back and guided me into the house. That felt... funny in places it shouldn't.

We moved toward the organized chaos of the living room, through the hallway lined with photos, past one particular photo that always caught my eye, the Kingman family, all together. A tall Bridger Kingman with strikingly handsome features that his sons had definitely inherited. A glowing, happy April Kingman with a radiant smile, holding a baby Jules, and eight boys surrounding them with a range from toddler to preteen. Chris was twelve when this was taken and already with that quarterback gleam in his eyes. It was a moment frozen in time, a testament to the family's tight-knit bond. And it always tugged at my heart.

Mr. Kingman gave me a friendly nod, and several of the boys shouted my name in welcome. If ever there was a big loud family I'd wanted to belong to, it was the King-mans. I may not be related by blood, but this very tight-knit clan had always made me feel like I was just another one of the kids.

"Two-man teams, people. We're playing Footballopoly. Let's go, let's go," Chris called, clapping his hands to gather attention. He winked at me, and I thought I saw a teasing spark in his gaze.

He plopped down right in the middle of one of the big couches, taking up half the room on the cushions, and left just enough space for me beside him. He patted the seat next to him. "You're mine, Beatrix."

Beatrix? He never called me that. Not unless it was something serious. And I almost always got stuck playing either with Mr. Kingman or Jules. Chris and his brothers were all too invested in winning to play with someone who didn't actually care whether they won or not.

"Jules, you're my wing woman tonight, kiddo." Everett grabbed his sister and yanked her clean across the room to sit adjacent to me and Chris.

The rest of the boys gave each other glances that looked about as strange as I felt about whatever was going on here. Declan grabbed Isak, the youngest of the broth-ers. "If you get the girls as your lucky charms, we get the lucky pillow."

A relic from Mr. Kingman's professional football days, it was hand embroidered by his wife with the words, "In this house, we bleed green."

Declan, Hayes, and both the twins all dove for the pillow, but Deck, with his best linebacker moves, blocked them all and came up with the prize, holding it over his head. He tossed it to Isak, who jumped about a foot in the air to grab it over the heads of Flynn and Gryffen faster than any human being should be able to move. "Fuck, yeah. Lucky pillow. We've got the home field advantage now."

The twins rolled their eyes and then simultaneously sat down opposite each other, so Hayes and Mr. Kingman were left picking either Flynn or Gryffen. Everyone settled into their seats while Everett and Jules spread the board game out, sprawling between us on the big square coffee table in the center of the room.

This was the only room in the house that didn't have a television, even though you'd think it would be the main room for watching the games. It had been Mrs. Kingman who insisted there be one room in the house that was football free, and even after more than fifteen years, they'd kept it that way. She might be gone, but they continued to honor her in a lot of ways, every day.

Although there was a whole movie theater with a bajillion inch screen, popcorn machine, drinks fridge, and fancy reclining theater seats in the basement that was the only place to be outside of the stadium on game day.

Everett was muttering something to Jules while they set up the board, and she tried really hard to pretend she wasn't flashing looks over at me. Hmm. Game play shenanigans being planned right there in front of us. The cheeky buggers.

Chris leaned in and whispered in my ear. "What's our strategy for winning, chickadee?"

His pitch was playful and low and... sensual, and the

air conditioner must have kicked on because I got goosebumps.

"Strategy?" I squeaked. "You mean besides blind luck mixed with some intuition?"

"Hmm. Then let's get lucky tonight," he said like he was some sexy version of a romcom movie star, then reached for the dice, gave them a toss, and started the game.

I sat there like a melting lump of goo while the rest of the Kingmans' chatter swelled into a loud, familiar soundtrack. What the heck was going on here?

Was he flirting with me?

Chris?

Chris Kingman?

Flirting?

With me?

No. No, no, nope. Couldn't be. This was my brain going wackadoodle, making up whole-ass romantic scenarios so I wouldn't feel weird about what I had to ask him to do for me later. Yeah. That sounded right. Chris could get any girl in the world, and he'd never been interested in me. He was my friend. And a good one at that.

That's why he would agree to be my date for the reunion even though we weren't even remotely in love with each other. Why he'd pretend to be my boyfriend. Because he was a really good friend.

It wouldn't even be awkward at all. Not asking him, not showing up at the reunion with him by my side, not dancing, or... ack. Everything was going to be normal and fine.

"It's your turn, Trixie, and Chris isn't allowed to throw

the dice anymore." Declan was determined to challenge Chris like any little brother should. I'd watched the two of them butt heads and support each other unrelentingly half their lives. "I don't trust this weird mojo he's rocking tonight."

Weird mojo indeed.

During the game, Chris was way more focused on me than the game. He must be sick. Have a fever. Drinking? Because he'd never let anyone else win a game of Footbal-lopoly. Or any other game for that matter.

His hand lingered in mine when he gave me the dice. On the next roll, his thigh casually rested against mine when there was plenty of room for him to spread out on the couch. His laughter echoed in my ears after every round we won on pure dumb luck. Each of his touches sent a buzz of energy up my spine, but I continued to laugh it off.

An hour into the game, and I was thirsty. Was it hot in here? With eight Kingman men strung out on winning and losing, who wouldn't be?

I glanced over at Jules during one of these moments, and she gave me a knowing look and a thumbs-up. I rolled my eyes at her. Jules and her teenage fantasies. It was just the game, the high stakes, the playful competition, the question I had to ask him tonight that he had to say yes to or I'd be forever humiliated in front of the mean girls that had me fanning myself.

The competition between Chris and Declan was as palpable as the odd tension between me and Chris. It was something I tried to ignore, telling myself it was the heat of the game, the pressure to win, my request I'd make at the end of the night.

As the game finally reached its crescendo, and I watched Chris move our game piece to crush Declan and Isak, I couldn't help but catch my breath. Despite all the teasing, the ribbing, the raucous energy of the Kingman household, something I'd been witness to dozens of times, the way Chris and I had dominated the board, destroying team after team together, had me way more excited than playing a board game should.

While Declan wasn't a sore loser, he wasn't above making a dramatic exit. He tossed the lucky pillow to Everett and Jules. "You'd better take him and Trixie down."

Then, with a smirk on his face, he stormed off to the kitchen, grabbed a couple of beers from the fridge and tossed one to Isak, leaving the rest of us laughing. Isak gave his father a quick look, twisted the top off, and chug-a-lugged. Mr. Kingman shook his head and rolled his eyes.

Everett and Jules were the only other team left. Everyone else lined up as cheering squads and-or Muppet hecklers behind our couches, picking sides to win it all.

We rolled and when we got snake eyes, Chris patted my leg, just above the knee. Even as Jules made their next move, his hand lingered there, his thumb making little distracting swirling motions on my skin. It was our turn again, and Chris leaned in. "Roll us a six or a nine, Trix, and we win the night."

The closeness was startling. The warmth from his breath tickled my neck, making me shiver involuntarily.

Shaking off the unexpected reaction, I nodded and shook the dice, then tossed them into the middle of the board. The room erupted into cheers and boos.

Laughing, Chris pulled me onto his lap for a hug. One in which I lost my breath. Because of his bear of a squeeze on me, not because I'd never sat on his lap before. "We make a good team. I'm not letting you play with anyone else ever again."

When he released me and I could breathe again, for a second, I was caught in his gaze, our laughter fading and our eyes locked on each other. His eyes were intense, his smile warm, and I licked my lips.

But then I blinked and looked away, right at Jules and Everett. The two of them exchanged a sibling communication glance and Jules nodded. Everett gave me a full eyebrow salute, stood up, and flipped the board game and all the pieces. "You two are the worst. No one can beat you. I'm calling unfair advantage."

Not a single Kingman could handle losing anything. Not even at Candyland. The room erupted and a full on dogpile on Everett ensued. Everyone except for Mr. Kingman, who simply sat there with a big ole grin on his face and took a long sip of his beer.

Chris pulled me away from the fray and dragged me toward the kitchen, and then out the French doors to the cool air of the back yard.

I was incredibly warm and took in long gulps of the cooler night air. I'd been lying to myself all night that it was only because of the game. Tonight of all nights, there was something more going on between me and Chris.

But I was also sure I'd manufactured it all in my head

because I'd been thinking about him pretending to be my boyfriend for the next few weeks leading up to the reunion. We were just friends. That's all. I was being silly, seeing something that wasn't there. Nothing more.

The world outside was a universe away, the din of the Kingman household replaced by the soft whispering breeze rustling the leaves in the back yard. He took a seat on the swing hanging from the far end of the pergola and, with a playful grin, patted the space beside him. "Come on, chickadee."

I hesitated for a second, then sank down beside him. A little closer than was probably necessary, but Chris didn't seem to mind. If anything, he leaned into me, our shoulders brushing with the slightest movement. I almost thought he was going to put his arm around me.

His voice was low, barely above the nocturnal sounds of crickets in the grass, and his words tumbled into the night air. "If we keep teaming up like this, they'll start thinking you've got a little Kingman in you."

There was definitely a dirty innuendo in there somewhere. I wasn't imagining it this time. I choked on a laugh and swatted him lightly. "That's ridiculous."

"Is it?" He leaned in closer, just enough so I could feel his breath tickling my cheek, my throat. Then his voice dropped an octave. "We were on fire tonight."

His proximity was throwing me off. I was sure it was my heightened awareness, nothing more. I'd spent all evening trying to pretend that my plan of asking him to play the role of my boyfriend was just a simple, friendly favor.

"Maybe, maybe not." My words trailed off, my mind

screaming at me that this was the perfect time to just ask him, but my courage to ask this outrageous favor was nowhere to be found.

The pause in our conversation was the kind where you can hear your own heartbeat echoing in your ears. Chris's hand came up and he cupped my cheek, turning my face to his. A moment stretched on as his eyes locked onto mine, his expression unreadable. Then, he leaned even closer, his warm breath ghosting over my lips, my heart pounding in my chest.

Was he going to...?

But then he simply ruffled my hair, that cheeky grin returning to his face. "Well, Beatrix, if you ever want some Kingman in you, you know where to find me."

A FAKE FAVOR

CHRIS

*T*rixie looked at me like I was on crack.

I'd been a half second away from kissing her. But Everett's advice not to move too fast, to let her see my love and downright need for her right alongside the fun we had, made me do a fool thing like ruffle her hair.

Fuck, I wanted to kiss her so bad I could practically already taste her lips.

That big soft mouth would be delicious. Her lips would feel so good against mine. Even better wrapped around my dick. There was no putting a little bit of Kingman in her. I had a lot of Kingman below the belt to fill her with. God, I was being such a dick.

And once again, I was lucky it was dark out and she wasn't looking at my lap, because that big bit of Kingman I wanted to put in her was getting bigger by the moment.

She was quiet for a minute, and it couldn't possibly be because she was nervous. Not my Trixie. But she cleared her throat, and her first word came out a little squeaky. "I... need a favor. It's kind of a big one too."

Uh-oh, this sounded serious and not the time for flirting. Shit. "Ask away. I'm here for whatever you need. You know that."

She nodded but also swallowed slowly. She was really nervous, and I didn't like it one bit. "I do know, and I still feel weird asking, but here goes anyway. But we've been friends a long time, and, umm, so I think I can ask you this. Umm, I need a date."

Why were my palms suddenly so sweaty? Be cool, Kingman. Be. Cool. I was a bona fide ring-wearing champion and not even a fourth and ten with three seconds left on the clock at the twenty-yard line, trailing by five made me nervous. Beatrix Moore asking me out on a date was no big deal.

Except it was. She was my girl and had been since we were ten and she yelled at me for calling a football a pigskin because pigs were people too. This was it. I could throw all of Everett's relationship coaching out the window because she had feelings for me too and we were finally going to—

"I need you to pretend to be my boyfriend at my high school reunion. I know, I know, it's cringe-worthy, but I have to go because I'm on the committee, of course I am, and I can't face Rachel, Amanda, and Lacey thinking I'm some lonely cat lady just like they said I would be. Or, uh, in my case, chicken lady. And maybe I accidentally told them you were my boyfriend, because they saw the picture of us in the paper and, you don't mind pretending for a couple of teeny tiny events at my high school, do you?"

Pretend.

The sweat on my hands dried the fuck up, as did the moisture in my mouth, and the blood that had been pumping from my brain to my cock.

Trixie wanted me to pretend to be her boyfriend.

What the shit?

"It's weird, I know. You don't have to answer right now, just think about it. Okay? You've got a couple of weeks before the reunion, so... yeah, let me know what you decide." She patted my leg, stood up, and walked toward the gate between my dad's house and hers. I just sat there like a second place trophy.

I hadn't even answered her. I let her walk away feeling awkward. Way to go, dumbass.

I almost blurted out that I'd do it. If I pretended to be her boyfriend, even for one night at some stupid all-girls Catholic school reunion, that would be one step closer to getting her to see how good we could be if we were more than friends. This fit perfectly into Everett's plan for me to spend time with her and show her how good we could be together, getting her to fall in love with me too.

Play it cool, asshole.

I needed a long run and then twelve cold showers. What I was getting was probably more family game night, while I tortured myself wondering what the hell just happened. Everett was going to have a field day with this shit, and I had to make sure I did everything I could to make sure Declan never heard hide nor hair of it or I'd never—

"Did Trixie Moore just ask you to be her fake date to the prom?" Declan leaned against the open French doors, arms crossed and a shit-eating grin on his face.

Fucking eavesdropping little brothers.

"No." I put my elbows on my knees and sank my head down into my hands. "It's her high school reunion."

Deck sat down next to me and the weight of two professional football players was almost too much for the bench. It squeaked, and still my giant of a little brother scooted his ass every which way trying to get comfortable.

He was probably just taking his time to come up with a hundred and one ways to fuck with me over this. That's what brothers were for.

"Dude. You have to do it. This is your fucking chance to show her how you feel about her, man."

My head shot up before my brain even knew what I was doing. Being the two eldest of the family, Deck and I never missed an opportunity to take each other down a peg. Except on the field. When it was important, we always had each other's backs.

"What, you thought I was going to razz you?" He shook his head at me. "Come on, brother. Not when it actually matters, you dickwad."

Huh. "How is it half the fam knows I'm in love with Trix? I've never said a damn thing."

Deck rolled his eyes and snorted like I was being a real dumbass. "First of all, everyone in the family knows. I mean, who among us hasn't been a little bit in love with

Trixie over the years? But everyone also knows she's your fucking soul mate or some shit."

The magnitude of Declan's words hung in the air like a Hail Mary pass waiting to find swift hands to catch it in the endzone. My heart pounded hard against my chest and the blood whooshed through my ears like I was actually on the field and adrenaline was pumping through me. My soul mate? Even thinking of her like that gave me a level of certainty I hadn't realized I was missing.

"Yeah, I think she is."

"All right, so what's the plan?" Deck asked, rising from the bench, making it squeak again. "We need to strategize this, and God help you if you bungle it, Chris. It's not just about you, it's Trixie. If you hurt her, you'll have to deal with all of us. We're all a little protective of her."

That was the last thing I wanted. I got up and punched Deck on the shoulder. I didn't have words to say thanks for being a cool little brother right now. A bruise would have to do.

"Finally, he gets it," Flynn said, rolling his eyes. He hopped down the step and joined us on the back porch, and Gryffen was only two steps behind him. Great, more little brothers to punch.

"Was everyone listening to our conversation?"

Hayes, Isak, and Jules all stuck their heads out from behind the curtains. They were grabbed by their shirts one by one and shoved into the yard by Everett. "Yes."

Jules shrugged and plopped down on the bench next to me. "Duh, of course we were."

Everett jerked his chin at Declan. "Deck was sent as the sacrificial lamb in case you were freaking out."

I could not think of the last time I'd been ganged up on by all seven of my siblings. "I don't freak out."

"Umm, yes you do." Hayes, who hadn't even played his first game with the Mustangs yet, side-eyed me. "If your game plan is even an iota off, you freak the fuck out, and we all just watched Trixie mess with the plan hard core."

"If this family is going to grow, we all want in on it," Jules said as if she wasn't dropping a fucking bomb on me. "Whoa, whoa, whoa." I held up my hands, ready to call a whole lot of flags on the play. "Nobody said anything about the family growing."

"Hey," Isak pointed at me in a move that looked exactly like the one dad pulled on us when he even suspected funny business. "If you think you're going to bang Trixie and then leave her high and dry, I'm here to tell you that is a career ending decision. Because you won't recover from the beating the rest of us will give you."

I dropped my head back onto my shoulders and stared up at the sky through the slats on the pergola. "You're all a bunch of dickheads."

"Except me. I'm a fucking lady," Ms. Bossypants Jules corrected.

The mouth on her. That's what she inherited from growing up with seven older brothers and no other woman in the house. I'd never tell her I thought it was adorable.

"Yes, pretty, pretty princess, except you. You're a fucking lady." I looked around at them all, making sure to catch every single one of my brothers' eyes. "Of course that's not what I'm talking about. But I haven't even gotten her to kiss me yet, much less gotten her into bed or asked her to marry me."

Declan nodded all sagely as if he wasn't about to say something to poke at me. I knew that look. "Mmm-hmm, right, right. You can't tell us you're not already imagining a white picket fence with half a dozen little Chrises and Trixies running around with their whole flock of chickens trailing after them."

There were murmurs of agreement from everyone. "Each and every one of you needs to get the fuck out of my head."

Hayes smirked and shook his head. "What fun would that be?"

"Lord save me." There were only two people missing from this impromptu family meeting. One was watching down on us always. "What's Dad think about this?"

Jules patted my arm. "Who do you think sent us to eavesdrop and intervene if necessary?"

Dad always did like Trix. He and mom had been good friends with the Moores. It made me wonder if our parents had ever had one of those weird *our kids should get married when they grow up* chats. But if even Dad was on the Trixie train, we were going full steam ahead.

"Fine. Huddle up. You lot are going to spend the rest of game night strategizing my grand love plan." I was going to be the best damn pretend boyfriend Trixie had ever seen.

"Dude, you need to be mysterious," Flynn suggested, to which Gryffen added, "Yeah, keep her on her toes. Girls love a little intrigue."

"Since when do you two know anything about girls?

Your last date was a joint disaster at your last sci-fi con," Jules retorted, snickering into her soda.

The two of them glared at Jules, but each shrugged, not really bothered. Flynn said, "This is the way."

Gryffen repeated it as required. "This is the way."

Hayes, who weirdly had a book on quantum physics in one hand, chimed in, "Gifts. Trixie likes unique things. Get her something nobody else would think of. "

"Like, hats for her chickens, or oh, arms. I saw those on FlipFlop. They're hilarious. Trixie likes to laugh," Isak suggested, while literally looking at his phone. Both he and Everett had ridiculously huge FlipFlop followings. I refused to even get the app on my phone.

Jules rolled her eyes, "Oh great, advice from the guy whose only relationship is with his online followers."

Isak just shrugged. "Hey, they love me."

"Guys, Chris needs to tell her how he feels." Declan's declaration caused a ripple of silence to spread through the lot of them. Jules sucking on the very end of her soda, very, very loudly, was the only sound in the yard.

Out of the corner of my eye, I saw Everett lean back in his chair, a bemused smirk on his face. As the family's resident ladies' man, who'd already told me what to do, he didn't join in the chaotic brainstorming, opting instead to watch us flounder like a barrel of monkeys.

"Isn't anyone going to ask Everett?" Hayes finally broke the silence, gesturing towards our silent brother.

"I thought we were saving the best for last." Apparently he hadn't let slip yet that I'd already spent all morning at his house going through almost exactly the same list of ideas they all had just mentioned.

Everett's smirk through this whole convo never wavered. "He doesn't need some game day style strategy."

He looked me dead in the eye. "I already told you, just quit hiding your feelings for her. Trixie's known you for years. Any attempts to be someone or something not a hundred percent you, will be as transparent as Flynn's and Gryffen's twin telepathy."

The twins looked at each other and then flipped Everett off in perfect sync.

"Besides, we've all been waiting years for you to make your move. Now that you've admitted you've got feelings for her, we're all anxious to push and shove you together, mostly to get you to quit looking like a sad fucking puppy whenever you think she's not looking." Declan raised his beer, saluting my years of misery.

Our family had always been tight. We had each other's backs, and we cared for each other a lot. Family was everything. But more often than not in the past sixteen years, I was the one helping the rest of them, and I was more than a little overwhelmed seeing how they didn't just say they supported me but were ready to band together to help me right back.

They all had punches in the arms and bruises coming from me. Except Jules, who'd get an embarrassing pinch on the cheek.

"All right, you cocky fucking Kingmans, this is by no means an actual plan, and I have no idea what I'm doing." I had to pause just a second and clear my throat. "But with you lot conspiring for me, I can't lose."

I could and would probably fuck this up three ways to Saturday several times. I wasn't used to letting Trixie see my feelings, but I was going to. The whole fake boyfriend for her reunion thing was just giving me the opportunity and excuse to spend even more time with her. I snagged Declan's beer and raised it, but I didn't have any words to express how these nosy assholes warmed my heart.

"For Trixie," Isak said. He was such a softie in wolf's clothing.

The rest of them, all suddenly serious, each lifted their own drinks. "For Trixie."

Bring it on, high school reunion. The Kingman team was ready to play.

I was going to win Beatrix Moore's heart or die trying. Ooph. My heart definitely skipped a beat. That had better not be a bad omen. I needed to go find my lucky socks to wear to this damn reunion.

PRACTICE MAKES FAKE PERFECT

TRIXIE

"Hold up," Lulu's face on my phone screen had me wishing I had just called instead of Facetiming her, "you asked him to be your fake date? Like you actually said the words fake date?"

"Yes. I don't understand why you're making such a big deal out of it." It wasn't a big deal. I mean, it shouldn't be. We really were just friends. It would be fine. Just fine.

"I don't understand why you didn't ask him to be your actual date. He's clearly into you. The entire Denver Metro area and anyone who follows celebrity gossip sites can see that." Lu shook her copy of the Denver paper at me, even though I'd specifically told her not to go out and buy one after the reunion planning committee meeting.

Right. The photo that Rachel and Amanda threw in my face had become the shot seen round the world. I was definitely going to ask Chris how to deal with the media who were now stalking me. I had about a billion new friend requests on FaceSpace and way too many DMs. Someone had even left a voicemail requesting an interview and naked photoshoot.

My mom would be so proud. Ugh.

"Because we're friends. It would be like if I asked you to be my date to the reunion." Which I probably should have done anyway. The mean girls had taunted the two of us relentlessly about being lesbians in high school. If Lulu wasn't already married to a lovely woman who I adored, and who she was pee her pants excited to bring to the reunion, I might have. It would have been less stressful than this lie I was getting myself tangled in.

"Mina says we can have a threesome if you want to." Lulu moved the camera so her wife, who was standing behind her in the kitchen, could wave.

"Thanks, but it's too late now. I'm already committed to the ruse." Unless, of course, Chris said no. He really didn't seem to like the idea last night when I asked him, and I hadn't heard from him yet this morning. I did say he could have time to think about it. But mostly so he didn't shoot me down right then and there. I planned to ply him with some of Paul Hollywood's jammy biscuits later to butter him up to say yes.

It's not like it was some long term thing. Two evenings and one picnic. We could even skip the picnic if he really didn't want to go. Honestly, we could skip the dinner and dance too. All I really needed him to show up for was the fundraiser. Which I still had to ask if he and any of his brothers would consider donating to.

No way I was hosting a freaking bachelor auction.

Yuck. Since Rachel had put me in charge of the fundraiser, we'd be doing what I wanted. So there.

God, she brought out the worst in me, and I hated that about myself. This wasn't high school, I wasn't a teenager still trying to figure out who and what I wanted to be, and I'd gotten over caring what haters thought or said a long time ago. Or at least I thought I had.

I could use some good old-fashioned words of wisdom from my mom right about now. She was the queen of having a barren field of fucks. But she and dad were on their way to some tantric sex retreat in the Himalayas or something.

"Well, what did he say when you asked him?"

Ooph. "He hasn't answered yet. I told him he could think about it. It was kind of awkward." Which I wasn't used to with Chris.

"I'm shocked. Shocked I tell you." Lulu was not, in fact, shocked. Her eyeroll and her deadpan tone were much stronger than her words.

I didn't know what I was going to do if he did say no. He wouldn't though. He couldn't. He might. Ergh. I hadn't been this awkward around him since the summer before college. I'd been angry and hurting back then and had taken it out on him when he was just trying to be nice.

We hadn't spoken much at all after that and pretty much totally lost touch when I went off to school in Wisconsin. But when I moved back to Thornminster a couple of years ago, we were like peas and carrots again, and he'd never mentioned how rude I'd been to him, not once.

Some people were just kindred spirits, as Anne of

Green Gables would say. Chris and Lulu were mine. Didn't matter if we didn't talk for a few hours or a few years, we just picked right back up where we left off.

But had I just quashed that kindred feeling by crossing the boundaries of our friendship? Probably. That was really dumb of me. Chris's friendship meant more to me than showing Rachel that I wasn't some crazy chicken lady.

"I guess I'd better call him and tell him to forget it." I could handle some disdain and taunts from girls who were stuck in high school better than I could feeling like I screwed up my relationship with one of my best friends. "I don't know what I was thinking."

"I do, but Mina says I should keep my thoughts to myself and let you figure it out on your own." I could still see Mina in the background, and she had her arms crossed and was simply nodding.

"Mina is a meanie." I stuck my tongue out at them both.

Lulu waggled her eyebrows. "I know. Isn't it hot?"

They were so fricking cute and in love, it made my heart both happy and hurt. Something I tried not to even think, much less say out loud, was that worry in the back of my mind that I might never get to experience love like that.

Except with Luke Skycocker. He loved me, even if no other man wanted me for more than bragging rights.

"I guess I'll call him and..." Say what? Kidding? He'd know I was lying instantly. And Chris hated lies. What a mess.

"Give him a chance to respond before you nope out on

the whole thing. He's probably going to say yes anyway. When has he ever said no to you?"

I didn't have to answer that because Luke started crowing and having a big old freak out. He was better than any guard dog when it came to alerting me to stranger danger at the house. "Gotta go, someone's here."

I waved at Mina and hung up before the two of them could call me out on more of my shit. They were good at that particular skill. And that's what friends were for.

I found Luke chasing Chris around the back yard. Chris pretended he wanted to cook my rooster up on a spit, but I think the both of them secretly liked teasing each other. Luke dived for Chris's shoes, and Chris jumped over him and sprinted for the coop. I'd seen them play this game a half dozen times before. Chris's goal was to trick Luke into the coop, and Luke's goal was to peck holes in any available clothing or skin. Or poop on Chris's shoes. Good times.

Chris had the upper hand today. He was carrying Princess Laya under his arm like a football, and that had Luke all riled up. I might be his number one girl, but nobody messed with his hens. I sat on the top step of my back porch and cheered them on. "Run, Luke, run."

Chris shot me a dirty look but turned right back to dancing around Luke's attempts to trip him up. Luke had something in his beak, and I couldn't quite figure out what.

Chris made a mad dash for the coop, and right at the last minute, set Laya down, giving her a little pat on the butt so she squawked and hurried through the gate. The other girls came over to greet her and Luke got caught up in their girl gang. He shot a look at Chris that clearly said 'traitor.' But Chris shut the gate and gave Luke a little salute. Just like the one he gave the crowd when he ran a touchdown in.

"Thanks." I leaned back on the step, no longer having to do that chore before I left. "I needed to put him away before I headed out."

When Chris plopped down beside me, he was panting and ruffled, like he'd been through a mini-war. There was a reddish orange smudge on his neck and another running down his forearm. Not blood, too brightly colored. I squinted at it. "Is that... lipstick?"

I did not like the weird feeling at the thought he'd been with a woman.

Chris touched his neck and then looked down at his hand and arm, noticing the red stuff for the first time. "No, it's wing sauce. I brought a packet along to taunt Luke with, and he jumped up and snatched it right out of my hands."

"You're telling me Luke Skycocker assaulted you with hot sauce?"

He nodded solemnly. "Ran at me, packet clutched in his beak. Shook it like a Polaroid picture. But don't worry, it's the mild kind. I don't think he's quite ready to upgrade to extra spicy yet."

I had to cover my mouth not to snort-laugh. He glared at me and rolled his eyes like the whole incident wasn't a hundred and twenty-seven percent his fault. "Where you headed? Not work."

I was dressed in one of my fave chicken t-shirts and jeans. Not library appropriate attire. "No, I'm doing some volunteer work this morning. Working the closing shift at the library tonight."

He just nodded and looked out over the lawn. It was a nice clear morning, and we had a magnificent view of the Flatirons and the Rockies today. We stared at the mountains for a bit, and it wasn't exactly awkward, but it also wasn't our normal comfy hang either. We were both waiting for the other to say something about last night.

I cleared my throat. This was Chris I was with, not some morning after a one-night stand. "You don't have to go to my reunion if you don't want to. I didn't mean to put you in a weird position."

I was this close to a full-on ramble of awkwardness, but he interrupted me. "Yes."

"Yes?" Yes, I had made him feel weird and obligated, or yes, he'd be my fake date? I don't know why I couldn't just ask him. Why was it suddenly hard to talk?

"I'll be your fake date, but, Trix," he paused and I already didn't like the 'but' I knew was coming.

Crap. I had made him feel weird, and I was going to be royally pissed at myself if this made our whole friendship different. He was such an important person in my life. My best friend. But lots of boy-girl friendships got ruined because of sex. Not like I'd asked him to have sex with me. Oh god, I was spiraling waiting for that but.

He glanced my way and then back out at the view, and I had to bite my tongue to let him say what he needed to before I made everything worse.

He moved his head from side to side, stretching his neck. He really was uncomfortable. I opened my mouth to renege on the whole thing and pray I didn't make everything worse, but he finished his thought first. "You know I'm a horrible liar, so if we're going to pull this off, we have to practice."

"Practice?" I'd apparently forgotten how to have an actual conversation with him because all I'd done was ask a question by repeating the last word he said. But my brain had gone into a tornado of things he could be asking to practice with me. None of them were football, and all of them were kissing. Friends didn't kiss. Not the kind you practiced.

Gah. See? Friendship ruined. What was wrong with me?

"Yeah. If I just show up with you on the night of and we have to dance and be together as if we're more than friends, we need to spend some time spending time together, acting as if we're actually, you know, together. If we don't, I'm gonna fuck it up."

"Oh. Like... you want us to go on a date?" I guess you could call the outing to Manniway's a date. But that hadn't been either my intention or his. Sure, I'd dressed up and we'd had dinner just the two of us, but it hadn't been romantic.

If that's what he was proposing, then I could do that. And it also meant I hadn't screwed up our friendship. Probably. He still wasn't looking at me.

"Yep. If we're trying to sell me as your boyfriend to the Queen Bees in a couple of weeks, we need to be all in. Staring deeply into each other's eyes and holding hands and... all the boyfriend-girlfriend stuff."

All? I was ignoring what that did to my lower belly. Probably I was hungry.

"Queen Bees? You do not remember that." Rachel, Amanda, and Lacey had self-styled themselves that in high school. Our school mascot was a bee, since our school was named after St. Ambrose, the patron saint of beekeepers. Those three had definitely ruled over the rest of their drones.

I'd likely complained about them back in the day, but I didn't expect him to remember them or how horrible they were to me. I wasn't sure I remembered who he was friends with back then.

"Of course I do. I would never forget the girls who made your life shitty. I don't want them getting even a whiff that what's between us isn't a hundred percent real or give them any fodder to talk schmack. So, we practice until being together is second nature."

Most days I felt that way being with him anyway. But that was when we were watching TV or playing board games or whatever. He was right. I'd been uncomfortable in the spotlight on that red carpet, and while there wouldn't be Mustang fans and press, there would prob- ably be a lot of people taking photos and scrutinizing our every move. Chris was famous after all. Especially in Denver. And I'd barely made it ten minutes in the spot- light before making a mad dash for cover.

"You're right. But maybe we could start with some- thing not so... public?" Not that I knew what that would be. He was a giant celebrity. Except to me and his family. Then he was just Chris.

His shoulders dropped and he blew out a breath I don't think I was supposed to notice. Had he actually been nervous about this? Chris Kingman wasn't nervous about anything ever. He was confidence and grace, like Miss United States. "Yeah. That sounds like a good idea. Especially after the way my phone blew up after the picture at Manniway's."

"Oh my god, mine too. I meant to ask you about that last night, but... uh, forgot." Since I was focused on asking him something else entirely.

I pulled out my phone and showed him the little red number that said I had fourteen voicemails. I never answered a call from any number I didn't recognize and had only listened to a few of the messages. They were all from journalists. Like I wanted my business all over the papers and internet. Gross. "How do you deal with people being all up in your business like that? And tell me it will go away."

He grimaced and shook his head. "Sorry about that. I've got the PR girl that works with my agent playing interference. I really didn't think we'd end up on the front page."

He looked directly at me now. "But they probably won't go away if we're seen together again."

"Oh. Yeah. Right. But you don't think the press is going to care about my high school reunion, do you?" Although, the other girls would probably have a heyday with that. Maybe I could actually use that to my advantage.

"Well, they sort of care about most everything I do. But I've been thinking about that." He took my hand and rubbed his thumb over my knuckles in a way that was meant to soothe. That's not what I'd say his touch did. "We could have the PR people tell them I'm dating a local girl. Unless that's too much press. But it does play into your evil plans. I need to talk to my agent about some car commercial he's got lined up for me anyway, and he'll be thrilled to spin some hometown love story."

Yikes. That was a whole lot more public than I'd ever planned to be about this fake relationship. The more people that knew about it, the more likely someone would find out it was all a ruse. But what choice did I have at this point? "Sure, that's fine. As long as the paparazzi don't start showing up at my house."

I brushed off my worries and his apology with a shrug, though in all honesty, it did put a nervous zing in my belly. But I was the one who had asked him to pretend to be my boyfriend in the first place.

"Nah, once they know you aren't also a celeb, except of course to the teenagers at the library, they'll just use that pic of us at Manniway's a hundred more times."

Phew. I'd never been happier the most public facing I ever had to be at my job was when the newest teen vampire novel came out. "That makes me feel better. So we should plan our first practice date then."

This 'date' with Chris, even if it was a fake one, hovered in the air between us, charging the atmosphere with a tension I hadn't felt before. I stole a glance at him. He was already looking at me, his expression unreadable. Suddenly, the air around us felt too warm, too close. I swallowed, feeling my cheeks heat up.

This was going to be more interesting than I'd thought.

"How about we go hiking?" he suggested. "We could

pop over to Chautauqua, maybe have a picnic? Out of the public eye, just you and me. Low risk, high reward."

I did love the park and open space tucked right up next to the Flatirons. "Maybe tomorrow? I promised I would volunteer at the Rooster Rescue today. Those poor guys need all the love they can get."

Chris laughed and shook his head like he was both surprised and not at the same time. "Alright, then. Rooster Rescue it is. But if any of them try to murder me, I'm blaming you."

FOGHORNS AND FLIRTING

CHRIS

"*L*ook at you, Foghorn," Trixie cooed, holding one of the roosters close to her. The bird squawked, fluffing its bright red feathers, and leaned into her, rubbing his face right up in between her breasts. Little fucker.

I watched the whole interaction from the barn since I'd been put on food tray filling duty. "That rooster is taking advantage of you, Trix."

I kind of wished I had some feathers sticking out of my ass with the way she was cuddling that guy. He was definitely getting the snuggles I wanted. So far, this pseudo-date was not going anything like I'd hoped. I was all for helping out an animal rescue, but this just felt like any other day hanging out with Trix.

Feeding chickens and picking up their shit wasn't the most romantic way to get up close and personal. But this was what she loved and so I was going to do it with a smile on my face. But I'd be keeping my eyes peeled for the opportunity to show her I was more than just a pal.

She looked up at me, her eyes sparkling with amusement. "They're sweet if you know how to treat them right." The rooster squawked again, almost as if in agreement.

God, she was adorable. Trixie could probably get a charging bull moose to give her some love just by batting her eyelashes at him. "They hate me, so clearly I don't have the magic chicken touch."

I'd been pecked at least a dozen times since we'd arrived. The trainers were going to have a field day berating me for treating my body as anything less than a temple. Today I was a shrine to why chickens made a better dinner than a pet.

Trixie carefully placed Foghorn back onto the ground. The rooster gave me the side eye and then pecked at some invisible bugs in the dirt before strutting away.

"Okay, next task," she pulled out the volunteer guide. "It looks like we're cleaning the coop next."

I had no idea how to flirt with her in this barnyard setting, and I was fairly sure I was failing miserably at my flirting task. She was paying way more attention to the roosters. She chatted to each one and checked them over, and for the thousandth time this morning, I was jealous of poultry.

My flirting skills were damn rusty, and it wasn't like I could review tapes of my previous attempts to pinpoint my weak spots, or practice under the watchful eye of my coaches. Maybe I should have made Everett or

Declan come with us so we could do a play-by-play afterwards.

But I was on my own and would have to come up with my own game plan.

"Yep, sure. But first, can you come over here and look at this?" I waved her over as if I'd found some problem. My libido was the real issue. When she got close, searching for whatever I was worried about, I threw a handful of straw at her like a four-year-old trying to get her to pay attention to me.

Yeah, real smooth. But it worked.

Trixie gasped, but then laughed and grabbed two handfuls of hay and threw them at me. I did a fantastic job, if I do say so myself, of pretending to be totally surprised and affronted. "Oh, it is on like Donkey Kong."

I grabbed two huge handfuls and dashed toward her, dancing on my feet like I was looking for a receiver, just to give her a little bit of a head start.

She squealed and jumped away. "Don't you dare, Christopher Bridger Kingman."

I dared. I definitely dared. Not only did I toss one whole handful right over the top of her head, I shoved the other handful down the front of her shirt. If I was lucky, I'd be helping her pick that straw out of her bra later.

"Oh my giddy baby Jesus, you are going down." Trix lunged and surprised the shit out of me by pulling on my waistband.

While I stopped and prayed that her hand was going down my pants, I got a fistful of straw in my shorts instead.

"Hey, truce," I called out, laughing and bouncing

around, trying to shake the straw out when a particularly sharp piece ended up down where the sun don't shine.

Trixie smiled at me, her eyes sparkling with mischief. But the mischievous glint in her eyes told me she was far from done. "You started it."

She was the only one who ever beat me at my own games. But this time I was going to win. Win her over. I gave her my best smoldering smile and wink. "Yes, I did. You ready for a roll in the hay now?"

Trixie snort-laughed. Like actually snorted. "That was the worst dad joke ever. Come on, let's go do the coop before it's time to go."

She walked away and waved for me to follow after. Which, of course I would.

How the fuck was I a university graduate, the star quarterback of the bowl winning pro football team, a multi-millionaire, small business owner, and loving older brother, and still couldn't figure out how to charm the sweetest, curviest, smartest, kindest woman I'd ever known?

Fuck.

Foghorn the rooster trotted over to me and stood by my side as we both watched Trixie's hips sway as she walked toward the coops. I looked down thinking I had a brother in... feathers, wings? The damn rooster looked up at me and then pecked me on the damn heels. "Okay, okay, you little dinosaur, I'm going. Trix, wait up."

We finished up the rest of the chores the sanctuary set out for us, still joking and palling around, but I needed some advice before I attempted to flirt with her again. I was questioning Everett's advice to just be myself. She already liked me, but she didn't love me. Hmm. Maybe I could stop for roses on my run tomorrow morning.

Trixie went to go sign us out, but returned with a slightly older woman in overalls and an old school camera. Nobody had made a big deal about who I was when we arrived, which had worked out perfectly for getting to spend time with her without anyone watching us. But maybe that wasn't the right way to go. If we were in the public eye these next few weeks, we'd be forced to act more like a couple.

"Hey, the owners wondered if you would mind doing a quick photo." She indicated toward the sign nearby with the name of the sanctuary, where Foghorn the rooster was perched. Because of course he was. "They could maybe post on their social media? You'd probably get them a ton of attention and that will bring in donations to feed and—"

"Sounds great." I pulled Trixie over to the sign, wrapped my arm around her and pulled her into the famous V-J Day dip, but didn't actually kiss her. I. Didn't. Kiss. Her.

I stared down into her sparkling blue eyes. I should have kissed her. I should have fucking kissed her.

Right on cue, the owner click-clicked away on her camera. I heard the flappity flap of chicken wings go right over our heads and the owner lady coo. "Oh, that's absolutely adorable."

It probably was the perfect shot, until Foghorn landed on my head and dug his claws into my scalp. I yelped, and he went flying again. Trixie and I tumbled to the ground, and I rolled to protect her, taking the brunt of the fall on my back and clasping her in my arms. She landed on top of me, and I held her against my chest a bit too long.

A tingling awareness of every inch of her curves molding against my body spread through me like fire. This was a sensation more potent than the adrenaline that usually surged through me on game day. Her hair smelled of hay and sunshine, her body warm and soft in my arms. This was Trixie, my friend, but she was also the woman I was utterly in love with.

In that moment, with her laughter still echoing in my ears, her body pressed to mine, the danger in this ruse hit me right in the gut, knocking the wind out of me as if I'd been sacked.

"Chris?" Her voice was soft, questioning. She straightened her glasses that had gone askew in our tumble, and looked down at me, her eyes wide and vulnerable. Did she feel it too? The shift in our dynamic, the crossing of a line we could never fully retreat from?

"You okay?" I released her a little too quickly and scrambled to my feet to help her up too.

"Yeah, I'm good." She smiled, but in her eyes was a flash of confusion.

A part of me wanted to confess everything right then and there, to tell her how I felt and what I wanted. But that wasn't the plan. I'd prove myself to her first. So instead, I brushed straw and dust off my clothes and forced a laugh. "Foghorn sure has it in for me, doesn't he?"

The owner, camera still in hand, looked between me and Foghorn, who was strutting around like he owned the place. "He's just an old romantic. Likes to make sure the hens he loves are protected," she said, her voice soft and thoughtful. "I expect you're the same."

Her words struck me like another sack before I even had my breath back. Was that what I was doing? Protecting what I loved, even at the risk of losing it? The stakes had never been higher, and the game had never been more real. I wasn't playing at being Trixie's lover. I was desperately, hopelessly trying to become her love.

I made a quick anonymous donation on my phone to their 501c3 to keep their animals fed for the rest of the month.

We drove back from the sanctuary, the easy banter and laughter from earlier in the day gone. The lines of what I was doing, the plans I was trying my damnedest to execute, had blurred, and the unspoken emotions between us were a fucking chasm. This wasn't what I wanted. This fake dating was supposed to bring us closer.

"Did you have fun?" I knew she had, but I was trying to gauge her feelings now in this uncomfortable silence we'd landed in.

Trixie looked over at me, surprise flickering in her eyes. "Of course. I had a blast, didn't you?"

"Sure." Damn. That didn't sound convincing. Shit.

"But..." She bit her lip in the cutest way. "It didn't feel like a date, did it?"

"Nope." Not my best flirting, or... kissing being done in the barnyard. Not by us anyway. "I'm not so sure Foghorn would feel the same."

Trixie tapped her finger against her mouth and I don't think she had any idea how she was driving me crazy with the way she kept drawing my attention to her lips. She made a thinking hum and said, "It's just too easy to be myself with you. Maybe I just shouldn't go to the reunion. I can tell them that—"

All right, I'd be analyzing the shit out of that whole too easy to be herself with me statement later with the boys. First I had to rally so she didn't give up on me.

"No way, sweetheart. We are in it to win it. This was just our first practice run, and clearly we've got some work to do. But I don't mind." Here goes nothing. "I kind of like flirting with you."

Trixie's cheeks went pink, and it wasn't from being in the sun. Good. If she was blushing at the thought of me flirting with her, maybe I wasn't as far off the right track. God, I was all over the fucking place. I hadn't ever been this wishy-washy on what to do in my fucking life.

"Did you flirt with me today?" She pursed her lips, trying to hold back a teasing smile.

See? Lips. Again. What I wouldn't do to kiss them.

"Guess I'm gonna have to try harder." I shook my head and chuckled, pretending I wasn't dying to taste her.

When I pulled up in front of her house, I didn't miss the hint of reluctance from her when we said goodbye. I drove away but not into my own driveway ten yards away. My mind was whirling with confusion and longing. A sensation similar to the jitters I used to get when I first got drafted, when I had to prove myself, skittered through me.

I had to work some of this out and doing something physical, but rote, gave me space to think. I pointed the car toward the training center. Camp wasn't for another two weeks, but that didn't mean I couldn't go get in a workout. Hard, sweaty exertion was exactly what I needed.

I just wished I was getting hard and sweaty with... no, the second I let my mind go south, I was headed for a cold shower instead of a workout.

Why wasn't I surprised to see Declan's truck at the training center? Of course he was already training. Probably had been for half the summer. Always trying to get ahead of me.

Declan wasn't alone, both Everett and Hayes were there too, each doing their own training drills. "Who forgot to call me to say we were working out?"

"Hey, lover boy," Everett called as I walked in, tossing a football in my direction.

What I should have caught easily almost slipped through my fingers. My mind was still on Trixie, and the way her lips were taunting me.

"Looks like someone's head isn't in the game." Declan threw a knowing glance my way and then at the boys. "How'd it go with Trix?"

"Don't ask," I grumbled, tossing the ball back at Everett. "I'm failing miserably."

Hayes tapped his hands, indicating for Everett to toss the ball to him. When he got it, he gave the ball a shake and pointed it at me. This kid was going to replace me one day with those hands and his quiet ass observations. "No, doubtful. Tell us what happened. We'll re-strategize."

"Yeah," Declan held up his hands and Hayes tossed the ball to him. "And tell you where you fucked up."

"I'm paralyzed out there. I don't know how to act around her anymore." I held up my hands and Deck tossed the ball to me. I sent it straight to Everett but didn't wait for his 'be yourself' advice again. "I did a shitty job making her see me as more than a friend today. I know you told me to take it slow with her, but I have to win her over soon, before the reunion."

Before this whole charade unraveled and I lost this one chance.

Everett shook his head, disbelief all over his face. Shit. This was why older brothers weren't supposed to ask for advice from their younger siblings. It was supposed to be vice-versa, and I was shattering their perfect big brother vision of me.

"I told you to be natural, not a fucking lovesick snail. Come on, Chris. You're the star quarterback." Everett patted the ball and sent it over to Hayes, but he continued telling me like it is. "You take charge on the field, you make decisions in seconds, you know how to play the game. You did the same with your real estate biz, you do the same when we play fucking board games. Why are you letting this situation intimidate you?"

"It's different," I protested, but I knew he had a point. "She's my friend. I don't want to ruin that."

Declan laughed. Fucking laughed at me. "Bro, you're treating her like she's made of glass. Stop walking on eggshells around her. Be you, be confident, be bold. If you want her, go after her like you go after a touchdown, or that house on the corner, or Park Place and Boardwalk with twelve hotels."

Hayes tucked the ball under his arm and nodded in agreement. "Stop playing defense, that's never been you.

You're Chris fucking Kingman and you play a mean game of offense."

Fairly sure that's not my middle name.

Declan grabbed the ball from Hayes, trotted over and shoved it at me. "You've been in the friend zone too long, and you're afraid of what will happen if you break out of it. But if you don't, you'll never know how good it could be, dumbass."

Jesus. When did my little brothers get so fucking smart? Their words hit me right in the solar plexus. I knew they were right.

Okay, yeah. I had to stop treating Trixie like she was some unattainable prize and just go after what I wanted. That's what I'd always done, and it had pretty much always worked out.

Except that one night when I asked her out ten years ago.

I palmed the ball and threw it in a perfect spiral all the way across the entire training center and right into the bin of balls fifty yards away. The cocky, confident guy that had taken me to the top of the football world was exactly who I needed to be to win her heart.

And this time, I wouldn't let anything stand in my way. "No more holding back, no more second-guessing. Either she falls for me or she doesn't."

The worry that I would lose her completely if she didn't want a romantic relationship with me absolutely had to be ground into the dirt beneath my feet. I wasn't going to lose her. I wasn't. She was my best friend besides my family, and best friends made the best lovers, and partners for life.

And yeah, I could definitely see us together forever.

"That's the Chris Kingman we've been waiting to fucking show up," Declan said, clapping me on the back a little too hard as only a defensive lineman would. "Now let's get in a real workout and get your head back in the game."

A few more Mustangs were in the training center, and we spent the next few hours running drills and pushing each other. This was going to be a great god damned season. Even better when I had Trix watching me from the fifty-yard line, or up in the box with the other wives and girlfriends.

Sure she watched our games, but knowing she'd be there especially for me and that I could come home to her afterwards and lose myself in her, that had me more excited to play than ever before. Play and win.

THE GOOD, THE BAD, AND THE UGLY LIBRARIAN

TRIXIE

*E*ven though I showered and changed into a work outfit after my first fake date with Chris, I was still finding pieces of hay poking me in places hay shouldn't be. I think they were planted as a reminder of how weird my morning had been. This was two days in a row where I'd honestly thought Chris was about to kiss me.

Kiss.

Me.

Nope, no, that was too weird. I'd chalk it up to him trying out the whole fake flirting thing. But he'd done it last night before I'd asked him to pretend to be my boyfriend. Did he really want to kiss me?

Did I want him too?

My computer dinged with an email notification and I just about fell out of my chair. Aw, crudmuffins. It was time for my evaluation with Karter. My head was not in the game today and Creepy Karter was the last person I wanted to deal with.

I gathered my notebook and pen, because at least if I pretended to be taking notes, I wouldn't have to see him staring at me like a piece of pie he wanted to stick his dick into. He was never overtly sexual, so I had no grounds to stand on if I wanted to call HR. But he still made me uncomfortable.

His office was just on the other side of the space where our cubicles were lined up, so he saw me coming. "Aw, Beatrix. I was just coming to find you. Come on in."

"Thanks." I sat and opened the notebook on my lap, clicked my pen and did my best not to take a deep breath to steel myself for this conversation.

"How's it going? How's your mom, your family?" He steepled his hands and leaned forward, his eyes flicking to my chest and back up.

Oh god. I had definitely never spoken about my mother to Creepy Karter. So that's what caused the gross vibe I got off him. Just like every other guy in my life, Karter had seen my mother's porn videos and thought I'd be a chip off the old BBW, hot mama block.

What the hell was wrong with men? This. This was why I liked being friends with Chris, and the rest of the Kingman boys. Friends.

Never once in all the years I lived next door to them did I ever worry that any of them thought they could get in my pants just because my mother had been a sex worker. To them, she was just another soccer mom, and one they appreciated and respected.

I did take that deep breath now. Maybe I was overreacting. I'd been overly sensitive about how people treated me because of my mother since she first had the sex talk with me and told me about how she made a living.

Never had I felt ashamed of her or what she did. I loved that she helped raise me to be both sex and body positive. But the rest of the world sure tried to make me feel weird about it at every turn.

"My parents are fine. Doing some traveling abroad. Shall we get to the evaluation?"

"Your family does seem to be remarkably interesting. I don't think my own mother has ever even left the state."

Okay, maybe he really was just making small talk. Fine. "Ah, well, Colorado is beautiful and there are lots of nice things to see here too."

"Right. So." He tapped on his computer and brought up something on his screen, but from my angle across the desk from him, I couldn't see what. "What's this I see about a nomination?"

Gah. Had Lulu forwarded that onto Karter too? The traitor. I had almost forgotten about the award with all the other craziness of the past few days. I didn't have the room in my brain to worry about everything, and nervousness about accepting an award was no longer number one on my list of anxieties. Maybe like, number five, and that was five too many.

"Yes, I've been nominated as the Young Adult Romance Writers Librarian of the Year."

Karter's head jerked back far enough he gave himself a double chin, and I did not miss the look of disgust. "Please tell me we do not have books about teens having," he looked around as if he expected the CIA to be listening in on us, "ess eee ex."

Good grief. How was this man actually a librarian? I clenched my teeth, holding in my tirade. He wasn't the only librarian I knew who thought the whole romance genre was mommy porn. He was a literary snob, and I wanted to slap him in the face with every book my favorite romance authors had ever written.

"That's not typically what young adult romance books are about." The fact that I had to school him about an entire section of our collection boggled the mind. How the hell had he gotten the promotion to branch manager? "Think more like the deliciously giddy feelings the first time you fall in love, which is even more fun when there are dragons and epic battles against evil, dystopian societies to thwart, or the patriarchy to dismantle, all while still going to high school."

He still looked at me like I'd sprouted a second head made out of penises. "Right, well, perhaps we should beef up the classics for our youth population, maybe some more mysteries, and—"

"Manga? Yes, I'll look into that. I've also applied for a technology grant that will give us some new money to upgrade the gaming system this fall." He probably didn't even know we had video games. This evaluation was not worth my time.

"It always looks good to the board when we get a new grant. Excellent job."

Yeah. Because I applied for the grant to look good for the board. Eyeroll. "Yes, thank you."

"You're not planning on going to this awards ceremony, are you?"

I may be freaking out about it, but, yeah, I was. "Yes. I was hoping the library might help fund the travel. The conference is in Texas."

"You can certainly use your vacation days for that, but I don't think it would look proper to fund a trip to, for, uh, I'm not sure there are funds for something like that."

The way he was fumbling all over himself because he was uncomfortable about books written by, for, and about women was one of the things that would have me forever thinking of him as Creepy Karter. In fact, I think I'd look into trademarking that. "No? They did fund two librarians' tickets and travel to the Sci-Fi and Fantasy con. I'm not sure how this would be any different except that I'd be representing us as an award nominee and not just an attendee."

I may need to stay civil because Karter was my supervisor, but I wasn't about to let a slight like that go. I knew I was an excellent librarian, had, in fact, increased the amount of participation in teens since I'd started here, and had done an excellent job promoting literacy, in part, because I did promote popular fiction like romance. I deserved that nomination, dammit, and the library and its board should be proud of this recognition and not try to sweep it under the rug like old, repressed, fuddy-duddies.

I had another word I wanted to call people like Karter, but I was a professional librarian and thus, had an excellent vocabulary that was filled with lots of 'F' words that were appropriate for the workplace.

Karter busied himself with searching for something on his computer again. "I'll look into it."

"Great."

"The rest of the evaluation is all pretty standard, and you've rated highly in all categories of course. If you'll just take a look and then sign at the bottom, we'll get everything all finished and filed away."

Coward.

"Glad to hear it." I took a quick perusal, but I'd done enough of these to know pretty much exactly what my performance was. I signed quickly and handed him back the papers. "If we're all done, I've got some programming to work on before my desk duty starts."

"Just one last thing, I thought you might like to know that the library website went a bit bonkers with hits over the weekend, specifically the page that lists our staff. Your profile was clicked on four-hundred and ninety-two times, according to IT. Looks like your date I saw in the paper yesterday is bringing in some new patrons."

Funny how I had some heartburn coming on even though I hadn't eaten since breakfast, six hours ago. "Huh. That's... interesting."

I literally didn't know what else to say. Not sure where all my bravado just went. Here bravado, come here girl, bravado, where are you girl?

"I think I hear my phone ringing." I turned and scooted across the office space back to my desk as fast as I possibly could. The second I sat down, I popped open Google, grabbed a screenshot of my profile pic on the library's website and did a reverse image search.

Yep, sure the Thornminster Library page came up. But

so did four-thousand nine-hundred and seventy-two other results. Oh blurgh. I was going to throw up.

Some of the very few pictures I'd posted on FaceSpace were next. No wonder I was getting friend requests left and right. Then there was the picture of Chris and I in the paper, which had apparently been picked up by several celebrity gossip sites.

Good god, I was in the tabloids. The headlines weren't as bad as I thought they'd be. A few couldn't help but play to society's disdain for larger bodies, but I knew better than to care what stupid people thought. It was pretty damn clear though that at least two-thirds of the internet were shipping the two of us hard.

They couldn't see we were just friends, and that meant, crap, my mother would be too. Quickly, I grabbed my phone out of my bag and popped open the messenger app. Yep, there it was.

> Hi, sweetie, just a quick note from the airport. You should have said you and that nice Kingman boy were together! How exciting. Be sure to use lots of lube as I'm sure he's rather large. Sending you two a little something fun I found in Thailand. Talk again in a few weeks!

Oh no. Okay, first of all, the story had made it all the way to Thailand? And trying to explain what was going on to my mother in a text message wasn't going to work.

> Hey, Mom, let's Facetime when you have a chance. Say hi to Dad for me.

That was way too vague-booky, but I really didn't

want to say more that could be construed as something it wasn't. It was too easy to read tone in text that wasn't there. Sigh. If ever a needed a chat with my mom, it was right now. She would have been able to tell me to pull my head out of my ass, but in her power mom who knew how to help me in the best I-love-you way.

Just as I was ready to sign off, my texts dinged again. It was from Chris.

> You, me, Mountaineers baseball game tomorrow night. You in?

Was this our next fake date? A pro baseball game was way more public than the rooster rescue. But maybe that's what we needed. A venue where we couldn't just be our same old goofy selves, but not entirely in the spotlight either. Then we could practice being boyfriend and girl-friend better.

I texted back.

> I'm in. Have you seen the pics of us in the tabloids?

The three little dots that indicated he was typing popped up, disappeared, and popped back up again. Either he had a lot to say about those pics or didn't know what to say.

> Nope. I learned not to look a long time ago. Don't pay them any mind. I promise they have nothing to say that you or I care about.

And that's what I adored about him. So famous he

should be on a box of Wheaties and didn't seem to even notice that the entire world wanted to know who he was dating. Or in this case, not dating, but nobody needed to know that.

That's when the realization hit me right in the gut like an icy hot patch had been plastered to my intestines. The entire world thought we were together. What was going to happen after the reunion? Would we have to pretend to stay together? Or, worse, did we have to stage a breakup?

Why, oh why, did my life sound like the plot to a YA romance right now?

Probably because I'd acted like a teenager trying to prove herself in front of the Queen Bees. If I was really the confident, smart, young professional woman I thought I was, I'd own up to my mistake and either resign from the planning committee or, even better, make the event a success regardless of my dating status.

But Rachel was expecting to see my final plans for the fundraiser at our next meeting on Saturday and after the whirlwind of a weekend, I hadn't even started. All I knew was that we weren't doing a gross bachelor auction. But I knew one way to make sure this year's event was the best the school had ever seen.

I sent another text off to Chris.

> Could you and the boys donate something to the fundraiser for St. Ambrose? I'm thinking silent auction type stuff.

Because somewhere inside, I was still that teased and

bullied high school girl trying to show the mean girls she was worthy.

God dammit.

At work, bring it on. In the rest of my life? Not so much. I don't know why I couldn't be Librarian Wonder Woman all the time.

> We got you, boo. Whatever you need.

Boo, huh? He must be practicing his boyfriend text skills.

> Thanks, honey. Nope, that's yucky.
> Sweetie? Babe? Shnookums?

Dot dot dots again from Chris.

> Oops, gotta go, on desk. Will ask teens
> for better sweetheart names. lol

I put my phone away before I could see his reply to my weirdo awkwardness about this whole fake dating thing. Why couldn't I just be normal with him like when we were regular friends?

A KISS CAM KISS

CHRIS

*C*ould I have called in a favor and gotten us into a box at S'mores Field? Sure. I knew at least half a dozen Mountaineers. But I didn't. Because I had a plan. I called in a different kind of favor, and we needed to be sitting in just the right place for it to all come together.

We arrived a little bit late, on purpose. Less people would be filing in through the turn stiles and into the stands once the game started.

We made our way up to the middle deck to where I'd bought our seats, and Trixie looked around at the people still milling about. We weren't headed up to the more private box seats where celebrities and big shots usually sat. "Here? Are you sure?"

She knew the Kingman family usually stayed out of public places simply because we were constantly getting mobbed by fans. I loved my fans, but today wasn't an appearance.

Seats right in the middle of the crowd were not something I'd normally do, but with my Mountaineers baseball cap pulled down low and just a plain t-shirt and cargo shorts, I wasn't projecting sports star vibes. I hoped. It was risky, because if I was recognized, it would draw attention to us before I wanted it to.

I had a contingency plan for keeping over-excited Mustang fans at bay though. A plan called Declan, Everett, and Hayes. They had seats strategically placed around mine and would swoop in if necessary.

"Yeah, it'll be okay." I shrugged and pulled my hat down a bit. "Nobody knows we're here and it's not like the paparazzi are going to be lurking behind every corner waiting to take pictures of us."

After our last fake date, we needed someplace public so we didn't simply fall into old friend zone patterns. It was too easy for us to just act like we did with each other on a daily basis. This had to push us both to behave like we were together.

"Let's get snacks, yeah? Dogs? They have the vegan ones. You want a beer?" I pointed to the concessions stand that was on the way to our seats.

"Yep, hit me with the good stuff. But no onions, this is a fake date. Can't have spicy breath." She was teasing, but the fact that she could possibly be thinking about kissing me did a number on all things south of my belt.

So far, so good.

"Right, so no nachos with jalapeños either, huh?" She

didn't even eat cheese. Which I knew. Why did I suck so bad at flirting with her?

Because this was more than just hanging out. She might be on a fake date, but I wasn't. And I knew what was coming during the sixth inning. Fuck, were my palms sweaty?

No. Dammit. I was romancing her, she was having fun, we were going to have our first kiss. Stick to the plan, Kingman.

I grabbed the snacks and had to tip the guy working the register a hundred bucks with a shh-finger to my lips when his eyes got big, recognizing me. With my cap pulled a bit lower, beers and dogs in the handy-dandy carrier, I grabbed Trixie's hand to walk to our seats.

She gave me a surprised look and the sweetest blush flashed across her cheeks.

"We're practicing, babe." I squeezed her hand. "If you gave me that look at the reunion, we'd get busted for sure. Couples hold hands, so I'm gonna hold yours."

"Oh. Right. Yeah. Practice." She looked down at our hands and gave mine a soft squeeze. "I just... I don't think any guy has ever held my hand in public like this before."

What the hell kind of fuckboys had she been dating? I'd like to smash every one of them under my fucking balls. That probably wasn't going to happen, so instead I'd concentrate on being such a great boyfriend that she'd forget the rest of them had ever existed. Fuckers.

"Out in the open?" she asked, when I pulled her down the steps to the very front row of the deck.

We shimmied past a nice looking family with a couple of kids, who all very kindly stood so we could get past.

They were fully decked out in Mountaineers gear, so hopefully they weren't big Mustang fans. Which was not something I'd ever hoped for in my life.

"Trust me," I said, grinning back at her. "These are great seats. Most of the foul balls come this way, and we've got a good line of sight to the jumbo screen to see, uh, replays and, you know, the mascot's shenanigans."

"Did you just say shenanigans?" Trixie sat and took the snacks from me.

"I'll have you know I love all forms of shenanigans and participate in them as often as possible." It took a minute to get my ass into the chair. These plastic fold down seats were not made for professional athletes. Which meant they weren't made for lush hips and thick thighs like Trixie's either.

I glanced at said thighs, and yeah, they were pressed against the sides, but she put her feet up on the railing in front of us and didn't seem bothered. I'd be more aware of the seating for our next date. I didn't want her uncomfortable just because the world wasn't designed for bodies like hers or mine.

If my plans didn't hinge on us being exactly where we were sat, I'd make a quick call and get us into a box upstairs. Fuck. Maybe I should anyway. I'd figure out another way to—

Trixie poked me in the arm and laughed in such a joyful and teasing way. "You're a shenanigan."

OK, she was fine. We were fine. I was still gonna be more cognizant of the spaces I took her though. "Wanna know what else is a shenanigan?"

She giggled again, because this was a game we'd played with each other since we were kids. "Your face."

"No, your face." I chuckled and handed over her dog and beer. Out of the corner of my eye, I spotted my brothers lurking under the shade of the deck, trying to look inconspicuous. I shot them a quick nod, assuring them that everything was under control. So far.

When I turned back, I caught Trix taking a huge bite out of her hot dog and needed an instant distraction. Or a program to cover my lap. The guy selling peanuts was nearby and I flagged him down. I passed some cash down the line, and he passed the peanuts back. The mother of the family reached across the empty seat between us and gave me a little wink.

Uh oh. I pretended I didn't see that. Hopefully she was a co-conspirator and not going to out me. The whole stadium would know I was at the game soon enough. I just needed to make it a few more innings.

"Peanut?" I asked, holding the bag up to Trix.

Her mouth was still full of hot dog, but she nodded and made happy, yumming sounds at me. Fuck. It took all I had in me to drag my eyes away from her mouth. I deftly shelled a peanut and offered it to her. "A gentleman always provides his lady with only the best nuts."

She laughed and pressed her fingers to her mouth, holding in the food she hadn't yet swallowed. I was lucky I hadn't been sprayed with half-chewed hot dog. After she shook her head at me and swallowed... something I watched rapt, she took the snack from my fingers. "Is that so?"

Once again, I couldn't tear my eyes from her mouth as

she popped the nuts in. "Uh, yeah. Definitely. Absolutely. Call on me for all your nut needs."

I'd chastise myself for that truly awful line later, but I got caught up in how the stadium lights made her eyes sparkle and forgot about the peanuts, the game, and how this was a fake date. All I wanted to do was lean in and kiss her. I wanted to pull her into my arms and taste every last inch of her. I wanted all of her.

Not yet. I wasn't going to scare her away.

Touchdown Jesus, I was in so much trouble. I'd buried my feelings for her for so long, and now that I was this close to having her in my arms, I was losing all control. Keep it together, man. This is the long game plan. I wanted her forever, not just right now.

The next couple of innings flew by, partly because the Mountaineers' new pitcher was a ringer and we went three up, three down two innings in a row. Didn't make for an overly exciting game, but it did get us a whole hell of a lot closer to the sixth inning. And the kiss cam.

We cheered for the Mountaineers and booed the opposing team, we played along with the silly games the mascot and the stadium media team put on during the lulls in the action. And I counted down the innings. At the bottom of the fifth, Declan, Everett, and Hayes quietly slipped into their seats. They were dressed as inconspicuously as I was, and no one, including Trixie, noticed their arrival.

When the kiss cam started, Trixie was cheering on the couples on the screen just like the rest of the fans, completely unaware of what was about to happen.

"And look at them," she laughed and pointed to the

giant screen across from us. "They didn't see that coming. She was so cute and shy. I think we just watched their first kiss. Adorable."

I turned to Trixie, fairly sure my heart was going to go careening out of my chest with each next beat. "If we're going to be a convincing couple, we should probably practice... that too, don't you think?" I tried to keep my voice steady.

She looked up at me and blinked a few times, the most innocent of looks on her face, her brow furrowing, before realization dawned on her face. "Kissing?"

I put my arm on the back of her seat and dragged my teeth across my lower lip. I was staring at her mouth again and this time, I couldn't fucking help it. "Exactly."

Right on cue, the camera found us. "Well lookie here, folks, looks like we've got Denver's own Chris Kingman and his pretty lady in the stands. Think we can get them to lock lips on the kiss cam?"

Trixie's eyes went wide, and she looked out to where we were dead center focused on the big screen.

"Looks like we're up," I said, my voice calm but my heart racing.

My brothers erupted into cheers behind us, good-naturedly urging us to kiss for the camera. "Come on, QB, don't be shy."

"Show her how it's done," someone else who wasn't a Kingman chimed in.

I barely heard them. Was I aware 50,300 and some people were watching and cheering on my first kiss with Trixie? Yeah. But I was good at tuning out a stadium full of people. Trixie didn't like being in the spotlight and I hoped she wasn't about to murder me on camera.

Without the entire world watching us, would she ever let me kiss her though?

The way she was looking at me right now said I should have tried, because I think she would have said yes. Her smile was a mix of shock and delight as she leaned in closer to me, and I scrambled to turn my hat around so the brim wouldn't be in the way.

"I think you'd better kiss me, Chris Kingman." Her voice was breathy, and she licked her lips.

"Yeah, I think I have to." I really, really had to.

The first connection of our lips was hesitant, and I thought for a second this was just going to be a quick peck. If that's all she wanted, that's what we'd do. But then something shifted. Trixie closed her eyes and she leaned in.

I cupped her cheek and parted her lips with my tongue, deepening the kiss. It became something real and unexpected, and so perfect, I got lost in the moment with her. I was finally kissing Beatrix Moore and she was kissing me back.

She finally broke the kiss, and the stadium was a mix of cheers and good-natured jeers. Trixie was blushing, her eyes twinkled dark with desire and then went wide with surprise. She touched her lips and then smiled, but looked away in the most adorable shy way, that I couldn't take it.

I pulled her back and kissed her again. Putting every bit of longing I had into just one more spine-tingling moment with her.

When we pulled away the second time, the stadium

was filled with cheers, the people all around us, including my brothers, leading the applause.

"I didn't see that coming," she admitted, her voice a little breathless.

"The kiss or how good it was?" I hadn't meant to blurt that out. But my brain and my mouth were not coordinating at the moment. And man, did my cock want in on the decision making going forward.

"Yes," She whispered. The kiss cam had done its job, but it was clear that something real was happening between us.

The game started back up, and I figured we had about thirty seconds before every Mustangs fan on the middle deck swamped us. But being seen in public was on the game plan to show up her mean girl bullies, right? And my agent's PR team would be delighted and have this all over the internet.

I glanced at my brothers, who were grinning like idiots, their thumbs up in approval. Trixie followed my line of sight and spotted two of them just a few rows away.

"What are you guys doing here?" She quirked her head to the side and raised an eyebrow at them.

"Wouldn't miss the game for anything," Everett replied, a twinkle in his eye.

Hayes gave her a little salute. "We're your get away plan."

They both stood up and went to either end of the aisle, blocking them off like they were my offensive linemen.

"Shit. We gotta go, chickadee." There was already a stream of fans moving in. I spun my hat back around and slapped the paper peanut bag I'd surreptitiously signed a couple of innings ago and handed it to the mom sitting nearest us. "Thanks, ma'am. You all have a good day."

They stood and let us pass by again, this time, the dad staring up at me slack jawed. I gave him a little nod and hauled ass up the steps, Trixie in tow. Declan stood at the top of the stairs, completely blocking anyone from even looking at us with his big growly presence. Never in my life was I happier that he was a grumpy bastard than right now.

"I owe you one, man." I slapped him on the back and pulled Trixie toward the elevator. Less chance of getting mobbed in there than on the next set of steps down to the ground level. Because we were mid inning and mid game, the elevator popped open right away and I pushed the button to close the doors at least twelve hundred times.

"You planned this, didn't you?" Trixie slugged me in the arm, but she didn't look mad.

Visions of me pushing her up against the back of the elevator and kissing her again, pulling her up to wrap her arms around my waist, and doing a whole lot more in this moment of privacy flitted through my mind. "Yeah. I thought we needed a little incentive to—"

"Practice kissing?" She touched her lips as if remembering mine in exactly that same place.

If the door to the elevator hadn't opened right that second, I would have practiced kissing her again, then and there.

RIDE OR DIE

TRIXIE

I insisted on blasting Taylor Swift the entire car ride home and singing along just so I could avoid talking about that kiss. Because whenever anxiety hit me in the head, heart, or anywhere else... like say my lips, the cure was always my girl, Tay. I kept the playlist to the upbeat songs, because I didn't need a love song making this whole situation more confusing.

We'd shared a lot of rides before, and plenty of playlists to sing along to too, but none that came after a kiss.

A kiss that had been preceded by hand holding, snack flirting, and a protective detail so I didn't have to deal with paparazzi-style fans and photos again. All seemingly carefully planned out by my now fake boyfriend.

That seemed like a lot of work for a fake date and a little bit of practice pretending to be a couple.

"Thanks for the, uh, practice date," I said a bit too loudly, seeing as the music came to an abrupt halt as I disconnected the aux cord and climbed out of his car.

"Right," Chris replied, and I could feel his gaze stick to me like invisible gobs of double-sided tape and school glue.

I fumbled with my keys, dropped them on the driveway, and about plowed into Chris, who'd somehow The-Flashed himself to my side while I was bent over to grab them.

"Let me be a gentleman and walk you to your door." He shut the car door, put a hand on my back, and it was a good thing too, because my knees were all wobbly. Probably from all those stairs at the ballpark and totally not because his hand was in that spot at the base of my spine that sent tingles up and down my legs and into my belly.

At the front door, I apparently forgot which key out of the three on my keychain unlocked the door, because I got it wrong, twice. Not because I was keenly aware of how close he stood, or the way he filled up the doorframe with all those muscles that were so clearly defined through his t-shirt, or the way he smelled like baseball, fresh air, and man. A manly man's man. The kind of man who could—

Oh god. What was wrong with me? This was Chris, my neighbor, my friend, my fake boyfriend. Who'd given me a fake kiss. Fake. We were faking. F. A. K... I could still taste him on my lips. What was I saying?

I looked up from the keys that must not be mine and had to tilt my head back just a bit to meet his eyes. He was leaning against the doorframe, his arm up all casual and sexy like, waiting for me to open the door so he could pin me against it and...

Gulp.

His eyes met mine, and the world held its breath. Was he going to kiss me? Again? My thoughts swirled, a sharknado of doubt and longing. Was I reading too much into this? Did he feel it too—the electric something that snapped, crackled, and popped between us? Or was he just practicing some more?

His eyes flicked down to my lips, which I accidentally parted and maybe I licked them. His eyes went all sparkly and dark and he leaned in closer "Trixie, I—"

My pants buzzed with the excitement of whatever he was about to say, and again because he really was going to kiss me again. Buzz buzz, buzz buzz. Oh shit. That wasn't me or my pants. That was my phone. I shoved my hand in my pocket to make it stop and epically failed.

"Beatrix? Hello? Is your camera broken? Why is it so dark? Beatrix?" My mom's voice sounded from the depths, and I had to fish the phone out.

"Saved by the international call," Chris said, breaking into a smile and taking a step back.

"Saved," I echoed, bringing the screen up so my mother wasn't left in the dark. Umm, saved from what exactly?

"Hello, darling. How's my favorite daughter?" My mom's cheerful voice was almost too loud, practically bursting through the phone from half a world away.

"Hey, Mom. Say hi, Chris."

"Hello, Mrs. Moore." Chris waved when I turned the screen and his voice tinged with amusement.

"Christopher, so good to see you," Mom said, clearly delighted.

"We're actually standing at my front door," I told her, avoiding Chris's eyes for fear of what I might read there.

"Well, I won't keep you two. I can call back tomorrow. Turns out the retreat here in Nepal is quite modern and we've got Wi-Fi."

"No, it's fine," I rushed to say. "Chris was just dropping me off. We went to a Mountaineers game."

I caught the subtle raise of his eyebrows, but he took it in stride. "Yeah, gotta run, Mrs. Moore. Nice to hear from you."

As soon as I heard his car pull away, I let out a breath I absolutely knew I was holding. Holding so I wouldn't blurt out that I wanted him to come inside, or that I was supremely confused, or cock-a-doodle doo for goodness' sake. I finally got my key in the door, stepped inside, and shut it behind me, leaning against it like it could support the weight of the confusion settling in my mind.

"So," Mom started in a vastly different tone than thirty seconds ago. "Chris Kingman, on your front porch. Your heart's been ride-or-die for that boy for a long time, honey."

"Mom, don't make it weird."

"Who's making it weird? I'm just stating the facts and opening up the door for the conversation you clearly are looking to have. We talk about feelings in this family, even if it's from seven thousand miles away."

I groaned. "I know. I just, I don't know what I'm feeling."

I kicked off my Converse and padded through the

house to the back door. I needed to check on the chickens, and maybe see if any of them wanted to cuddle. Luke was usually up for an evening snuggle before they all bedded down. Especially if it came with treats. I grabbed a container of cut strawberries from the fridge along the way. I could use a sweet treat myself.

Mom chuckled. "I can tell. So what's going on with you and Chris? It sounded like I interrupted something."

I hesitated, then spilled. "We kissed. At the game. He got the kiss cam to point right at us, it was supposed to be fake, but it was impulsive and thrilling, and I don't know."

Crapballs. I knew it the second it came out of my mouth. My mother would glom on to the fake kiss part and dig into it like an archeological find of the heart.

"A kiss is a powerful thing, sweetheart. Sometimes it's just a kiss, but other times it's the start of something more. Did it feel fake?"

Wait a minute? Who was this person I was talking to on the other side of the world and what had she done with my mother who'd ground into me to always be open and truthful with my feelings and my dealings? Faking it was not in her vocabulary.

"You're not going to grill me on the fake part?" I opened the gate around the coop and the girls came clucking out into the yard. Luke was perched on the top of the coop just staring at me.

"You were going to tell me anyway."

Dammit. She was right. It was a simple question, but the answer was anything but. "No, it didn't feel fake. And that's what's confusing. Exciting? Weird? Awkward, but also, not at all. See? Confusing."

Mom hummed knowingly. "Ah, a confusing kiss. Classic symptom of having feelings you're not quite ready to acknowledge for the one you're kissing."

Me? Feelings for Chris? I'd never allowed myself to consider a thing like that. He was my friend and I liked having him in that safe space in my heart. Anything else might ruin it. Ruin everything. "It just feels strange. He's supposed to be my fake boyfriend for the reunion, but the way he's acting doesn't feel fake. None of it."

"Ahh, I should have known this had something to do with the Queen Bees." A million and twelve times I'd heard my mother lament that I chose to go to her alma mater instead of the public school the rest of the kids in the neighborhood went to. Especially when I was getting bullied. But my mama didn't raise no quitter who ran away from a body shaming fight. "You already fought those battles, Beatrix. Why don't you just skip the reunion and explore this budding relationship with Chris?"

"Lulu dragged me onto the committee and now they're counting on me. I'm in charge of the fundraiser." What I didn't say was the part where I worried that this really was still just faking it, practice, whatever, and that the kiss wasn't real.

Wouldn't be the first time that had happened to me.

But no. No, no, and no. I didn't want it to be real. I wanted it to be fake. Needed it to be.

"You need to ask yourself what you really want, sweetheart. Only when I got a bit selfish and started taking care of my own wants and needs did I start to embrace the true authentic life I was meant to have. And the greatest sex too."

This was not the first time I'd heard this story or this advice from my mother.

"Yeah," I sighed. "I need to figure that out."

"And until then, maybe have some alone time with yourself to explore your feelings about Chris."

I laughed because she did not mean time alone with my thoughts. She meant masturbating. An orgasm a day keeps the blues away. "Noted, Mom."

Oh no. Oh. Now I was imagining doing all the fun and pleasurable things I normally did to myself in my bedroom alone, with a partner. A certain very muscled, charming, neighbor who had just kissed me and made my insides turn to jelly.

Crap.

"Okay, darling. Let me know how it goes, with Chris, not the reunion. Those Queen Bees can suck it as far as I'm concerned, and I'd be happy to know you told them so."

"I know you would." But I wasn't going to say anything to them about my mother. I'd never blame her, but her former profession had caused me plenty of problems in high school and beyond. I'd found it best not to mention her until someone was in my inner circle.

Although somehow so many guys I'd dated, or rather tried dating, over the years always seemed to know.

"We're off to the first session of the retreat. I'll post all about it on Insta later. Wish us luck."

"I don't think you and Dad need luck, Mom." Not in either the love or the great sex department. I could use a little of that kind of luck right now though.

"Love you, kiddo."

"Love you too, Mom."

Just as I was about to corral the chickens back into the coop and maybe go inside and find one of those toys from around the world my mother had sent me, my text notifications went crazy. Like bananas bonkers. At this rate, I could use my phone as a vibrator.

Glancing at the screen, my stomach plummeted. Notifications from social media were rolling in like a tide. I didn't even want to look, because I knew it had to be pics from the game today. Chris had warned me on the way home that there would likely be a few and not to let them bother me.

They bothered me.

I clicked. I shouldn't have, but I clicked. Someone... ugh, several someones, including Rachel, had tagged me in the comments of a snapshot of our appearance on the kiss cam at the ballgame.

The caption read *"Mustangs hottie QB Chris Kingman looks like he's off the market, ladies!"* followed by a whole row of crying face emojis. I also had about a gazillion more followers too. I doubted a whole bunch of people suddenly were interested in my YA book recommendations.

My stomach switched places with my heart. That moment was supposed to be private, a break in the armor I so carefully maintained. And here it was, shared with the world, open for interpretation, and worse, for judgment.

But Chris had said this was the best way to establish our relationship, very publicly. No one was going to question whether he was with me after seeing this. Including

Rachel, Amanda, and Lacey. He was using his fame to help me, and I couldn't be mad about that.

Just then, an email notification popped up, cutting through my spiraling thoughts. From Rachel, the head of the reunion committee and a master at thinly veiled insults.

"Urgent: Auction Complications."

My eyes narrowed as I read the email. According to Rachel, several auction items had "mysteriously disappeared" from the inventory at the school's gymnasium, including the signed jerseys Chris and his brothers had donated. "I don't know how this happened under your watch," her message read, "but you need to find a solution ASAP. This fundraiser better be the best St. Ambrose has ever seen, Bee. If you can't make it happen, I will."

Yeah, she'd spelled my name wrong on purpose. I eyerolled that so hard, I about gave myself an aneurysm.

It was sabotage, plain and simple. But as much as I wanted to call her out, I knew it wouldn't solve the immediate problem. And there was no way I was letting Rachel ruin this.

My phone buzzed again—this time, it was a text from Chris.

Hey, just saw the photos hit. You turned off your notifications like I told you to, right?

Okay, okay. Breathe. It wasn't like I had to see any of these people in real life. I was in a fake relationship with a major Denver celebrity, and while I hadn't really thought it would blow up like this, I wasn't going to freak out that something that should have been a sweet and private moment was now splashed all over the internet for the entire world to see and comment on.

I put my head between my knees, closed my eyes and took several long, deep breaths. A gentle caw-caw and the soft feathers of Luke's head tickled my cheeks and I reached for him. Sure, sure, chickens weren't meant for snuggles, but Luke was not a normal chicken.

Another message, this one from Lulu, buzzed.

> DO NOT LOOK AT THE COMMENTS.
> REPEAT - STAY OUT OF THE
> COMMENTS SECTION ON THAT POST.
> BITCHES BE BIG MAD ITS YOU AND
> NOT THEM.

Oh geez. It had to be really bad if Lulu was text yelling at me. My morbid curiosity really wanted to look, but my sense of self-preservation won out and I deleted Insta from my phone without delay. And FaceSpace, and Flip-Flop, and that weird one that the space-car guy bought and ruined. I never checked most of those that often anyway. I would miss the chicken memes though.

My phone buzzed again with a follow up from Lu.

> Also... you KISSED Chris?! I want all the
> details on Monday.

Another message from Chris.

> You okay? I'm coming over. I promise to
> murder anyone who says anything even
> remotely unkind about you on the internet.

That made me smile for some dumb reason. I typed out a quick reply.

> You know I don't condone murder. But feel free to block them all so they cry more tears that you're my...

I almost typed that he was my boyfriend. Delete delete delete.

> —that they don't get to see your sexy ass in their feeds anymore.

There, that was better. And, umm, a little flirty? Better follow that up before he decides to come over for more than my mental health.

> No need to come over. It's no big deal, I'm not even paying attention. But Rachel is.

I'd barely hit send before his reply came back.

> Do I need to kill and-or block her?

Yes.

In a split second, my anxiety about the auction, Rachel and the Queen Bees, and even the other mean girls on the internet melted into an odd sense of clarity. Maybe, it was the universe's way of showing me that Chris was someone I really could count on. Because before I even asked, I knew he would say yes. He would be there for me, just like he'd been all this time.

Was I scared that our relationship might change? Yep.

Double yep, with a cherry on top. But did I think I'd lose him from my life?

No. Well, mostly no.

For the first time, I didn't shy away from the thought that we could be more than friends. Instead, I welcomed it.

> lol - no. But I could use your help with something tomorrow. Remember that charity auction?

BBQS AND BALLERS

CHRIS

*T*rixie was fidgeting, and it was cute as fuck. Not that I wanted her to be nervous, but she was different with me today, and I had to believe it was because she was developing feelings for me. We'd just pulled into the big circular driveway at Manniway's, and she was stalling getting out of the car.

I'd happily stall by making out in my car before we went into the barbecue. On the drive over, I'd caught her peeking up at me through her lashes more than a few times, and I'd bet my champions ring that she'd been staring at my lips.

She was thinking about that kiss.

I'd only thought about it eleventy-billion times. Which is about how many times I'd come in my own fucking hand last night reliving every second of kissing her. Her lips were so damn soft and delicious, and I wanted to kiss her again and again until she forgot about anyone else who'd ever touched her lips before.

And I was not allowing myself to think about all the other things I wanted to do to and with those lips because excusing myself to go jack-off in the bathroom so I didn't have a hard-on in front of all my teammates and their families today was not an option.

"You're sure you want to bring me to this for our, you know... practice? Isn't this a just the team thing?" She tugged at the hem of the number seven jersey I'd given her to wear today. There was something so incredibly hot about seeing her wearing my name and my number that I couldn't risk seeing her in anyone else's jersey today.

"It's team and family, babe. You absolutely belong here with me." No more pussyfooting around what I said to her. Today was about taking our fake relationship to the real level. I took her hand, pulled her out of the car, and guided her to the back yard of Manniway's sprawling estate tucked up against the foothills. That's what sixteen seasons and two championships got you.

While I absolutely expected to not only play as long as he had, I was also going to win more bowl games. Was I cock sure about that? Yep, cockier than Luke Skycocker. But I'd keep my house tucked away in my neighborhood in Thornminster. I liked having my family surrounding me. Like a good offensive line.

Even with everything that had gone public about me dating a local girl, no one, not reporters, not photographers, not even a fan or two, had come knocking on my door or Trixie's. My company's security detail made sure of that.

"Are there other people who are going to see us together?" People I wanted to introduce her to. Girlfriends and wives I hoped she could make friends with. "Yeah, sure, but this isn't public, and there won't be anybody taking our picture and selling it to the tabloids. You can relax and have fun with me today."

The Denver Mustangs' pre-season barbecue before training camp started was an annual tradition hosted by Manniway for the last ten years. Because that's when he'd married Marie and she'd made his life fucking baller. I'd heard the tales of pizza and beer before the team headed to training camp. This barbecue was a hell of a lot better.

I looked forward to this every year, because it signaled the start to a new season. It was like my New Years. I set intentions for the season, checked in with the teammates I hadn't seen in the off season, and took one last minute to relax and refresh before my whole life became football once again.

But today's barbecue was different. This one wasn't about me and my team. My intentions for this year included one more particularly important factor in my life. Something that was on the verge of make it or break it.

Trixie.

This was my last shot to win her heart before the reunion. I wasn't going to be able to spend as much time with her this week. She had work and I had to do that car commercial in L.A.

Today's fake date was my Hail Mary play to be able to show up at the fundraiser, the dance, and her class picnic as her real boyfriend, not her fake one. No fucking way I was headed to training camp in two weeks without knowing she was my girl. Or not.

The more I thought about this whole fake relationship, the more I hated the idea. She was mine. Not in the gross 'I own her way,' but at a soul deep level. If this wooing her, trying to get her to fall in love with me too didn't work... nope that wasn't the winning attitude and I refused to let myself even think it.

I was setting the intention and making it happen. Trixie belonged with me, and I belonged with her. End of story, happy ever after.

We walked hand in hand, our fingers laced together almost naturally now. The back yard was already filled, with the grill sizzling, balls being tossed around, and a gaggle of kids were splashing in the pool. Trixie looked around with wide eyes, taking in the families, the players, and their wives and girlfriends.

"You good?" I asked.

"Yeah, just preparing myself for the inevitable questions of why you're here with me, you know?" She smiled, her eyes meeting mine. It felt different, warmer, flirtier.

Before I could dwell on it, Johnston approached, clapping me on the back. "Chris, my man. And you must be the infamous local girl."

Trixie's smile widened, and she shook his hand. "Hi, yeah, that's me, Trixie, local girl extraordinaire. Nice to meet you, Mr. Manniway. Chris speaks highly of you."

Manniway grabbed his chest as if wounded. "Trixie, Trixie, you're killing me. Please, Mr.? Call me Johnston or we can't be friends. Let me introduce you to Marie."

Manniway waved his wife over. It wasn't like Trix

didn't know who these people were, but she'd never been introduced. I couldn't believe I hadn't ever done this with her before. She'd been to team events with me, but nothing this inner circle.

Marie immediately wrapped Trixie into a big bear hug. "Forgive me, I should have checked to see if you were a hugger first, I'm just so excited he brought you. Christopher, nice to see you again, I'm stealing your girlfriend a little later to introduce her to the other cowgirls. Mostly because you've done a shit job of telling me you even had a girlfriend and I want all the details."

Marie's and Manniway's attention was immediately drawn away by some kind of hot dog emergency and that left Trixie giving me an oh-shit-what-did-you-get-me-into look. I bent down and brushed my lips over her ear and whispered, "Just tell her the truth. That we've been friends for years, but that I've had a crush on you all that time and finally got up the nerve to do something about it."

I didn't give her a chance to respond to that, and instead dragged her through the yard to the safety zone of Everett, Hayes, and a couple of our other teammates gathered around the giant barrel of ice filled with drinks. She wouldn't question what I'd just admitted to her in front of them. I hoped. "Come on, let's get a drink and you can meet some of the other guys."

As I introduced her to my teammates and she saw that no one was going to grill us on our relationship, Trixie's fidgeting calmed down and her regular playfulness came out again. She leaned close and whispered, "Your teammates have cute butts. Do you think they do special workouts?"

I chuckled. Was she actually flirting with me? "Are you trying to make me jealous?"

She looked over at me with wide, innocent, who-me eyes. She was fucking flirting. Hells to the yeah. I loved when a game plan came together.

"I'd love to show you the secret Mustang butt workout later." I meant to make that sound playful, but my voice had come out a little too husky to be anything besides the invitation I truly meant.

Her cheeks flushed, and she stared up at me with a sparkle in her eyes that had me wanting this barbecue over so I could take her home right now. She swallowed and then pulled one side of her bottom lip between her teeth and smiled at me like she was imagining my ass and what she'd like to do to it.

Fuck. Time to go. Right the hell now.

Even if I had to pick her up and throw her over my shoulder cave man style, I was taking her home and doing all the dirtiest most delicious things to her that she'd let me. As long as she would look at me the way she was right now, I'd get on my knees and worship her for the rest of my fucking life.

"Deal," she said so quietly, it was for me and me alone. And so was that cheeky grin.

"Trixie," Marie's voice broke in through the tension between the two of us, as did her body. She wrapped an arm around Trixie, claiming her from me. "I want to introduce you to some of the cowgirls."

Marie looked between the two of us and pressed her

lips together in a suppressed smile. "Oops. I think I just interrupted something, but you two will have to wait. We have pressing cowgirl business. Why don't you help Johnston with the horrible blobs of cow he's trying to make edible, Christopher?"

I stood there like a muppet as Marie dragged my woman away. Shit. I did want Trix to meet the other wives and girlfriends, the gang Marie referred to as the cowgirls, but fuck... did she have some horrible cock blocking timing.

I watched as the women welcomed Trixie instantly, pulling her into their circle like she had always been a part of it. One of the women said, "We're so glad you're here. Chris has needed someone to keep him on his toes."

They had no idea.

I looked over at Trixie, catching her eye. For a moment, it was just the two of us, even in the crowd. She smiled at me, that sparkle in her eyes still there for me.

Everett stepped up to my side and pushed a beer into my hand. Since it looked like we were going to be here for a while, I accepted it and took a long swig, needing the frosty drink to cool me down. "You just got fucking cock blocked by Marie, didn't you?"

"Fuck yeah, I did." That was twice in as many days that I'd missed the opportunity to have Trixie in my arms. I wasn't letting it happen again.

"So, looks like your plans to win her over are going well." He shrugged and took a swig of his beer and stared out over the pool like he was looking into the universe.

It did seem that my plan was working. But was she just

having fun while I was putting my heart on the line? Tonight would tell.

"Did I just hear a wistful tone there, Ev? You looking to find a girl for more than one night?"

"Dude. Shut up."

That wasn't a no. Hmm. I gave him a side eye, but he continued to stare anywhere but at me. Instead he avoided the subject all together. "Where's Deck?"

I'd beat the story out of him later. "Grumping around over by the grill. You need to make him your next project and get him a girl."

"I can get him laid, which would probably help his attitude, but he's not interested in settling down. That's just you."

Was it?

Did I want to settle down with Trixie? Yeah the fuck I did. I wanted what Manniway had with Marie. I wanted what my parents had. I was really the only one of us kids who was old enough to see and remember how they were together before she died. They loved each other so damn hard, and if she would let me, I'd love Trixie that way too.

"Man, you gotta quit eye fucking her. This is a family event. There are kids here." Everett tapped his beer against mine. "I know you're trying to woo her and all, but make your move already. Take her home, straight up tell her how bad you have it for her, and bury your face between her thighs."

He was the one who'd told me to take it slow in the first place.

"And if she's just really good at faking that she's into me? I made her practice pretending we were together.

She's a fast learner." He was right though. I had every intention on straight up telling Trixie tonight. I couldn't keep up this fake shit anymore. Didn't mean I didn't have my concerns. I assessed situations and made snap decisions for a living.

And if I thought Trixie wasn't ready to hear how I felt about her, I'd make the call not to say anything. Yet. "If she is faking it, then I won't have just blown my shot. I'll have wrecked her reunion for her."

"You're the one who said she's worth the risk." Everett shook his head at me. I hated when little brothers got all upstarty and smart.

"She is." I'd already admitted to her that I'd had a crush on her for years. Whether she believed me or not, I didn't know. She'd know later.

"Then what the fuck are you waiting for?"

Nothing. Except someplace with some privacy so that when I told her how I felt, I could show her too. All night long.

COWGIRLS RIDE

TRIXIE

*W*hen Marie stole me away from Chris, I both felt like I needed a chance to take a breath, and also wanted to stomp my feet right back to him and... what? Kiss him right here in front of everyone? No. One super public kiss was enough until I actually worked through these squidgy feelings I was having. I wasn't ready to go jump his bones, even if the flutters happening all up and down my spine said I was.

She introduced me to the women, but there was no way I was going to remember even half their names, because my head was still on the other side of the yard staring into Chris's eyes and having a swoony moment.

Marie cleared her throat, and I realized I was staring at him and not paying attention to her. Every eye in the circle turned on me. A woman, whose name was maybe

Kelli, waggled her eyebrows. "Girl, we bow down to you for landing yourself a hot Kingman."

Oh. Ha. That was not what I expected the wife or girl-friend of one of the other players to say. I was almost always on guard in a new group of people, but these ladies weren't reserved or restrained. I loved it.

And at least half of the women were big girls like me. That was surprising and unusual for fitness fanatic Denver. I full well knew that the average American woman was a size sixteen, and that size didn't equal athletic ability or health, but it felt like most of Colorado didn't get the memo.

But these women, they were everything my mother had taught me to be. None of them were holding them-selves back, which, more than anything, made me feel comfortable. Sometime in the last few weeks, basically since I'd had to confront Rachel and the Queen Bees again, I'd reverted to those old insecurities I'd thought I'd packed away a long time ago.

It helped seeing other confident, curvy women out in the world and reminded me who I was.

The woman sitting next to Kelli, whose name I had no clue of, smiled so big I could see all her teeth. "You have to tell me if he's as well hung as we've heard."

She was clearly teasing, but so many of them looked at me and I could see they actually wanted an answer. I took a long, long sip from my bottle of water. They waited. They. Waited. I swallowed and carefully set the bottle down, all nonchalant like. "Oh, we, haven't…"

"Are you kidding me?" Another woman, maybe named Elisha, basically squealed. "With the way you two were just looking at each other, I thought for a minute there he was going to haul you upstairs right now."

I mean, I don't think Chris and I had gotten that crazy making eyes at each other. Besides, he was just faking it, because we weren't really together. I needed to remind myself of that. Here I was catching feelings for him, and he was just being fun and flirty.

Right?

"Don't get me wrong, I love my husband," another woman whose name I didn't know said and put her hand over her heart, "but I would drop him like a bad habit to be a fluffernutter cream filling in a Kingman sandwich."

The ladies all erupted it into squeals and giggles. They were clearly all super comfortable in each other's company, and every worry I'd had on the car ride over here of feeling intimidated was gone like Donkey Kong. I sort of felt like part of the cool kids' crowd. And that hadn't ever happened to me in my life.

Fluffernutter woman gave me a wink and what could I do but nod my head in agreement? The Kingman boys were hot. There was no two ways about it. Although, I couldn't actually imagine being with more than one. That one in particular who'd kissed me yesterday. In front of the known universe.

"Since Chris is now attached and off-limits, the women of Denver will be crying themselves to sleep," Marie said sagely.

All the ladies nodded and hummed their agreement. I wouldn't be a little surprised if a few of them shed some tears into their pillows later. Elisha pursed her lips and raised a finger. "Until of course, they decide to make Declan or Everett their new most eligible bachelor."

Kelli scoffed. "What about Hayes?"

Fluffernutter—gah, I really needed a refresher on names—I think it was actually Fern, shook her head and rolled her eyes. "Girl, he's like twelve years old."

Not that I thought it mattered, but that was a little too much of an exaggeration. Besides, Hayes was a cutie patootie and deserved to be lusted after just as much as his brothers. Which was a really weird thing for me to think right now. "I'm pretty sure he's twenty."

"He's like that kid from that musical high school movie." Kelli glanced over to where the boys were standing together having a beer, and then lowered her voice all conspiratorially. "Adorable, sure. But in a few years, he's going to be so fine that the shes, theys, and gays around the world are going to be in love with him. I wanna set him up with my niece."

"Okay, okay, that's enough lusting over the Kingmans." Marie looked at me, took my hands in hers, and said, "Now, Trixie, how serious is this thing between you and Chris? Like, are we saving you a seat in the box at the games? Or is this a summer fling?"

Gulp. My mouth was suddenly very, very dry and I wanted to reach for my bottle of water again. I could be confident, cool Trixie, until we had to talk about my fake relationship with the man I may or may not be newly crushing on.

Was it new? Yes. Right? No. Gah. I was confused and was going to fuck this all up, wasn't I?

"Ooh, Marie going in for the kill from the get-go," Kelli said and gave a little snap-snap of her fingers.

"I'm a little protective of the boys." Marie sat a little straighter and looked a couple of the ladies dead in the eye. But not once did she let go of my hands. I wasn't getting out of this, and the right answer was not forthcoming. She turned that killer gaze back on me. "And I don't want to see anybody's heart broken. I'm all for some fun times, but that boy is in love with you, and I wanna know if you're in love with him too."

"Geez, Marie," big toothy smile lady said and fanned herself. "Initiation by fire."

"She did the same thing to me," Elisha offered.

Another woman nodded and said, "And me."

At least four more women, maybe five, raised their hands and nodded too.

I wasn't prepared to examine the weird feelings I was doing my best to pretend didn't exist. If I couldn't handle these questions from women who clearly liked me and who I felt more comfortable with than ninety-nine percent of my graduating class, I wouldn't have a chance at the reunion. Chris was right, we did need to practice. More than just kissing. I chose my next words really carefully. "He and I have been really good friends for a long time."

"And he just asked you out, like, all of a sudden?" Elisha asked. She leaned in closer too, and I got the impression Marie wasn't the only woman who felt protective of Chris. "What changed?"

Chris had said tell them the truth. So that's what I was gonna do. Well, most of it anyway. "Actually, I asked him."

To be my fake boyfriend. And that had turned into something more. Something confusing.

"Girl, you have some steel ovaries." Fluffernutter, I mean Fern, shook her head at me. "I've never asked a man out in my life. And someone you're long-time friends with? Mmm-mmm. I'd be all kinds of afraid to ruin a friendship. I didn't even like Derek when he asked me out."

I almost threw my hands up and declared that I'd worried about that exact thing. In fact, I was already worried that I'd changed our friendship as it was, and that put a kibosh on the idea of exploring these feelings, and Chris's lips.

"Wait, was this before the restaurant opening the other night?" Marie asked, squinting her eyes like she was recalling that night.

The truth. "No, we really did go to that as just friends."

"But that's where you realized you had feelings for him, right?" Elisha asked. "Because we all saw that picture in the paper."

What was the universe seeing in that picture that I wasn't? "I just asked him if he would go to my high school reunion as my date."

Marie's squint got infinitely squintier. Like she was reading between the lines, and I didn't want her to see what was there. Or what wasn't. "So you just wanted to show off to your high school pals?"

Crap. Kind of. Which made me a giant asshole, didn't it? I guess I already knew that. But then this whole pretend dating thing had gone, so... different than I expected.

"Umm, if I'm totally honest, a little bit." I made a regret-smile and shrunk down a little. "I swear I'm not normally that girl. Don't hate me."

"I see you." Kelli put her hand on my arm. "You had bullies in high school you want to show up, huh?"

Wait, how did she know that?

"Yeah, your face tells all, sister." She laughed, but it wasn't an entirely humored kind of thing. There was some bitterness there too. "I get it. I was chunky in high school, and that shit's traumatic. Kids are dicks to each other. It took me a long time and seeing myself through my husband's eyes and the way he loved me to face some of those demons. I get it."

Almost every other woman there nodded and ruefully smiled at me in solidarity.

I put my face in my hands and shook my head back and forth. "They are the worst, and I am on the reunion committee with them."

Lulu was the only other person that ever understood any of this, and to a certain extent, my mother. I definitely never expected a group of women I'd never met before to see me the way my best female friend did. I'd always been the kind of person that just had one or two close friends. But maybe I had been missing out by not trying to find myself more a part of a community of women.

Marie's squinty glare had lessened, but she still wasn't ready to let this go. Even though I was the one going through the AITA gauntlet, I had to be happy that Chris had someone like this looking out for him. She clearly grilled all the women the players brought around. "Does

Chris know about these bullies, and why you asked him to go?"

"Absolutely, one-hundred percent." I nodded vigorously. That was the truest thing about this whole relationship, besides the being friends for a long time part.

Marie gave one simple dip of her chin and that seemed to be her stamp of approval. She clapped both her hands down on her legs and said, "Well, then, that settles that. So then I think you should take the mustang by the horn, so to speak, and ride him like a cowgirl."

"Marie!" Several of the girls all squealed at the same time.

But several more practically battle cried out "Ride 'em, cowgirl."

Marie simply shrugged and smiled at me. "We don't call ourselves the cowgirls for nothing."

Oh my god. I got it now. Because cowgirls ride mustangs.

Chris came back over with several of the other players in tow, all of them with plates of food. He had a little bit of a frown on his face, and if I was reading it right, he was worried about me. Either that, or he'd overheard too much of my conversation with the girls.

"Hey, chickadee. I brought you some food." He handed me a plate loaded with things I liked to eat. Although, those portobello mushroom kabobs were burned all to hell. Johnston must have been on grill duty.

"Oh my god, why are you two so adorable?" Fern said. "If you start feeding each other right now, I might throw up from cuteness overload."

I picked up a carrot from the plate, swirled it in a little

bit of ranch, and held it up to Chris's mouth. He grinned and grabbed my hand, pulling it even closer, put the whole carrot and the tips of my fingers into his mouth. And sucked.

And my ovaries exploded. Was I pregnant now? I think so.

Someone nearby made retching sounds. But I didn't see who, because I couldn't look away from Chris's lips on my fingers.

I also couldn't ignore the tingles low in my belly. Every instinct I had said that this wasn't for show, that he was flirting with me and being seductive for real.

But my instincts hadn't served me well in past relationships, and it was hard to trust them.

Marie coughed and said "cowgirl" and coughed again.

Maybe I didn't trust my own instincts, but my mother and Marie and every other woman at this barbecue seemed to think Chris had real feelings for me. So maybe I could trust their instincts instead of mine.

No one, especially a man I knew hated lying, play acted that well. Chris Kingman wanted to do naughty things to me with his tongue. I had no doubt of that whatsoever. And I wanted him to.

But there was one more complication.

For the first time in my life, I didn't doubt that a man wanted me for me, and not because I was the daughter of a porn star. The fact that every man I'd ever considered being intimate with before had turned out to be a disgusting sleaze had ruined any chance I'd ever had at having sex. After the last guy, who I had to break up with because he literally called me by my mother's name when he'd seen my breasts really messed with my head, I'd given up trying.

That had been college. Four years ago. Before I moved back to Thornminster and back to my old house, in my old neighborhood, to start a new career. Before Chris Kingman had come back into my life.

I may have been raised to understand that virgin and whore were social constructs that were outdated and had little bearing on my self-worth. But not everyone had a former porn star turned sex positive educator for a mother.

Would it even matter to Chris that I didn't have any experience? I had a feeling I was going to find out later. Even my worries that I might lose him as a friend if we took this step weren't enough to stop me from taking this chance with him.

I wasn't going to be chicken, and that meant, hopefully by tomorrow morning, Luke Skycocker would be the last virgin standing.

AND THEN SHE KISSED ME

CHRIS

*I*t's funny how a few days changed my whole damn life. A week ago, I was still pining after the girl next door, and now I was leaning against that same door, staring down into the eyes of the girl I had loved for far too long to have never told her.

She looked up at me, only the streetlight, the little bulb on her porch, and the moon providing the lighting that had her looking so gorgeous. I felt like a fucking teenager again, wanting so badly to kiss her and waiting for her to say it was okay.

"This feels a little like deja vu. Weren't we doing this same thing last night?" Her voice came out as a wistful sound, barely more than a whisper.

Tonight's warm air felt different, the evening around us was charged, the sexual tension between us palpable. It was as if the universe had turned up the volume on the song of us, each note reverberating in the space between Trixie and me.

Her phone buzzed in her bag, but she ignored it, even dropped it to the wooden slats below. We were both lost in each other's eyes, neither wanted to break our gaze.

"Yeah, we were. But we were interrupted before I could do this." I put my hands flat on the door, either side of her head, and lowered my lips to hers. A millimeter from kissing her, I felt her tiny gasp. I whispered against her mouth, "Tell me you want this, Trixie. Say you want me to kiss you."

My head and heart and stomach and cock were about to riot, demanding I take what belonged to me. But without her enthusiastic consent, her need for me too, I didn't want it.

I'd lusted after this woman for so long, but even more than her body, I wanted her heart. I needed her to want me back.

"I want you to kiss me." Her breath warmed my lips, her words, my heart.

"Even if it's a hundred percent real? No more faking?" No more pretending. This was either real, or it wasn't going to happen. "Tell me you want that too."

"I... don't know. What if it's not fake, and—" Her breaths were shallow and mine matched, waiting for her to tell me to back off. Just like she had ten years ago.

That should have been my cue to back off. But I couldn't. Not this time. Either my play was completed, or I lost the game, right here, right now.

A beat of silence stretched between us, both of us teetering on the edge of something big, something life altering. Her eyes flicked down to my lips, just for a moment, but it was enough to send every nerve in my body into a frenzy.

Screw it. I'd been holding back for far too long, burying my feelings under the guise of friendship and fake dates. But there was nothing fake about how my heart raced when she smiled, or how my thoughts kept drifting to her when I should have been preparing for training camp. I had mere weeks with her before I had to leave.

I searched for the right words but found none that seemed worthy of the moment. So, I went with the truth. "Trix, I want you. Not as a friend. I have for a long time. And these 'fake' dates we've been having? They've been incredibly real to me."

Her eyes widened, her lips parting slightly as if to speak, but no words came out.

"I don't want to presume anything about how you feel," I continued. "But I can't keep pretending that I'm okay with being just friends."

Her eyes searched my face as if trying to decipher the truth behind my words. I prepared myself for rejection, willing myself not to recoil... but instead, she stood up on her tiptoes, raised her hands from where they'd been pressed against the door at her hips, and cupped them around my neck.

I sucked in a sharp breath at her sudden touch and stared into eyes that were so full of emotion, but also what I hoped was lust and need. I never wanted to look away. This gorgeous, amazing woman had become such a part of me, I didn't know how to breathe without her on my mind, in my heart.

"Then let's not be just friends anymore," she whispered softly before she pressed her lips against mine.

Trixie Moore kissed me.

Trixie. Kissed. Me.

My brain fucking exploded and sent a shockwave right past my heart and straight to my cock. There was nothing else in the world now except her lips, her mouth, her tongue, and my absolute and utter need for her. I leaned in, pushing her body against the door, and took her face in my hands. My blood pounded, whooshing through my ears, dimming the sounds of the night to only the sweetest little whimper she made when I kissed her back.

This time, there was nothing fake about it.

She molded her body to mine, our mouths and tongues crashing together. I kissed her not as if it was our first kiss, but like it could be the last time she'd ever let me this close. I'd waited so long to have her in my arms, and I was not letting go until she made me.

I couldn't get enough of her and groaned with the frustration of this being so much more than I ever hoped for and still needing increasingly more from her. She wrapped her leg around the back of mine as if she could pull me closer to her, but our bodies were already mashed together. I dropped one hand from her hair and wrapped my arm under her thigh, bringing her leg up to wrap around my hip.

That opened her up to me, and dammit, if it wasn't for our jeans in the way, I'd fuck her right here against the door. The erection I'd been trying to hide from her for weeks, or rather years, was bulging against my fly, and I ground my hips against her, practically ready to dry hump her for a little relief.

The air around us grew hotter and Trixie finally pulled away, breathing heavily, while still holding onto me with an iron grip that matched the desire in her eyes, so dark, like midnight.

"We should take this inside," she said softly into my lips. "This should be just between us, and not the whole neighborhood."

She dipped down and grabbed her bag, slid her key out, and turned to unlock the door. A move which put her plump, soft ass right up against my dick. I bent and kissed her neck and wrapped my arm around her waist, sneaking my thumb under her shirt and pushing it up to touch her bare skin.

"You're making it hard to concentrate, and I may never get the door unlocked if you don't—" her words shuddered and she fumbled the key when I gave her neck a little bite and ground my cock against her ass.

"If you don't get that door open, I'm going to shove your jeans down and take you right up against the door, babe." I would too. My body would shield hers and I'd punch that tiny light she had right the fuck out so it was nice and dark.

"You're distracting me too much. Either help me get the door open or just kick it down for goodness' sake." Her key scraped right across the wood and missed the lock entirely. I grabbed her hand and brought the key to the lock and helped her push it in. Together, we turned the handle and tumbled inside. That was fine. I had no problem fucking her right here on the floor.

Between more kisses, she flung her hand toward the open entryway. "Shut the door. Knowing my luck, a raccoon or something will wander in and want to watch."

I caught the door with my foot and kicked it shut. Now we were all alone.

"Rrr-rrr-rrr-rrr-rrrh," Luke Skycocker crowed from the top of the couch. Then he flapped his wings and flew right at my head.

"Luke, no," Trixie squealed.

All my years of combat with this bird were about to come to fruition. I snagged Luke out of the air and rolled, tucking him under my arm like I'd just gotten the game winning touchdown pass. "Sorry, buddy, but you're not cock blocking me. She's my girl tonight."

Luke squawked and wriggled, obviously mad I'd thwarted his plans to dive bomb my face and scare me away from Trixie. He definitely thought she was his. I scrambled to my feet, pointed at Trix with my free hand and said, "Don't you move, unless it's to take off all your clothes while I put him in his coop."

Trixie huffed out a laugh and rolled her eyes, but she also had an adorable grin on her face, heat to her cheeks, and well-kissed, plumped lips. Yeah, I wasn't leaving her side for long.

I sprinted to her back door, thought about shoving Luke out the doggie door, but had a feeling he'd come right back in. He was a jealous guy when it came to Trixie. I could relate. I wasn't having any of his ruffled feathers in my way tonight.

I plopped him into the little fenced-in area and made sure the gate was latched tight. I grabbed a handful of chicken treats from the box next to the coop and tossed a handful in to him. He gave me another little weird rooster cluck, and I'm fairly sure he was side eyeing me and telling me off.

When I turned back toward the house, I saw that Trixie hadn't followed my order not to move. She was propped up against the door and the light from the kitchen illuminated her like a god damned curvy angel. It was a good thing I was in peak shape, because my heart was taking a beating tonight and working overtime.

I jogged back to the house, grabbed Trixie up into my arms like my own personal princess, and this time, I kicked the door shut behind me.

"Chris, what are you doing? Put me down, you can't pick me up like this." She wrapped her arms around my neck, but also looked down at the floor like I was going to drop her or something.

"The hell I can't. Not only am I going to pick you up, I'm going to carry you upstairs to bed."

Trixie smacked me on the shoulder. "Christopher Bridger Kingman, I know I'm a big girl, and you are going to hurt yourself trying to carry me up those stairs."

I liked that she didn't deny we were going up to her bedroom, only the fact that I had the ability to carry her there. Just to prove the point, I took the stairs up two at a time. "Sweetheart, I am a highly trained athlete and it's the fucking off season. What the hell else do I have all these muscles for than to haul my girl, lush body and all, to bed?"

A sweet, slightly surprised smile turned her face into something that once again made me think she'd never been with a man who'd made her feel special. "Your girl, huh?"

I shouldered my way into her room and over to the big, lush bed covered in about a thousand too many pillows. "Yes, you're mine, and I've waited a long time for you. So be a good girl and kiss me again like you know you belong with me."

If I thought Trixie had blushed before, it was nothing like the crimson that lit up her cheeks this time. Her mouth made a cute little oh, and then she bit her lip and looked down and to the side as if she could hide her reaction from me.

My sweet librarian next door liked being called a good girl. I was definitely down for some praise kink. I just about tripped over the bed wondering what other kinks she might have.

I laid her down on the bed, crawled over her, and grabbed her hands, sweeping them up and pinning them over her head. Her breath whooshed out, just the tiniest bit shaky. Yep, my girl was dirty in all the best ways, and we were going to have so much fun in bed.

Not that I expected anything else. Everything about being with Trixie was a good time. From the way she laughed to the way she kissed.

She bit her lip again and that was something I couldn't resist. I took the other side of her bottom lip between my teeth and pulled it into my mouth, giving her a little nip, which made her do a sexy as hell whimper-groan. She had me so hard already that I was going to be lucky to last more than a minute inside of her.

And that meant I had to make sure I got her off at least two or three times before I even let her touch me. I kissed along her jaw and found a spot behind her ear that made her shiver. "Tell me what you like, Trixie. How you want me to touch you, what you want me to do to you to make you feel good."

She grinned up at me, but there was something else in her gaze that I couldn't quite identify. "I'm quite sure anything we do is going to be great. But you should know..."

There was insecurity in her voice that I wasn't used to hearing from her. I wanted to make sure she knew how much I wanted her, but also that this wasn't just fucking around for me. "There's time for us to get to know everything, babe. I'm not going anywhere. I don't only want you now, tonight, I want a whole lot more."

Her lips parted but froze in a half gasp, and she hesitated, her words caught in the surprise of my declaration, held hostage in her throat by her tangled feelings. Her hands, which usually animated her thoughts so freely, were still clasped in mine over her head, and her fingers danced, wanting to clench, but she didn't fight against my hold on her.

For a split second, her eyes darted away, scattering her thoughts, and I could almost see her trying to collect them from the far corners of the room. But then she locked onto my gaze again, her eyes not just meeting mine but clinging, as if she found something there she didn't want to let go of.

When her mouth finally opened to respond, she arched into me ever so subtly. She was stepping over some invisible line inside her, crossing from what she'd always thought would be into what could be. With me.

Instead of words, she pressed her lips to mine again and squirmed out of my hold, reaching for my shirt and yanking it up and over my head. Oh, hells to the yeah. I went straight for the button on her jeans, and together we got them down her hips. She lifted her ass, and I tugged them all the way off.

"Are... are those roosters on your panties?"

She propped herself up on her elbows and looked down and laughed. "Yeah. And the back says cock blocked."

I threw her jeans over my shoulder with the intention of rolling her over to see. But something behind me crashed. Trixie's eyes went wide and I turned to see what the hell I'd broken. Some kind of laundry hamper had fallen off a small stand inside her closet and the contents were now scattered across the floor.

The debris wasn't her dirty laundry. But it was dirty though. Dirtier than I ever would have imagined for my sweet, nerdy, curvy girl.

There were at least a hundred very interesting sex toys, including dildos, vibrators, and a few things that I couldn't identify.

Trixie jumped off the bed and dashed toward the mess, diving for the nearest toy like she was going to clean them up. "Oh god. Pretend you didn't see any of this."

I basically tackled her, gently taking her to the floor and wrenching the already buzzing vibrator shaped like a tentacle right out of her hand. She squeaked and tried to cover her face and she snort laughed and turned every shade of red.

I grabbed that hand away from her eyes and brought the toy down between her legs. "Later, you're going to tell me why you have a whole menagerie of sex toys, but first, I'm going to make you come with at least a dozen or more of them."

TENTACLE PORN

TRIXIE

*T*his was my own damn fault, but I also wasn't even a little bit sorry. I certainly never expected to have a literal quarterback throw my jeans into my closet and knock over the secret stash of sex toys my loving, but weirdo mother had sent me over the last four years.

Chris had probably already figured out where most of these had come from. He knew my mother and her body and sex positive platform. He also knew that she and my dad traveled the world. I hope to god that he didn't care that was why he had a vibrating, Japanese tentacle-porn sex toy in his hand and was making his way down my body with it.

Because I was not going to bring up my mother right now. Especially since he was the first man to touch me like this who hadn't even mentioned her once.

"You're a little too excited about that tentacle." The grin on his face was far too entertained to just be about getting in my pants.

"I know a good wingman when I see one. Good squid-man? Either way, I can't wait to see your eyes roll back in your head when I make you come the first time."

"First time? How many times do you think—oh god, oh, oh god." He pressed that tentacle monster right to my clit, and even with my underpants as a barrier, my eyes were already rolling back in my head.

"Yeah, the first time." He stroked the vibrator up and down, teasing me with it. "And it's going to be through your panties, since they're cock blocking me."

At this point, I was so turned on that I had no doubt he could make me come with my panties on. But that's not what either of us really wanted.

I bit down on my lip, trying to control myself before finally taking the initiative and tugging at the waistband of my panties with one hand while Chris still had his other hand pressed against me with the toy.

I shifted around on the floor beneath him, and I slowly began slipping one side of the underpants down my belly and hips, then the other side. I was not a thong kind of girl, but you'd have thought I was wearing fancy lingerie with the way he watched eagerly as I slowly started to pull them off.

When I couldn't move them down any further due to the vibrator pulsing against the fabric, he set the toy aside and leaned down, pressing a kiss to my belly button, then the lower part of my rounded stomach, before he grabbed the panties with both hands and pulled them all the way down my legs.

I was revealing a part of me no man but him had seen in a long time. Not since college, when my new boyfriend Tate had tried to get in my panties and failed epically.

Chris's eyes met mine and he winked as he grabbed hold of another toy from the pile. This one was a little less kitschy, and more, umm, useful. The hot pink, rabbit-style vibrator was from Italy, and the base was decorated with Swarovski crystals. But despite its fancy appearance, when he turned it on, the buzzing promised to be more powerful than the last one.

"Do you use these when you masturbate, Trix?" His voice had gone dark and husky and that sent more tingles through me than the damn toy.

I shook my head. "No. I have a normal vibrator that doesn't have all these bells and whistles."

He traced over each of my thighs with the pulsing bunny head and then lifted both my hands over my head while keeping full eye contact. Way, way too slowly, he moved the toy closer to my pussy, still not yet touching me where I needed him. "Later, you're going to show me exactly how you use that one."

"And what are you going to be doing when I'm playing with my toy?" I'd found a little bit more confidence, mostly spurred on by the way he was so visibly needy for me, but still hadn't even taken off his own pants. This wasn't just about him wanting to get off.

Never in all my adult life had anyone asked if they could pleasure me with what felt like pure love and affection instead of intensely trying to just get off—or worse yet because they wanted to see what a porn star's daughter was like in bed. ·

"I'm going to be fisting my cock just like I do when I imagine you touching yourself. But this time I want to watch when you come, Trixie. I've fantasized about what you looked like when you're coming so many times, and I need to see it for myself."

He'd imagined me having an orgasm. That sent my imagination into overdrive, because if he'd been imagining me coming, what had he been doing? I knew the answer to that, but I was still surprised. How had I not known?

Because I hadn't wanted to. Since the day I moved back here after college, Chris has been my friend, my safe space, and hadn't once made me feel like... the porn star's daughter who was nothing more than a sex object. And after my last break up, I needed that.

Here he was, making me feel sexy and like I mattered and was wanted. I didn't think he would even care that I had extraordinarily little experience or about that stupid virgin label. Because this wasn't about anyone or anything else in the world except for the two of us finding out that maybe we did belong together.

"You're not going to get to see anything if you don't touch me soon." I gave him what I hoped was a dirty smirk. I didn't want to get all up in my head, but just foreplay with Chris was so incredibly different than any other sexual experience I'd ever had.

And I liked it.

I assumed he'd do something to flirt back, but instead he bent to me and took my mouth in another one of his soul deep kisses. I tugged at my hands, still held in one of his, wanting to wrap my arms around his neck again. He held me tight and licked my bottom lip, then pushed his tongue into my mouth. At the same time, he slid the toy between my legs and found the exact right spot, putting my clit directly between those vibrating bunny ears.

I moaned into the kiss and tipped my hips up, instinct pushing me to get closer. The way he slid his tongue across mine, mimicking the slide of the toy across my clit, was going to have me coming way too soon. We were just getting started. Maybe he was going to get those touted multiple orgasms out of me.

Chris broke the kiss and stared down at me and he pushed me closer and closer. "God, you're fucking sexier than in my wettest dreams. Now be a good girl and come for me, because I want you dripping when I taste your wet cunt."

I clenched my fists, wanting to grab at anything, but he wouldn't let me, and it surprised me that I loved this lack of control I had. I was the one responsible for my own orgasms my whole life. Never once had anyone else even come close to getting me off. But here on the floor, with Chris taking charge, taking control, I was having one of the most erotic moments of my life.

And I was about to come. In under a freaking minute.

"Oh god. I'm..." I shivered and gasped, not even able to finish my sentence.

"That's it, babe, let me see you come for me." It wasn't just his words, or the way he knew exactly what to do with my body, but the needy, husky tone in his voice that pushed me over the edge. He needed my pleasure.

My body clenched hard, and the orgasm rocked through me, quite literally taking my breath away. I bucked against the toy, needing more and feeling like it was too much at the same time. "Chris, yes, god, yes."

He kissed me again and dropped the toy, using his fingers to stroke through my wet folds, drawing every bit of the orgasm out of me. "That was so much fucking better than I even imagined, babe."

Yeah. It was.

Like... I knew how to give myself an orgasm. But Chris was a god damned master.

And I wanted to tell him that. I wanted to tell him that he was the first man to ever do that for me. And I would, just as soon as I could breathe again.

Except he dropped down and buried his face between my thighs, and I forgot about anything but his mouth licking his way around and around my clit. And the sounds he was making? If they were any indication, I wasn't the only one getting mind-blowing pleasure from this.

And the manufacturers of the toys that said they emulate tongue action are lying liars from liarsville, because nothing came even close to Chris's tongue. That rose toy with the flickity-flicking petals? Going in the trash. The real thing was god damned magical.

I didn't know if he wanted me to keep my hands where he'd left them above my head, but there was no way I was keeping them to myself. I pushed my fingers into his hair and held on tight. He popped his head up and licked his lips as if he'd been having the best snack of his life.

"You're fucking delicious, and I'm going to be spending a lot of time with my face between your legs."

"Like I'm going to," I gasped, getting cut off mid-sentence because he slid a finger inside of me and gave it a little swirl, "say 'no thank you' to that." I'm not even sure how I got those words out of my mouth.

"Mmm. I'd rather hear a 'yes, please' from you." He dipped his head back down and sucked on my clit as he pushed a second finger inside and wiggled his fingers against my inner walls, finding my g-spot, and maybe my h, i, and j-spots too.

Yes, please I could do. "Yes, yes, god yes, please."

My pleas turned into full on whimpers, and then I basically lost the ability to make sound at all. This time, it built up slower, but so much deeper. I could literally feel my pussy fluttering around his fingers and my clit pulsing, pulsing, the pressure growing as he pushed me into yet another earth-shattering orgasm.

Once I could breathe again, I just floated in a spacey afterglow. Somewhere in a galaxy far, far away, Chris came up over my body and hovered there. I didn't have the strength or the will to open my eyes yet.

"You're gorgeous when you come, sweetheart, but I like this blissed-out look you've got just as well." He brushed his lips across mine and lingered, giving me a taste of myself that had my senses waking back up.

I wrapped my arms around his neck and took my time exploring his mouth and what I tasted like to him. He moaned and in a second flat, he was up, with me in his arms, and moving us toward the bed. My eyes fluttered open, but all I could do was smile like a fool.

In just a few hours and a couple of orgasms, I was a fool for Chris Kingman.

That was more than the oxytocin talking. I knew it was easy to get really intense feelings from a sexual encounter. I was raised understanding how my body and mind worked, especially when it came to sex. But I'd never actually experienced any of it for myself.

I wasn't about to kid myself and say that I was totally in love with Chris, but the feelings I had for him right now? These weren't feelings of friendship.

I was falling for my best friend.

GOYKATTDLAGG

CHRIS

*S*eeing Trixie come apart for me was the best fucking thing I'd ever seen in my life. Every inch of her was so fucking gorgeous, and even though she was clearly nervous, she still had this delicious underlying confidence that I couldn't get enough of.

The way she leaned into my touch and came like she'd been turned on for ten years and just needed my touch to push her over the edge, had me close to coming in my jeans like a teenage boy seeing his first tits in real life.

And now I had her under me, and while I wanted to take my time and savor every moment, I knew once I was inside of her the first time, I wasn't going to last. That meant I needed to make sure she was close to coming again before I got my cock inside of her.

She already had this soft, hazy look on her face, and I

couldn't help but give her another long, languid kiss as I pushed her thighs open with my knee. God, I would never get tired of kissing her. Those little whimpers she let out and the way she tasted, matching my every attempt to control her mouth with her own need for me.

We'd been in such a hurry to play with her insanely extensive toy collection, that we weren't even fully undressed. I hadn't even gotten to see her big, full tits yet. I planned to spend a long time worshipping them. I'd had one too many fantasies about fucking them. I shoved the hem up and was this close to just ripping it open. "Take your shirt off, sweetheart. I'm dying to see how sensitive your nipples are."

She got the shirt over her head and her bra followed. It was simple and plain, and thank fuck, wasn't covered in roosters. I snagged it while it was still over her arms to pin her to the bed. I got that same flush as before, and later I was going through the rest of that hamper to see if she had handcuffs or some other kind of restraints, because she definitely liked losing a little of her control to me.

For a minute, I got completely lost staring at the tight little nipples and the soft mounds of her breasts, just waiting to be teased and tasted, and...

"Hello? Christopher? They're just boobs." She gave a small laugh, which made said boobs jiggle, and I forgot everything else I'd been thinking.

"These are not just boobs, babe. These are the tits I've imagined fucking, and I think my brain is glitching seeing them in real life for the first time."

She swayed side to side just to tease me and laughed again when the movement made me moan.

"If I didn't want to be inside of you so badly right now, I'd suck on your nipples and fuck these tits."

"Hard to do any of that with your jeans on." She jerked her chin toward my legs. "Not fair that I'm naked and you aren't."

I leaned in and braced over her nipples. "We make sure you're close again before I get my cock out."

And then I did what I'd been thinking about for the last ten years. I wrapped one elastic strap of her bra around the finial on her headboard and secured the other around her wrists. Then I grabbed a pillow, propped it under her back so she had to arch for me, and started teasing both of those sensitive points with my tongue as if they were soft little berries meant just for me to eat up.

Trixie arched and whimpered into every touch and suckle, moans coming faster each time as I alternated between sucking on them, pulling them gently between two fingers, and going back with my tongue again. Then I did the exact same thing between her legs, sucking on her clit, twisting it between my fingers, and going back again with my tongue.

I so wanted to be that guy that could just give his girl a dozen orgasms and then fuck her like a fucking porn star, but with every touch, I was losing my own god damned control. The more she moaned and whimpered, the harder I was getting. I was already dry humping the fucking mattress as it was, and the only thing saving me was that I wasn't naked.

If I had been, I'd be inside of her, coming already.

I wanted this night to be the one that she'd remember for the rest of our lives.

One more quick tease and then I'd crawl back over her and fuck us both into oblivion. I dragged my tongue over her clit and, whoo boy, my girl was a live wire. She cried out my name and her knees clenched around my head as she came apart again.

Well, damn. I couldn't help but laugh. And cry a little that I wasn't going to get to fuck her yet, but I loved how she came apart from me over and over and over.

I popped my head back up and stared up at her. She was panting, eyes closed, with a full-on look of bliss on her face. That was almost as satisfying. Almost.

I crawled up her body, dropping little kisses to all her curves and soft spots along the way, until I made it to my very favorite curve of hers. The curve of her smile.

This time I just gave her a soft kiss, gentle, to help her come back to me from that little nirvana she was floating in. I undid the makeshift ties holding her arms over her head and kissed the inside of her elbow.

She peeked one eye open and her smile got even brighter. "Is it my turn to touch you, make you feel this good?"

"Babe, I promise, fucking you will definitely feel good."

She sat up and gave me the sweetest kiss, stroking her hand down my cheek. But her other hand went to the button on my jeans. I helped her unbuckle them, and then quickly stood to shuck them. She hopped off the bed at the same time and gave me the cutest little shove, trying to make me sit or maybe lie on the bed for her.

I didn't move at first, because, what, like she was going to tackle me? But she gave me a smirk and a one eyebrow raise that did me in. If she'd look at me like that wearing some kind of naughty librarian outfit, I'd be a goner.

Once I was sat at the edge of the bed where she wanted me, she leaned forward, putting her hands on my shoulders and her lips to my ear. "But I want to hear you call me your good girl again while you fuck my mouth."

How the hell had I gotten so lucky to get a woman like Trixie? I reached up and cupped her chin in my hand, kissed her hard, and gave her what she wanted, because we were both going to enjoy it. "Then get on your knees and take this dick like a good girl."

Her eyes went dark and she hissed in a breath. Yeah, my girl definitely had some kinks that I was more than willing to have some fun with.

She dropped to her knees and put her hands on my thighs. For a minute she just stared at my cock, and I didn't know whether she was sizing me up like a tasty treat or was worried. I wasn't the biggest guy in the locker room, but I was larger than the average, umm, mustang.

I fisted my cock in one hand and pushed the other into her hair. I was going to say whatever she wanted to take was fine by me, or something, but then she dipped her head and took my head between her lips, and for the hundredth time tonight, I forgot my own fucking name. "Jesus, fuck, Trixie. Your mouth is so god damned hot."

I wasn't going to last long at all, which was a crying shame, because the way she was swirling her tongue around, exploring every fucking centimeter of my cock, was fucking amazing. I fisted her hair and guided her head up and down. She groaned, and the vibrations sent me so close I had to grit my teeth and take several harsh deep breaths to keep from coming.

She looked up at me through those gorgeous lashes, and I had to pull her off my dick or come without delay. I bent forward and kissed her swollen lips, then whispered against her mouth, "You are so fucking good at this, baby."

Did she blush from that? She was sucking my dick and a little bit of praise had her blushing? God, the innocence of her mixed with the pure eroticism of having her on her knees for me was damn near perfect. I gripped her hair tighter and growled into her ear. "I want you to touch yourself while you suck my cock. Make us both come, sweetheart."

She nodded and her eyes darted to the side. That hilarious tentacle vibrator was within reach, and looking at it now, it wasn't a fucking dildo. It was meant for her to grind her pussy on. I snagged a pillow from behind me and dropped it between us. "Put that thing on this and let me hear how good it makes you feel while you suck my dick."

She pushed the little button, straddled the pillow, and slid the toy underneath her. Her eyes fluttered shut for a moment and I grabbed her face between my hands. "That's it, baby, ride that thing, and when you're close, come put your mouth on me again, because I've been this close to coming since I first touched you, and I'm not gonna last long in your hot mouth."

She nodded and bit her lip, swiveling her hips.

"Look at me while you play with your toy, Trix. I want

to watch you get yourself off." I tipped her face up so she was forced to look directly into my eyes. Her pupils were blown, her eyes so dark I think I could see into her soul. She was so beautiful, and I was so god damned in love with her.

This wasn't the sex talking.

I was so fucking in love with Beatrix Moore.

Getting to finally touch her, taste her, claim her body, was just the cherry on top. She was the ice cream, the chocolate, and the sprinkles, and I would never get enough of her.

I wanted to tell her, wanted to shout out how much I loved her. But I didn't want her to think it was something said in the heat of this moment.

Tomorrow, when we were wrapped up in each other's arms, cozy, warm, and well sated, that's when I would tell her I love her. I had for so long.

Her sweet little gasps turned into full-on pants, and after three orgasms, I recognized the signs now. "You're close again, aren't you, baby?"

She nodded. "Yes, ooh, yes. God, I've never come this many times before."

Hell yeah. "I'm gonna want at least a couple more out of you tonight. Now come here and put that pretty mouth on my cock again."

She continued to rock her hips and it matched the up and down movement of her head. My balls were already tightening up, and I was going to come so hard. "That's it, take my dick deep. I'm gonna come down your throat."

Her body shook and she lost her rhythm as she came,

and fuck if I could hold back for another second. "Fuck, Trixie, fuck. That's my girl, fuck. I lo—"

I almost yelled that I loved her as I came into her hot wet mouth. But I clenched my teeth and groaned out my release. My whole body tingled, and I couldn't stop from thrusting just a little bit deeper, feeling her throat working to swallow every drop I was giving her.

When I didn't have anything left, I pulled out, and she practically collapsed onto the floor. I'd be worried except she started giggling her ass off. I crawled down there next to her and wrapped her in my arms.

"You doing all right there, chickadee?"

She waved her hand around, not communicating very well at all, giggled a little more, but snuggled into me. "Sorry, I think this is a reaction from too much oxytocin, serotonin, and dopamine, from all the orgasms."

"You're fucking adorable. Anyone else would have just said it was from great sex."

She was quiet for a moment, and then another giggle popped out. "I'm overly sex educated."

"I think tonight you're over sexed. Come on, giggly. Let's get you cleaned up and into bed. Where, if you give me just a little while, I'll fuck you nice and slow later."

"Mmm. That sounds just as fun." She didn't move from my arms, and so I once again picked her up, but this time carried her to the bathroom where we went straight into her nice, big walk-in shower. "Oh, geez, you really don't have to carry me everywhere."

"I don't have to, I want to, I love to." I love you. The words were on the tip of my tongue, but I didn't say them. Instead I slid her down my body and turned on the water.

She was basically a noodle woman at this point, and I soaped us both up quickly, and we were back out of there before the water even got hot.

She had nice big, fluffy towels, and I wrapped her up in one, grabbed one that I swung quickly around my waist, and led her back to the bed. She practically collapsed into the billion pillows, and I threw a couple of them off so I could wrap my body around hers.

I didn't need more pillows because her whole body was like one big soft pillow, and I could so easily fall asleep holding her right now. I yawned and let the contented satisfaction of having her in my arms wash through me. "We'll just take a little nap. I think you maybe sucked the life out of me back there."

"Oh." She yawned too, and I loved the sleepy sound of her voice. She was well satisfied, and I'd done that to her. "I didn't, umm, suck too hard, did I?"

Her words were already fading into sleep.

I dipped my face to her neck and gave her a dozen little kisses. "No, you were a very good girl and sucked me all too well."

"Good. Because I haven't ever done that before." Her voice was so soft, I almost didn't hear her.

What? Like... what? "You mean you've never gotten off while sucking somebody's dick?"

Her answer was the cutest little snore. I closed my eyes too. I'd ask her about what she'd said when I woke her up later. And I was definitely not waiting more than a few hours to have her under me moaning my name again.

Except the next thing I knew, Luke fucking Skycocker

was crowing and sunshine was streaming in through the open window.

Trixie jerked awake, looked at me like I was a serial killer in her bed, fumbled around for her glasses, and looked behind me. "Oh shitbuckets. I didn't set the alarm last night. I'm late for work."

She flew out of the bed, smothering me in the covers. By the time I found my way back out, she already had her bra on and was pulling on her panties and trying to put a dress on at the same time.

"I'd help, but I might just get in your way."

She got the dress on, ran over to me, gave me a fucking hot kiss, and then ran for the bathroom. I heard the sink turn on, the fastest teeth brushing in the west, and when she came out, her hair was up in a cute ponytail. "I'm so sorry. I wish we could snuggle and have breakfast, and do... some other things, and talk, but I'm on opening duty and the library is supposed to open in, oh god, fifteen minutes."

"Do what you gotta do, babe. I'll see you when you get off work. Then I'll get you off some more."

She grinned at me, kissed me one more time before she flew out the door, and I heard her race down the stairs and slam the front door.

Jesus, she'd gone from dead asleep to out the door in less than five minutes. Here I was, still in her bed. Which I liked. I'd stay awhile. Maybe jack-off thinking of everything we'd done last night.

My jeans buzzed from the floor, and I reluctantly rolled out of bed and grabbed them. There was a message from Trixie asking me to feed Luke and the girls. And another one from Everett.

You might want to close the windows the next time you fuck your new girlfriend's brains out.

MONSTER ROMANCE?

TRIXIE

*I*t took all I had in me not to call Lulu the moment I had a free second at work. But this convo was NSFW, and I didn't need somebody reporting me for having inappropriate conversations in the teen section of the library. But I played out what I was going to say to her about a hundred and seventeen times in my mind before lunch.

In zero of those scenarios was I calm, collected, or cool about it. In fact, maybe I was having a heart attack? No matter how many times I wiped it away, a bead of sweat kept forming at my hairline right near my temple.

I had sex with Chris. Well, oral sex. With Chris. Sex. With. Chris.

"Ms. Moore, are you doing okay? We can come back later if you're not feeling well." A mom wearing a shirt that said *The book was better* and her teenage daughter were standing at my desk. How long had they been there?

"Oh, I'm fine." I pulled myself together and put professional Trixie in the game. "Not enough kick in my coffee this morning. How can I help?"

"We have an appointment with you to work on Zenia's college applications."

"Right, good. Let's see what we can do." This was the perfect distraction. If I hadn't become a librarian, I might have become a guidance counselor. I loved helping teens pick out schools and do their essays. My favorite was once they got in and we perused the class list, making strategies for what they'd take and when.

"Where are you applying, Zen?" Four years ago, when I'd first gotten the teen librarian position at the North branch of the Thornminster Library system, Zenia had hated reading and was failing a lot of her classes. She'd thought she was dumb, and that broke my heart. But her Freshmen English teacher, Mrs. O'Hare, had figured out that Zen was dyslexic and had done something about it when no one else had.

I loved Mrs. O'Hare. She spent about as much time perusing the YA section as a lot of my teen patrons, and we talked books and which ones would be great for her different students all the time. Plus, by night she was a romance writer. But that was a secret and I'd never tell. As long as she kept writing and telling me all the hot goss going on in Romancelandia.

I was such a dork for gossipy stuff. As long as it wasn't about me. I wanted to know a hundred and ten percent of the drama but didn't want to be involved in any of it. I'd just be over here, drinking my tea.

Zenia smiled like I'd asked her which kind of ice cream she wanted. "I want to go to Denver Sex. I know it's a big one, and it's hard to get in."

"Wait, where?" A big, hard... oh lord, what was wrong with me?

Zenia's face fell a little bit, and I kicked myself for making her doubt. "Denver State? I'm taking two AP classes this year, so I think I have a shot. You don't?"

I put my hand on hers and gave her my most sincere smile. "You have a great shot, Zen. My brain literally misheard what you said, and it took me a minute to process. Sorry about that."

"What did you hear?" She gave me too-knowing side eye.

Teenagers couldn't tell when you'd recently gotten laid, could they? "Never mind. Now, let's look through the requirements and figure out what you want to write your essay about."

"Oh, I know what I want to write." She glanced up at her mother who gave her a smile and a nod. "About how books and reading saved my life."

Oh my god. I was going to cry. I had to blink a couple of times to make sure nothing leaked out of my eyes. "That's awesome. I'm sure the admissions people will love it."

With her grades, she was a shoo-in anyway. I could hardly wait to tell Mrs. O'Hare what Zenia said.

Zenia's mother added to my emerging emotional outburst by saying, "You and Mrs. O'Hare and the library changed both of us. I didn't do great in school, and I wanted better for Zenny, but had no idea how to help her. But now, we buddy read books, and I have a whole Book-Flop following."

"Yeah, but she only talks about her spicy books on there." Zenia rolled her eyes, but it was easy to see she thought it was cool but could never admit to it as a card-carrying member of the teenage girl club.

This. This was why I loved what I did.

We spent the next forty-five minutes going through the application, and I promised Zenia I would proofread her essay when she was done. I also promised to lend her mother the latest Molly O. book, of which I happened to have an advanced copy.

I texted Lu once I was finished with the appointment and my other morning tasks.

> Can you do an early lunch? I missed breakfast and I'm starving.

It took her a few minutes to reply back.

> I can, but you probably can't. Karter just left here, and he is all bent out of shape. He thinks your newfound fame crashed the library's site over the weekend.

What the fuck? I opened the browser on the computer at the teen desk and opened up our website. It looked fine to me. Maybe a little laggy, but we'd needed a new server for a while now.

I looked around before I texted her back just to make sure Karter wasn't lurking somewhere and ready to jump out at me for being on my phone while I was on the desk.

WTF?

She just sent back the shrug emoji and the raised eyebrow irritated face emoji. That said it all.

Before I put my phone away, I decided to send a quick text to Chris. I hated that we didn't get to talk or anything this morning. But what to say? *Thanks for all the orgasms last night* didn't feel quite right.

If I thought about it too long, I was going to need a fan and maybe a change of undies. In the end, I just sent a kissy face. Gah, I hoped that wasn't too corny. It wasn't like he was actually my boyfriend.

I didn't know what he was. Which was why I needed to talk it all out and overanalyze everything with Lulu. Friends with benefits? But we'd both said we wanted to be more than friends. Did sex count as more?

He immediately sent back the smiley face sticking its tongue out emoji and followed it up with:

Thinking of what I want to do to you later.

Oh man, lunch could not come soon enough.

Karter did indeed show up while I was putting together my *Books for Back to School* display. It was mostly stories about kids in high school situations, but I threw in a few study guides and our flyer about our school supplies drive. He literally just stood there and silently watched me.

If he wanted to be weird and awkward, I was going to let him. It wasn't my responsibility to help him with his social skills. Should he really need to talk to me, he would figure it out eventually, or send me an email. Even better.

When one of the other librarians came to take over the desk, he left, and I practically bolted for my car. There was a cute little locally owned coffee shop in between the library and the central office where Lulu worked, and we met for lunch there at least a few times a week.

When I got there, Lu was already at a table, my standard cinnamon oat milk latte and their to-die-for peanut butter and jelly scone, waiting. Thank god. She closed the book she was reading on the history of sapphic literature, and looked over at me as I sat and shoved half the scone in my face.

"Spill." She narrowed her eyes at me and raised an eyebrow while I chewed.

I did not finish chewing. Gross, but I couldn't hold this news in any longer. Crumbs tumbled out and right down my shirt when I blurted out, "I had sex with Chris last night."

"Wait, what?" I was pretty sure I'd almost gotten latte spit on me just then. "Like P in the V, as in you're no longer a virgin?"

I rolled my eyes at her and made a face. "You know I don't like that moniker, it's outdated and—"

"Are you, or aren't you?" She tapped the table with one finger, so hard it rattled my plate. That had some of the other patrons looking over at us.

"Technically," I lowered my voice to near a whisper, "he did not put his penis into my vagina. But he did put his fingers and his tongue in, and then his tongue again, and there was that tentacle while I gave him a blow job. That did not taste like what I thought it would."

Oh man. I'd swallowed too. Did that mean I wasn't a vegan anymore?

"Hold up." Lu gave me a bombastic side eye and used her latte to point at me. "Tentacle? Did your life just become a monster romance? Like, by day he's the quarterback for the Denver Mustangs, and by night, he's your tentacled lover?"

"Not the point. It was a toy my mother sent from Japan. He accidentally found my stash, and we, uh, played with some of the items."

"Okay then." She took a sip. "Continue."

"That's it. That's what I got. I slept with Chris and left him in my bed this morning." And I really wished I was there with him right now.

My heart did an extra little kerthump.

"Harsh, Trix. Did you at least leave him a note and a flower on the pillow?"

I answered that by taking another bite of my scone.

"Well, was it good? Are you in love with him now? Can we all stop pretending the two of you are just friends?" She did finger air quotes when she said the just friends part. "Are you going to get married and have lots of little football players of your own? Ooh, can I plan the wedding? We can have it during halftime. Do they allow weddings at Mile High?"

I love Lulu so much. I was ready to go out of my mind wondering about every aspect of what had happened last night, and she was already planning the wedding. That gave me just enough peace of mind to not freak out like I had all morning.

"Yes?"

"To which question?"

"Well, the first one at least. It was, well, not that I have anything to compare it to, but four orgasms is a rather good night, right?"

"Jesus, Mary, and the other Mary. Yeah. I'd say four orgasms is a good night." She gave a small laugh-huff. "Although, to be fair, my record is seven, but Mina couldn't walk the next day, so I generally just go for a couple now."

"Please do not tell Chris that." Or maybe do. No, bad. Although, based on last night, he could do it. "You know how competitive he is, and I would like to remain gainfully employed at my job, where I do, in fact, need to walk around."

"No promises." She paused for a second and took a long sip, like she was contemplating what or how she wanted to say next. "So are you really more than friends? No more of this fake dating stuff?"

This time a double thump hit my sternum from behind. "I think so. Yes."

"And he took the whole V-word that shall not be named thing okay? Guys are weird about that, even if you aren't and don't want them to be."

I choked on my scone. "I, uh, didn't tell him."

Lu's face went cartoonish with her astonishment. But I held up a hand to stop her onslaught.

"Not on purpose. I meant to, I started to even, but,

then everything started going so fast, and I think I literally forgot how to talk at some point."

"Yeah, but you know how to now. Talk to him. Immediately, if not sooner."

"You're right, I should have already, but... no, no. I've got a lot of excuses, and that probably means I'm not as cool about it as I think I am." Or as enlightened as I was raised to be. "But shouldn't that be a face-to-face conversation and not a text?"

"I'll grant you that. Yes." Lu grabbed my bag and fished out my phone. "Text him and tell him you have something you want to talk about tonight and don't want to forget, so he should ask you about it as soon as he sees you."

Geez. "You're mean."

"Only to the ones I love." She winked and took another sip of her coffee looking like the mastermind that she was.

I tapped out the text and sent it before I could lose my nerve. Oh yeah, definitely some inner feminist work calling my name in the near future.

His reply dinged back right away.

> If it's about how you have a praise kink, I already know. Feel free to tell me all your kinks and fantasies later, babe.

While I was trying to decide what to say to that, an email notification popped up. From Marie Manniway. I read it, my mouth dropped open, and then I read it again.

"What? Is he mad? Did he freak out?" Lulu growled and frowned at my phone. "Do I need to beat him up?"

"No, no, he made a cute joke, and I'll tell him everything later tonight." I stared at the message in my inbox

THE C*CK DOWN THE BLOCK

again, still a little flabbergasted. "I just got an email from Marie Manniway."

"Ooh, you fancy now." Lulu stuck her pinky finger out for her next sip of her latte.

"I told her about Rachel, and how I think she's purposefully sabotaging me for the fundraiser so she can swoop in and save the day last minute or something." I had no doubt she'd orchestrated the missing jerseys, which were, of course, the only donations to have been mysteriously taken from the gym. I knew she didn't want the actual fundraiser to go badly, because that would reflect on her. But making me look bad and then taking over to make herself look like a hero and me a zero? Yeah, that was high school bullshit at its finest.

"A. I didn't know about this, and as second-in-command of your fundraiser committee, I should have been told immediately, so I curse Rachel with pillows that are hot on both sides." Lu waved her finger around like a magic wand. "And B. What did Ms. Fancypants say? Doesn't she do all kinds of fundraiser philanthropy stuff for the Mustangs?"

"Sorry, and yes. She wants to host the fundraiser at the Manniway estate." If I could get the rest of the reunion committee to approve of the move, which, really, who wouldn't want to be able to go to a party at the Manniways', we'd have to get a notice out to the rest of the class, transfer the donations we'd already gotten from the gym, and a whole logistical nightmare.

But the look on Rachel's face would be priceless. Even she couldn't pretend she was a big fish in Marie Manniway's pond.

"Do it, do it, do it. Rachel is going to die, and then her buzzy little worker bees will... oh, shoot, don't they just, like, go find a new queen?" Lu stood up and raised her arm to the sky like she was holding a sword aloft in some kind of fantasy novel. "I shall rise as the new queen and free all the workers to live their happy little lives without tyranny."

"You're so weird." I quickly tapped out my reply to Marie, gushing with thanks and a promise to call her when I got off work to coordinate, and then a second to the reunion committee with the subject line: Amazing Update!

Lulu grabbed her phone and replied immediately with a hell yeah, and I got several other excited replies right away too. But of course, silence from Rachel and her minions, Lacey and Amanda.

Oh, no, wait. Lacey replied, and strangely voted yes. She even said she was excited. With her affirmative, I had enough of a majority to go for it.

"Ooh, Lacey is gonna catch hell for that later. Trouble in the ranks of the Queen Bees." Lulu swigged down the last gulp of her latte. "Delicious tea."

Tea indeed. "I gotta run, don't want Karter to catch me getting back from lunch late."

Right when I got back to the library, a new message from Chris pinged.

Hey, call me?

I had all of one minute before I had to go work the front desk for the next two hours. I typed back quickly as

I walked up the stairs from where the staff offices were in the basement.

> About to be on desk. But I can go hide in the bathroom for one min if it's an emergency.

He sent a laughing emoji and then a reply that I didn't really know what to do with.

> No. But I've got some bad news.

Bad news as in he was breaking up with me? No, silly. Ridiculous. He wouldn't have sent a laughy face. And we hadn't even decided we were officially together. And no one texted to say they had bad news and then broke up with you. Right?

BAD NEWS

CHRIS

*M*y agent made me a lot of money, but I was ready to murder him at the moment. "God dammit, Maguire, can't we push it to next week?"

I'd fucked up. The commercial I was slated to star in was the same fucking weekend as Trixie's reunion. I hadn't even thought to check when I told her I would go with her. Of course I was going to go with her. But I didn't like breaking professional commitments.

The best Maguire had been able to finagle was for me to leave today, shoot this week, and be back in time for the fundraiser on Friday. Which meant I'd spend the whole week away from Trixie. And then training camp started right after that, and I'd barely have time to sleep, much less make my girl feel special, wanted, needed, and all the other things a smart boyfriend did at the beginning of a relationship.

I was not fucking letting Trix slip though my hands by not being available for a month just when I'd finally... won her heart? No, I wasn't sure I'd gotten that far with her. But I had plans to. Which was why I was pacing Everett's living room while he and Declan watched me like I was either a predator about to start foaming at the mouth or a dumbass.

"During training camp? You don't want that." He was right, the fucker. "They weren't even happy you can't film this weekend. It's now, or the deal is gonna go south."

Damn it all to hell. I glanced over at Declan. "Hey, man, go be in this car commercial for me."

He gave me the finger and shook his head. "No. I don't even fit in their cars."

True. He was bigger than most sports cars. It was what made him one of the greatest defensive linemen in the league. That, and how flat out scary he was to opposing quarterbacks. Dude was mean when he wanted to be.

Like now.

"Ev?"

He shook his head and rolled his eyes while laughing like this was the most hilarious thing he'd ever heard. "They don't want a wide receiver, man, they want the quarterback."

Shit. I'd made the commitment and I was going to have to go. Because I didn't go back on my word. It was just the shittiest of timing.

"Fine. I'll call the jet crew. But they weren't expecting this so it'll probably take them a few hours to get it ready." Which would give me time to explain to Trix, and maybe even talk her into going with me. Surely she had some vacation time.

Shit. I'd take care of her if she'd let me. She never needed to work a day in her life again if she didn't want to. But I knew how she loved her job, and she'd never want to quit to be a kept woman.

"I already called them. They're ready to leave now," Maguire said. "I'm in the car on my way to the airfield in Broomfield. We take off in an hour."

The advantage of having three brothers who were at the top of their games and had multi-million-dollar contracts like mine, was that we had our own Kingman family jet. We'd make Hayes start paying his fair share once he had a few seasons under his belt. It's not like he even knew what to do with the money he'd been offered as a first-round draft pick rookie anyway.

What sucked is that my agent knew I could be at Rocky Mountain Metropolitan airport in under twenty mins if I had to, and anywhere in the continental US in a matter of hours.

I had no time to even pack, much less see if Trixie could go with. She was still at work, and I knew better than to bug her there. I'd probably land before she was even off.

At least I could take a nap on the plane. It wasn't like I'd gotten a lot of sleep last night. And I wasn't even a little bit sorry about that.

I glared at my brothers. "You guys suck."

"I think you're the one who sucks. At least based on what I heard coming from Trixie's upstairs window last night." Declan gave me a smirk.

"Oh, Chris," Everett put on a fake high-pitched voice. "You're a sex god. Do it to me, big boy."

I loved having my entire family living all around me, but there were disadvantages to having your shitty little brothers so close.

I flipped them both off as I left. "I curse you both with delays to your weekly condom delivery order."

"Hey, thems fighting words," Everett called out to my back as I walked out of his house.

I was just as much of a grump on the plane, and Maguire even moved to the seat farthest away from me and got out his laptop to do some work.

The second we landed, I saw the message from Trix asking where I was. My thumb hovered over the screen, debating what emojis could possibly encapsulate my mix of frustration and regret. We had a minute, because the car that was supposed to be waiting for us at the FBO wasn't here yet. I decided to just call her.

"Hey, you," her voice was light, maybe a little too cheery. I had warned her I had bad news.

"Hey, you're home? I'm gonna Facetime you." I forced myself to sound more upbeat than I felt. Her adorable face popped up on the screen, and I could see she was in the back yard letting the chickens out. "So, listen. Something's come up."

"Whoa. Where are you?" She examined the screen. "Because I do not see Rocky Mountains or golden fields of grain behind you. Is... is that smog?"

"I'm in L.A." I told her about the commercial and how Maguire had rearranged the schedule so that it didn't overlap with her reunion. "It's crappy timing, I know. I'll

be back in time for the fundraiser on Friday, but it's just...
I wanted to spend the next twenty-four to forty-eight
hours in your bed."

There was a brief silence, but when she spoke, her
voice was warm. "Well, that's the job, right? It's not like I
don't know you get busy at the end of the summer. And
I'm not going anywhere. You know where to find my bed
when you get back."

She gave me a cute little eyebrow waggle. That's my
girl, flirting and making me want to hop right back on the
jet and... I couldn't do that.

"Yeah, I do." I flirted right back, because it was the only
thing I could do. "I just hate that we finally figured out
how good it is to be together, and I already have to leave."

"Me too. So," her voice took on a playful note, "what
are you going to bring me from this fancy trip of yours?"

I chuckled. "Are you asking me to bring you home a
toy, naughty girl?"

Not that I could compete with what she already had
hidden away in her closet. Maguire looked up from his
phone and rolled his eyes.

"It's the least you can do for abandoning me." She
threw her arm across her forehead like she was swooning.
"I'm going to have a serious serotonin drop and be
depressed the whole week."

"Well, we can't have that." I knew what would make me
feel better. But I couldn't have that, so I'd have to settle for
the next best thing. "Wanna have phone sex later?"

She laughed, and for a moment, everything felt right in
the world, even with a week-long gap stretching out in
front of us. "Umm, kind of. I've never done that before."

This was at least the third time she'd said something similar to me. I was fucking giddy that I was the only man who'd gotten to do these things with her. But at the same time, I wanted to take all the men she'd dated out back and beat their asses and send them to how to please a woman school.

I hated that she'd had shitty experiences with her past boyfriends. I knew she had a bad breakup in college, mostly because she hated to talk about it. I was going to do my best to erase every bad memory she had and replace them with our own. "Hmm. Then I can't wait to call you later, babe."

"I'll be waiting. Probably naked. Just so you know."

God she was so fucking perfect. "That's my good girl."

She grinned and got that cute slash of pink across her cheeks. We hung up, and the big black SUV arrived to take us to the hotel and apparently some kind of story board meeting later tonight.

How fucking complicated could a car commercial be? Get in the car, drive the car, look cool driving the car. Sold.

"That's the hometown girl I'm selling to the press right now?" Maguire didn't look up from his phone for this question, and he seemed all nonchalant about it, but there was something in his tone I didn't like.

"Yeah. That's her."

"You two have been a pain in my ass. Got the PR team working overtime to keep her info out of the grubby hands of the tabloids. But man, are the Denver fans eating it up. You've gotten almost ten thousand new followers on IG just over the weekend."

I'd been living in one spotlight or another for so long that it was all mostly meaningless to me. Maguire cared how many followers I had because it was his job. I couldn't give two shits. I didn't do any of my own posting. The PR team did.

"She's gotten a few too. She handling this newfound fame thing all right?" That question did garner me an actual look in the eye from Mr. Face-Stuck-In-His-Phone. "Do you want me to get her some media training?"

"Trix? She's fine. She mentioned her accounts had gotten some attention, but if it's not about a celebrity baking show or books for teens or FlipFlops about chickens, she doesn't really care." Besides, I had doubled up the security detail in the neighborhood for the past few days. Most of the journalists knew better than to try and hang around my house.

I gave them plenty of access during the season and was happy enough to do press conferences and I even did the social appearances Maguire wanted me to. That was enough access into my life, thank you very much.

Now that I had Trixie in my life and on my arm, I wouldn't be going on anymore of the dates he tried to set me up on with models and starlets. I knew it was all to give me a good image and all that, but I never cared about any of them.

"She'll be on my arm at any other events you want me to attend too. I'll ask her later if she wants any prep for that kind of stuff. She doesn't love being in the spotlight."

"Yeah, I wouldn't either if I was her. The internet is brutal on women, but more so on ladies with some junk in their trunk like your girl."

What the fuck? "Don't talk about her body like that, man, and what the hell are you talking about?"

For the first time in hours, Maguire actually stopped doing whatever the hell he did on his phone and laptop all the time. "Right. I'd recommend two things here, Chris. First of all, do not go scrolling through the comments of any post with the two of you in it, or even the ones with just her. There are a lot of trolls out there, and like I said, they aren't kind to women in general. But the two of you are getting a lot of attention because of the, uh, differences in your, let's say attractiveness."

"Don't make me punch you in the face and then fire you. Because I will do both."

"It's not me, man. It's society. If you're going to publicly date a bigger girl, you're going to learn firsthand how ugly people can be, to both of you, but mostly her."

Publicly? Like I should be fucking hiding that I was in love with and lusted after the most gorgeous, kind, smart, amazing woman I'd ever known in my life? "I am close to punching you right now. What's the second thing?"

"Make sure your girl has thick skin. It's better that she isn't into social media. But eventually she'll probably see something. And I can tell you from experience, that can be devastating to anyone."

I narrowed my eyes at Maguire and studied him for a minute. "Your wife is a plus-size model, isn't she? That's the firsthand experience you've had. How she's had a challenging time?"

"Yeah. But Sara Jayne has had a fuckton of media training, and she's done a lot of inner work. In fact, she took a workshop from your mom when she first started in the business, and she still uses the skills she learned then to this day."

Fuck. If ever I wished my mom was still around, it was right now. Not only could I use her advice, but I also wished to god she could see just how much in love with Trixie I was.

She'd been a plus-size model way before that was even a thing, and I'd heard her tell stories about how hard that was. After my dad had taken the defensive coordinator position at Denver State, she'd started a non-profit to promote body positivity and inclusivity in the fashion world, helping young models navigate the industry and empowering them to challenge the status quo.

I'd grown up with powerful, beautiful, plus-size women being the norm in my life, not the exception. But, because of my mom's work, I also knew that Denver wasn't the most body positive town, and that she'd worked tirelessly to fight fatphobia in big and small ways nearly every day. Especially in the media.

"Right. Trix is pretty solid in her confidence. Her mother was Sunshine Babcock back in the day, but now she's a body and sex positive coach, so it's not like Trixie won't have had some background in shit like this. But maybe Sara Jayne and Trix could have coffee and, you know, exchange notes. I'll ask her if she wants that when I talk to her later."

Maguire was very rarely shocked. But his mouth hung open so long that I poked his chin to see if it was stuck. "Uh, Sunshine Babcock... the porn star? That's Trixie's mother? Oh fuck. Way to bury the lead. Do not let that get out."

BALLGOWNS AND BASTARDS

TRIXIE

J was about twelve minutes from having a complete and total breakdown. Chris would be here in less than ten to pick me up and take me to the fundraiser, and all I had on were frilly new panties and a matching bra. Every dress I owned, a couple of Lulu's, and one new one I'd splurged on when I probably shouldn't have were strewn across my room. Lulu and Jules each held up the dress they thought I should wear.

"Come on, Trixie," Jules said, holding out the slinky red number I'd just bought. Very Jessica Rabbit, minus the sequins. "This dress is daring, it's vivacious, it's just so you when you're not being the buttoned-up librarian."

"Hey, I'm a super cute buttoned-up librarian." I reached into the front of my bra to give my boobs a little lift so they were actually where they were supposed to be.

"Yes, yes, we all know you're a snack. But I swear this is going to make my brother—"

I held up a hand. "Do not finish that sentence."

Lulu interjected, raising her choice higher, a more sophisticated burgundy gown that made me think of holiday Barbie. It was, in fact, what I'd worn to the Adams County Employee Christmas ball last year. "This one is timeless. Elegant. You can never go wrong with a classic."

I glanced from one dress to the other, biting my lip, then thinking better of it because I'd already had to reapply my lipstick twice. This wasn't just because I wanted to look good when I got to see Chris for the first time in four days. Four exceedingly long, horny days. Which I did. But I was going to be in the spotlight for most of the night. I hated being the center of attention.

"Chris is gonna think you're a goddess no matter what you wear. He always has." Jules was all for this relationship between me and her oldest brother. It was cute.

Lulu chimed in, "Look, the Queen Bees are gonna be buzzing with jealousy regardless. Because you're you, you're amazing, and they can't stand it. So stop worrying about what they're going to think about what you wear, and I know you are, and pick what you're going to feel fabulous in."

I wish Lulu wasn't right. I hated that I cared what they'd think. I didn't care what the rest of the world thought. Ninety-nine percent of the time, I was not only fine with how I looked, I loved my body. I was a fricking snack. But one word from Rachel or Amanda or Lacey, and I ridiculously felt like a moldy, old snack that made you wrinkle up your nose when you discovered it in the back of the refrigerator.

Sigh.

"Okay, fuck it. Let's go bold. The red it is." I held out my hand for the dress and pretended to ignore Jules's triumphant grin. Yes, even the Kingman daughter had that competitive streak in her and would take the win.

I slipped it on over my head, and the too expensive fabric did feel amazing gliding across my skin. I turned and said, "Zip me up?"

"Allow me." Chris walked into the room, his eyes sparkling.

As soon as I laid eyes on him, all the worries I was clinging to vanished. He looked up from checking out the cleavage this dress showed off rather well, our eyes met, and for a moment, the world stopped. His expression was a mix of awe and something deeper, something I hadn't even known I needed. But I did need him. I might even love him.

He stepped behind me but didn't immediately zip up the dress. He slowly ran his fingers up my bare spine and kissed my shoulder. Then he whispered in my ear, "If my sister and your friend weren't here, I'd be stripping this dress off you instead of helping you into it."

Jules cleared her throat and handed me a pair of golden hoop earrings. "But we are here, so you're going to have to tell your hormones to cool their jets."

"Don't you have some homework to do or something, brat?" Chris acted the part of the put upon older brother, but it was so evident how much he loved his baby sister. Although, she wouldn't be a baby much longer. She'd turn eighteen this year, and I pitied any guy who tried to ask her to homecoming or the prom.

Jules stuck her tongue out at Chris. "School hasn't started yet, butthead."

Chris finished zipping me up, and I did a little twirl.

"You look incredible." His voice had gone all husky, and I sort of wished we didn't have to go to this thing tonight. Maybe we could leave early.

"You look pretty great yourself." I reached up and straightened his already straight tie just because I could.

"Your hot ass boyfriend is giving Brendan Fraser in the Mummy, but in a tux," Lulu said and then recoiled. "Holy Egyptian Gods and Goddesses. Am I bi? Excuse me while I go find my wife and bang her real quick in your guest bathroom."

Chris was sporting some five o'clock shadow, and it was sexy as hell. I didn't blame Lu one bit for lusting after him. I certainly was.

"Your friends are weird," he said. We watched Lulu bolt from the room. "I like it."

I pulled him closer by the lapels of his jacket. "Aren't you my friend? Does that make you weird too?"

"I'm more than your friend, chickadee." He brought his lips down to mine and kissed me softly, but then gave my lip a little bite.

"You too are both gross and cute at the same time. I'm leaving. But Christopher Bridger Kingman, if you mess up Trixie's hair and makeup that we just spent the last hour on, I will pee in your Cheerios."

Chris took a step back, laughing, and shoved his hands

into his pockets. "She'll do it. She has before. Granted, she was two, but still."

We followed Jules down the stairs, because if we didn't, Chris might have ended up with yellow Cheerios. She gave us a little wave and was out the front door. Probably so she didn't have to see anymore gross cuteness from us. Lulu and her wife, Mina, were arm in arm, waiting in the living room. Nobody looked as though they had banged or been banged, so I guess Lu's half a minute of bi-curiousness was over. Mina gave me a wink. "Great choice on the dress, Trix. Sure we can't talk you into that threesome?"

"Ooh, sorry." I shrugged and put my arm through Chris's. "Wish I could, but it appears I'm now taken, girls."

"Don't let me stop you." Chris had that giddy look all men get when presented with the idea of women doing sexy stuff.

I smacked him for it. "That is not what loving boyfriends are supposed to say."

That boyfriend thing just slipped out. Was he my boyfriend now? What was I, twelve, waiting to ask him if we were girlfriend-boyfriend? We hadn't defined anything, but we had said we were more than friends. My brain was full-on ready to go into a tailspin of overanalyzing what I'd just said while waiting for his reaction.

He looked at Lulu and Mina. "You two should go on ahead. We'll see you there."

They left, giggling all the way out the door. When he turned back to me, I swear he was murmuring, "Cheerios, Cheerios, Cheerios."

But the moment the door shut behind my friends, he

pulled me into his arms and kissed the breath right out of me.

I could have happily kissed him all night and said fuck it to the fundraiser. He left me all woozy and swoony and feeling well-kissed. "Whew, what was that for?"

"Just because I like when you call me your boyfriend." He rubbed his nose along my jaw, sending all kinds of shivers across my skin. "Do it again."

"I think I'd better not." Yeah, that was my voice that was all breathy, and sounding more than a wee bit needy. "I wouldn't want you to have to throw out all your Cheerios."

"I'll buy more. Hell, I'll buy General Mills if it means I can kiss the rest of that lipstick off your face and mess your hair while I push your skirt up and bend you over the couch—"

"Next time we decide to be more than friends, can you not then leave for almost a week?" I ran my fingers over that bit of scruff on his chin. That was going to feel really interesting rubbing between my thighs later. "But I don't want to be late, and we have to stop by the library really quick."

"Fine. But we're leaving early."

We were not, because I was in charge of this fundraiser and there wasn't a chance that I was letting anything go wrong, even if I did want to come home and, uh, bang my boyfriend.

"Lemme just pop out and give Luke and the girls a little treat. I haven't gotten to spend as much time with them this week, and I think Luke is pouting." My days this week had been long as hell trying to make sure everything was set and perfect for the fundraiser to happen at the Manniways'.

"I can relate. I was grumpy without you too."

When we got out to the coop, all three of the hens were in a cozy little circle, but Luke was perched on top of the little structure, facing away. Who knew a rooster could get mad like this? I tossed some treats into the pen but didn't want to do much more because I could not show up to this party smelling like a chicken.

"Did Luke just huff at you?" Chris frowned at my stroppy rooster. "I didn't know that was a thing he could do."

"Told you, he's big mad." After this stupid reunion was over, I'd see about getting him a new girlfriend or two.

"Well, I'll chase him around with some hot sauce and threaten to turn him into dinner tomorrow and see if that perks him up."

When we got in the car, Chris turned on the music, and maybe my heart melted a little, because this was definitely a Taylor Swift playlist.

"Oh, how was the rest of the shoot?" While we had indeed tried phone sex, which was fun but not half as satisfying as when he was the one making me come, the other nights we were both so tired that we'd just talked for a few minutes before bed.

"Nobody told me that there would be actual mustangs. Do you have any idea how hard it is to get a shot when a big ass horse keeps trying to eat your hair?"

"I do not, but it's nice to know that it isn't just roosters who like to harass you."

It was only a couple of minutes to the library, and we

parked right in front since it was almost closing time anyway. "I'll just be a minute. There's a donation from one of the moms I worked with this week who is a travel agent, but I wasn't able to get into my work email from home to print it out."

Chris insisted on coming inside with me, but I think he just wanted to stare at my butt while I led him down to the basement where our offices were.

Unfortunately we ran into Karter, who was on closing duty tonight. He got that awestruck look in his eyes that almost every Denverite did when they realized they were face to face with Chris Kingman. Crap. I was going to have to introduce them.

It would have been fine with me if Chris never had to experience Creepy Karter. He'd heard everything about him, of course, but they'd never met.

"Hey, Karter. I'm just here to print something out really quick."

"Uh-huh." He said that with his mouth still hanging open and his head tilted back since Chris had a good seven inches on him.

Sigh. "Karter, this is my boyfriend, Chris. Chris, this is Karter, the branch manager." I'd be damned if I called him my boss.

Chris held out his hand to shake, and it took Karter a full ten seconds to remember his manners and actually take the offered greeting.

I mouthed 'sorry' to Chris and bolted over to my desk. Luckily the setup of our cubicles allowed me to keep an eye on that awkwardness while I logged into my desktop.

It took me three tries, and in the end, I had to change my password. Weird.

But finally I found the email and sent the fancy looking certificate for a trip to Vegas to the printer we all shared. Which, of course, was all the way on the other side of the cubicles.

I rushed over and tapped the thing with my fingers like that would make it print faster. It didn't. Just as the machine whizzed to life, I swear I heard Karter say, "So, uh, you hit that?"

Did he just say... and mean what I think he did? Why were men so gross?

I turned and yeah. By the look on Chris's face, that's exactly what Karter said and meant. I'm sure he didn't mean for me to hear it, but what the actual fuck?

Chris's eyes went wide and he blinked a few times, and I could practically see his brain processing the same questions I'd just asked myself. His gaze quickly narrowed and he turned to Karter in what seemed like that movie-style super slow mo.

"What did you just ask me?" His words came out all snarly, and his fists clenched.

Oh god. I was going to lose my job because my boyfriend, yes, my actual boyfriend, not my fake one, murdered my boss for being a sexist asshole.

And I hadn't even paid my school loans off yet. How was I going to do that without a job? Well, at least I'd read enough thriller and mystery novels to know how to hide a body.

JACKASSES

CHRIS

This jackass didn't seem to notice that I was about to beat him to a bloody pulp.

"Because, you know, her mother was a," he lowered his voice to a whisper, "porn star, the kind for the fat fetishists."

I'd known these kinds of guys my entire life. The kind that thought being a sexist ass made them some kind of cool guy. They tried to buddy up to me, assuming I'd be a man's man since I was a sports star.

This guy was her god damned boss. He should be her biggest supporter at work, and not thinking about her sex life.

"I had my reservations about keeping her on as a children's librarian when I found out, but you do kind of have to use some deep dive Google Fu to discover that, so I figured the general public would never know, and she really has been a model employee. If a bit too—"

Oh, and he was cyber stalking her? He was fucking going down.

"Karter. You need to shut, and I emphasize this next part, the fuck up." No way I was passively standing by while anyone acted like this. I literally started reciting the play-book in my head so I didn't just lay him out flat right now.

He held his hands up and smirked like this was all a big joke. "Oh, I'm not making a move on your territory or anything. I've just always wondered if she was any good in bed. Her mother sure was flexible for a big girl."

This absolute piece of shit was not worth ruining my career over or I'd already be calling my insurance agent for the damage to my hands from beating him senseless.

But Trixie was worth it, so maybe I'd be making that call anyway.

Trixie rushed at me and grabbed my arm, pulling me away from my impending beat down. "Violence is not the answer."

She sing-songed the words, and I did not understand how she was so calm and collected. "You need to let me teach that guy a lesson."

"He wouldn't learn it, even if I did let you murder him, and then both you and I would lose our jobs, and I don't even know where the supermax prison they'd put you in is located, or if conjugal rights are granted to murderers. So let's just go about our night and pretend this never happened."

"You need to file a sexual harassment suit, or worse.

He's been cyber stalking you and knows about your mother's former career."

She paused outside when the glass doors slid shut behind us and took a deep breath and sighed. "I suspected as much."

"And you didn't do anything?" She knew? How long had this kind of harassment been going on?

"What am I supposed to do?" She shook her head and frowned at me. "If I tried to fight everyone who found out my mother was in sex work before I was even born and wanted to know if I was a chip off the old block, I'd, I don't know, probably be a top MMA fighter instead of a librarian."

She walked to the car, and I could very clearly see the defensiveness in the set of her shoulders and how ramrod straight her spine was. Karter might be a creep, but I'd fucked up pushing her on this. I'd admit I was feeling a whole lot protective of her. "Trix."

"No, don't." She stood next to the passenger side car door waiting for me to unlock it and wouldn't look at me. "I know what you're going to say, and trust me, I've heard it. Pretty much every man I've ever known is just like that."

I didn't unlock the car for her. I went right up to her side, turned her around, and pressed her body against the car. I took her jaw in my hand and forced her face up to look at me.

I may be a pretty fucking enlightened dude, growing up with strong, powerful women like both her mother and mine in my life, but I wasn't perfect. I hoped Karter was fucking watching us right now, because I was going to lay claim to my woman. "That man is a predator, and the fact that he even thinks about you and your mom in that way is revolting. I won't stand for it."

Did I know I was making an asshole move right now when she probably needed to exert her feminine independence? Yeah, I did. And I didn't fucking care. I'd care later, I'd apologize on my knees with my face between her legs later.

Right now, she was mine, she'd been threatened, and I was going to prove to her and any creep watching that I would stand in the way of anyone who hurt my girl. My girl. Mine.

I pushed my hands into her hair and kissed her so god damned thoroughly that anyone watching would think I was about to fuck her up against the side of the car. She stayed stiff in my arms for a moment, but then she wrapped her arms around my neck and her foot around the back of my calf.

I broke the kiss and pressed my forehead to hers. "If you'd said yes when I asked you out that summer, you never would have had to deal with shitty men who treated you like nothing more than fodder for their wank bank."

I was one to talk. She was the reason I masturbated every day.

"What?" She blinked up at me, cutely dazed from my claiming of her mouth, lips, and tongue. "When did you ask me out?"

Huh. I'd kissed her brains out. Because how could she not remember? "The night you graduated."

"No. No, you did not."

"Trix, I swear to god. You were going off to school in

Wisconsin, and I couldn't stand the thought of not seeing you, so I finally got up the nerve. You not only turned me down flat, but you also told me to fuck off."

So I had.

She'd gone off to the Midwest, and I'd banged every cheerleader, sorority girl, and ball bunny trying to get her out of my system. If they were the opposite of Trixie, with her lush curves and nerdy glasses, I'd fucked them. I thought it had worked too. Until she'd moved back. The first second I saw her, I'd fallen right back in love with her again.

But she hadn't wanted me.

"Oh no." She shook her head and had a horrified look on her face. "God. I remember seeing you, but that was the night I broke up with Asshat Anthony. Because... proving my point that too many men are exactly like Karter, he wanted me to have sex with him while watching a Sunshine Babcock video."

"Are you shitting me?" I hadn't even known she had a boyfriend, but now I had one more bastard on my list to kill.

"No."

No wonder she'd told me to fuck off. Men are pigs.

"And that's not the only time something like that has happened."

"Jesus Christ, Trix. Is... is this why you haven't, why you keep telling me you haven't done... things?" I was trying hard not to be an absolute ass right now, but this had me in a fucking tailspin.

She pressed her lips together and her eyes went looking everywhere but at me. "You, you figured that out, huh? I should have said something, but, you know, you had a tentacle vibrator between my legs and I sort of forgot. It doesn't bother you, does it?"

"Bother me? I'm god damned thrilled that there are so many things that will always be just between you and me. I'm going to make you forget any other man who ever touched you, looked at you, or even talked to you, sweetheart."

She smiled up at me and put her hand over my heart. "You already have."

I was this close to just blurting out how much I loved her. "You sure we have to go to this thing tonight? We could just skip it and I could donate however much you wanted to raise."

"Shit, shit, shit." She gave me a little push and turned to grab the handle of the car door. "We are going to be late, and now I have to fix my hair and make-up in the car on the way. Get in and drive like the devil, Kingman."

We made it to the Manniways' well in advance of the event, because Trixie was a smart cookie and decided we needed to arrive an hour before everyone else, which meant we pulled up to the valet attendant a good half hour before any guests were scheduled to arrive.

Marie greeted us with champagne, which Trixie down in two gulps. "Are the rest of the cowgirls here?"

"Yep, ready and waiting. Don't worry, doll. This ain't my first rodeo, everything will go simply fine, and if anything goes a little off kilter, we'll be able to manage it. I promise. Your Queen Bees won't know what hit them."

She was right. This place looked straight out of a Hollywood movie, with lights twinkling all around the yard, the pool filled with some sort of floating lanterns, and a stage set up with displays for all the items being auctioned off.

I'd bet tonight's fundraiser would not only pay for the programming and extracurriculars, but it would also probably pay off the mortgage on the buildings. It would help that a good third of the Mustangs and their wives were here and would be happy to bid on items, most of which had been donated by them anyway.

It filled my soul with gratitude that I had a team and a family who would pull together to help pull this off at a moment's notice. This was why I'd never leave Denver if I could help it. This was my home, my people, my family. And Trixie was my lynchpin in it all.

Lulu and her wife waved from the stage and Trixie moved to go meet them. I grabbed her arm and pulled her in for one last kiss before I lost her to the night. "I'll be here if you need anything, but you're going to kill it, chickadee."

I let her go and went in search of Johnston. He was standing in his usual place near the barbecue grill, which was thankfully closed up for the night, and my dad was there with him. "Gentleman, nice night for a party."

"Dad." I gave him the usual handshake-half hug. "I didn't know you were coming tonight."

"Wouldn't want to miss Trixie's big coup. I donated a pair of Dragons season tickets."

I whistled. The Denver State Dragons football season tickets were hard to come by. But I guess if you were the five-time national championship winning coach that they'd named their new stadium after, the university would give you whatever you wanted. "In your box?"

He chuckled and shook his head. "No. Wouldn't want to end up hanging out with some dickheads I don't know all season. They'll get midfield and like it."

My dad kept his circle of trust just about as tight as I did. He was the one who suggested I start buying up the homes in our neighborhood as they came available. A real estate investment, he'd said. But he liked that we could have a say about who lived near us, and who couldn't, just as much as I did.

It had worked out perfectly when Trixie had moved back to town and found out the house she grew up in was available to rent. Right next door to me.

"They will indeed. I'm sure that will be a big-ticket item tonight. Lots of DSU fans around."

"I might bid on those," Johnston said. "Don't let it get out, but Marie loves college football more than professional. She is a Husker, after all."

"Then the tickets are for every game except the one against Nebraska." My dad had a long-standing rivalry with the Cornhuskers. Especially since they'd won the National Championship the year he hadn't.

Johnston laughed. "Go Big Red."

The guests started arriving, and I kept my eye on Trixie first, and the entrance to the back yard second. I wanted to know the second Rachel walked in so I could see her face. She might think she was a Queen Bee, but she was no cowgirl.

The crowds filed in, and Trixie got up on the stage to welcome everyone. Still no Rachel. Was the bitch actually going to skip out? She probably couldn't take how badass this whole thing Trixie had pulled off was going to be.

Well, good riddance to her.

"Hello, my fellow alumni of St. Ambrose and special guests. I'm pleased to welcome you to this year's Honeybee Fundraiser."

There were claps all around, and the crowd seemed genuinely excited. For most of them, this was their chance to meet some local celebrities, and there were some pretty damn cool prizes that had been donated. I'd probably bid on a few. I wouldn't mind taking Trixie on that Vegas trip just so we could have obnoxiously loud hotel sex without the consequence of my entire family hearing.

"Special thanks to Johnston and Marie Manniway for hosting us, and my personal thanks to her and the wives and girlfriends of the Mustangs for their help this week in organizing." More applause, then she got the main event started. "Please welcome Marie as our first auctioneer of the night."

Marie stepped up to the stage, gave her wave and smile, and waited patiently for the applause and the camera clicks and flashes to die down, and she presented the first item of the night. While she did an excellent job of cajoling the attendees into raising their bids, Trixie made her way back to where I was standing.

"Did I do all right? I was so nervous." She smoothed her hair and her dress, even though nothing was out of place. "There are way more people here than I expected. I think the entire class came and they all brought a guest."

I wrapped my arm around her and pulled her to my

side and kept her there. "You were great. This is all everyone will be talking about for years, I'm sure."

Everett finally showed up, fashionably late. "Hey, Trix. This place is hopping. Now show me who your single classmates are. I do love that Catholic girl school vibe. So many opportunities for debauchery."

"I don't really know who's married or has partners." Trixie laughed and shook her head, shrugging. "I haven't really kept up with most of them. I'm only here because Lulu made me be on the committee."

"Gimme your phone then. I'll just lightly peruse your FaceSpace." He held out his hand like Trix would actually give him her phone. I smacked him hard enough that he had to shake his hand out.

"Oh, sorry. Can't. I deleted it. I was getting too many weird messages."

"Fine, you two are no fun. I'd be less bored hanging around with grumpy butt." He jerked his chin toward Declan, who was surrounded by a group of women with that fawning-over-a-football-player aura about them. "Damn. How'd he do that so fast? I'd better get in there before he does something dumb like growl and scare them all away."

Looked to me like Ev had gotten his groove back this week.

"Did you delete your account because of me?" Maybe Maguire was right about his PR team and the media training thing for Trix. I hadn't brought it up yet, but this was the first she'd mentioned about weird messages.

"Yes, but it's okay, I really didn't go on there much

anyway. I'm more of an Insta girl, and those DMs are way easier to lock down."

"I'm up next to auction off the next item. It's your Mile High workout with the quarterback prize."

After the physical donations we'd made went not so mysteriously missing, Trixie had suggested experiences for the auction instead. She came up with the idea of an insider's access tour of the stadium and a chance to work out with me. Sounded easy to me.

The cowgirls had already rotated through auctioning off about half the prizes, and the highest bid so far had gone to dad's DSU season tickets, a whopping eight thousand dollars. Although, Hayes's video game night had gone for seventy-five hundred, which was insane to me. I mean, I liked Madden or Fortnite as much as the next guy, but geez.

"Okay, ladies and gentlemen, item number seventeen is up next. A Mile High tour and workout on the field, donated by Mustangs quarterback, Chris Kingman." Trixie grinned at me as the oohs and awws rippled through the crowd. "Do I hear a thousand dollars?"

"Twenty thousand dollars for Chris Kingman," a woman's voice rang out over the crowd and all eyes turned to see who bid something so ridiculous.

THE QUEEN BEE STINGS

TRIXIE

*T*wenty thousand dollars? That was half my salary for the year. I couldn't even fathom that amount of money.

"Twenty thousand dollars from Rachel," I said, my voice steady despite the emotional tornado swirling inside me. "Do I hear twenty-one?"

I glanced toward Chris. He looked almost as shocked as I felt but he was still calm, his eyes locked onto mine, as if willing me to keep my composure.

This was more than just a high bid. It was a power play. Rachel knew this fundraiser was going to go gangbusters despite the way she'd tried to ruin it. Her little trick hadn't worked, so now she was trying to show me up in front of the whole class. God, this was just like high school, and I couldn't stand it.

I wanted to say I was the bigger person and that I'd

outgrown this bullshit. But if that was true, I wouldn't have even shown up to be on this committee, and I certainly wouldn't have pretended Chris was my boyfriend.

I was just... so tired of her and people like her who didn't think I was worthy. Of love, of a guy as amazing as Chris. From the get-go, she'd questioned whether I could even have a relationship with him. She'd thought I'd won a date with him. Now she was using her money to do exactly that, as if that would prove the point that Chris could be bought.

Selling my boyfriend to my nemesis.

Ugh. This was exactly why I hadn't wanted to do her stupid bachelor auction. It's not like I could bid against her, I was the auctioneer for goodness' sake. Not to mention, I didn't have that kind of money, even if it was for charity.

"Twenty thousand. Going once—"

Lulu's voice sliced through the tension in the room. "Twenty-two thousand!"

A collective gasp filled the air.

She was holding her phone in her hand and the screen was lit up. She better not have been checking her bank balance to see if she actually had that much money. I glanced over at Chris, and if I didn't know better, I'd think he didn't actually care what was going on, because he was staring down at his phone.

Please, please let them be conspiring together.

He glanced up for the briefest of moments and gave me the tiniest of head nods. My grip on the gavel relaxed a fraction.

"Twenty-two thousand dollars from Lulu," I announced, unable to keep the relief out of my voice. Except to play the part, I still had to ask, "Do I hear twenty-four?"

Rachel's eyes narrowed, a mixture of annoyance and disbelief coloring her features. "Twenty-three thousand," she bit out.

The room buzzed. This was going to be the tea even more than getting to go to a fancy fundraiser at the Manniway estate. I looked back at Lu and pleaded with my eyes for her to go higher.

She winked at me and then put on a show of her own. "Whew, this is gonna hurt, but yep, let's go to twenty-five thousand."

Like we were watching a tennis match, every eye in the place swung to Rachel to see if she'd counter again. She wasn't in a position to have seen Lu's facial expression communications to me.

Rachel raised her chin and rolled her eyes as if twenty-six thousand was beneath her. "Let's just end this. Thirty thousand dollars."

Sweet baby Jesus.

"Thirty thousand? Wow, Rach. When you want something, you really go hard, huh?" Lulu retorted almost instantly. "But when I said this was going to hurt, I meant you more than me. Fifty thousand dollars."

Rachel hesitated, her eyes darting from Lulu to Chris to me, gauging whether there was a conspiracy going on between the three of us. But Chris was still staring at his phone like he was totally bored, and I was literally standing in the spotlight, so it's not like I could do anything. I shrugged, and trying so hard to keep the smile off my face, I asked, "Do I hear more?"

She narrowed her eyes at me but turned her back and sauntered over to the bar and grabbed a glass of champagne.

"Fifty thousand dollars." Gah, that was a lot of money. More than I made in a year. But I supposed it was just a Saturday night for someone who literally made more than that by playing a professional sport for a living. Still, I was going to have to come up with a way to say thank you. I had more than a few ideas. And none of them involved pants. "Going once, going twice, sold to Lulu for fifty thousand dollars!"

The gavel hit the block, and the room burst into applause. That one bid was more than any other class had ever raised at one of these Honeybee Alumni fundraisers in the history of the school as far as I knew. I handed the microphone over to Marie, who was due up to auction the next item. She gave me a smile and a wink.

I stepped off the stage, and Lulu rushed over to me.

"What was that all about?" I kept my voice low, so the others around me wouldn't hear. I pasted a fake smile on my face so it would just look like I was congratulating her. "Tell me that was Chris, because you don't have that much money, and I'm pretty sure Rachel will notice if you don't pay."

Chris came up behind me and grabbed me around the waist, pulling me against his chest. He bent and whispered softly in my ear. "Some things are too important to leave to chance."

Lulu grinned and did not speak quietly at all. "Sometimes, you've got to put your money where your mouth is. Besides, Mina is a huge fan. Aren't you, honey?"

Mina snorted. "Huge."

I caught sight of Rachel weaving her way through the crowd toward us, and more of them were paying attention to us than the next item up for bid. Her lips were curled in what looked like a congratulatory smile, but her eyes... well, they still had that razor-sharp glint I'd learned to be wary of.

"Wow, Lulu, that was some aggressive bidding," Rachel said, once she reached us. "You must really want to hang out on a football field."

Lulu grinned. "Oh, you have no idea."

"Congrats to you then," Rachel said, her eyes suddenly shifting to Chris, who had his arm wrapped protectively around my waist. "It's going to be quite an experience, spending that much time with such a talented quarterback."

Her voice oozed insinuation, and she took a step closer to Chris. "I'm sure he could teach you quite a few... techniques."

My stomach churned, but I clamped down on the surge of insecurity that tried to rise.

"Oh, I'm sure we'll have a great time," he said, his eyes never leaving mine.

Rachel's lips tightened, the veneer of her gracious-loser act cracking just a bit. "Well, enjoy your prize. I do hope it doesn't strain your pocketbook to pay. And you will pay, won't you? I'd hate to have to inform the school administration how much we raised, but then only give them a small portion of that number."

226   AMY AWARD

With a final, lingering glance at Chris, she walked away, joining Amanda and Lacey, a few yards away.

Chris leaned into me as one of the cowgirls announced the next auction item. "I had my eye on that Vegas trip for us. A romantic weekend getaway, maybe during our bye-week. Unless you want to go up to Bear Claw Valley with the rest of the family. What do you think?"

"You don't have to bid on something else. I think maybe you're already on the hook for a huge donation to St. Ambrose. But remind me to put in for that week off, because I'd love to go to Bear Claw with everyone." Mr. Kingman liked to take his whole family back to his home-town, now a ski resort, in the mountains for his annual charity 5K. We'd gone up to the resort a few times with the Kingmans when I was younger, but I hadn't been in years.

"Sweetheart, I promise I can afford it. Besides, I'm betting you haven't tried hotel sex yet."

Oh geez. I swatted him but mostly to distract from the blush rising up my cheeks. "Shh. How about Vegas to cele-brate your next championship win?"

I was manifesting both that we'd be together then and that he'd win the big game again this year too.

He gave me a little boop to the nose. "I like how you think, chickadee."

"A luxurious weekend in Vegas, ladies and gentlemen," Cowgirl Stephanie announced. "We're talking a suite, fine dining, and a top-rated show. Starting the bid at five thousand dollars." She waved toward her husband and pointed toward the certificate like she wanted him to bid on it.

"Five thousand," Chris called out without hesitation, his eyes never leaving mine.

A giddy kind of warmth washed over me. It wasn't about the money or even the trip. It was that look in his eyes—the excitement, the intent—that made me feel incredibly special.

"Six thousand," Rachel piped up, her voice dripping with faux sweetness.

I felt my heart sink momentarily. She couldn't outbid Chris. She knew it and so did everyone else. He'd just proven that. She was running up the tab, just to spite us for thwarting her plans.

Chris gave me a playful wink. "Ten thousand."

"Fifteen," Rachel smirked, convinced Chris would take the bait. How far was she going to push this? I had a feeling it would be more than that fifty grand mark from before.

Chris looked at me with that competitive glint in his eye that I knew all too well. "Watch this. Twenty."

Rachel countered immediately. "Twenty-five."

Oh no. I knew he had money, but this was getting ridiculous, and he hated to lose more than I hated Rachel's devious ploys.

Chris closed his mouth with an evil grin and fell silent. Oh. Oh no. Ha. I buried my face in his chest so no one would see the absolute gleeful giggle I was holding back.

When I peeked over at Rachel, expecting another counter bid, looked increasingly uneasy as the seconds ticked by. Stephanie called out, "Twenty-five thousand going once, going twice—"

A tense pause filled the room.

"Sold! For twenty-five thousand to Regina." Stephanie gave me a sorry-not-sorry look for saying the wrong name that had me holding in another laugh.

The room erupted into both applause and a round of chuckles and murmurs, but Rachel looked less than thrilled. Chris leaned down to whisper in my ear, "Sometimes the best move is not to play."

"Good job, Rachel, you're going to Vegas!" Lulu called out, her voice sugared with faux enthusiasm.

Rachel turned, pasting a smile on her face as if it were an accessory. "Thank you. It's always nice to have a little vacation," she said, although her eyes couldn't hide her resentment.

"Congratulations, Rachel," Chris said, the words wrapped in a layer of irony so thick it could smother a lesser man.

"Why thank you, Chris," she replied, drawing his name out like they were old frenemies, making eye contact for just a second too long.

Her eyes slid to mine, and then she gave Lulu a once-over, as if assessing. "Funny how everything seems to work out, isn't it? We all think we know how things are going to play out, and then, surprise."

"Surprise is my middle name. Didn't you know?" Lulu took a step toward Rachel and Mina grabbed her arms, holding her back.

Rachel's smile tightened, just a little. "I love surprises. Keeps things interesting. Don't you agree?"

Before anyone could respond, she turned toward me and pointed. "See you tomorrow night at the dance. It's going to be a truly surprising evening."

And with that ambiguous yet somehow menacing statement hanging in the air, she pivoted and retreated, leaving me with a sense of unease that lingered like an uninvited guest.

She dragged Amanda and Lacey, her trusty sidekicks, with her, and they huddled together near the exit. Though I couldn't hear a word from our spot near the stage, their body language spoke volumes.

Amanda seemed eager, almost gleeful, as Rachel talked to them. She'd always been a sycophantic echo to Rachel's malevolence. But it was Lacey who caught my attention. Her eyes flicked toward me for just a moment, meeting mine before dropping away. She seemed less animated than Amanda, her face inscrutable. Was that hesitance I saw? Discomfort?

Rachel said something sternly to Lacey, and for the briefest moment, I saw her mouth tighten. But then she fell back in line, nodding along with whatever nefarious plan Rachel was cooking up. Rachel and Amanda finally walked away, and their exit felt like the lifting of a dark cloud.

Lacey was joined by a nice-looking man in a suit. He cupped her chin, and, I wasn't totally sure, but there might have been tears bubbling up on her lashes. He gave her a soft kiss, and then they left too.

The last few items of the night were auctioned off, and there were no more crazy bids. After the auction ended and the crowd began to disperse, Marie and a few of the other football wives gathered around Lulu, Mina, Chris, and me.

"Oh my god, Trix, you did so well up there," a cowgirl named Orma said.

"You looked amazing, and you were so composed, even with all the drama," another cowgirl named Jeanette gushed, hugging me tightly.

Marie chimed in, "I have to agree. Tonight was fabulous. You've set the bar pretty high for fundraisers. I will definitely be recruiting you to help with the other ones we do for the Mustangs and their foundations this year."

"And let's talk about that Ramona, the Pest." said the cowgirl Melissa, with a satisfied grin. "You let me know if she doesn't actually pay up for that trip. I wanted my hubby to take me for our anniversary, so we'll buy it."

They all full-well knew her name was Rachel and I was completely tickled they all collectively kept calling her the wrong name. It would drive her insane. If I didn't love Beverly Cleary so much, I'd probably call her Ramona, the Pest for the rest of my life.

I couldn't help but smile, their utter support made me feel all fluffy and nice on the inside. "I really appreciate all the help, you guys. I couldn't have pulled this off without all of you."

Chris pulled me in closer to him, his arm wrapping around my waist. "You're the star tonight and I'm incredibly proud of you for facing that particular demon."

Lulu gave a mock salute to Chris. "Well done, Quarterback. But I'm keeping my eye on you. Bring your A-game for my girl, or I will take you down when we're on that field together."

I thought he'd just grin and tease her back. This was the standard *be good to my friend and don't break her heart* talk that BFFs were required to give. But he didn't even smile. He got all serious and said, "She's my girl now, Lu, and I promise to take care of her with everything I have for the rest of our lives."

Was that a proposal?

Because if it was, I think I'd say yes.

INTO THE HIVE

CHRIS

*T*rixie fell asleep in the car on the way home after the fundraiser, and she was so out, that I literally had to carry her inside and up to bed. I stripped her out of her pretty red dress and groaned when I saw her matching bra and panties. They were frilly and gorgeous, and it would have been a hell of a lot more fun to talk her into a strip tease for me instead of carefully taking them off and tossing them in her laundry hamper. The one for clothes, not the one for toys.

But she was fucking exhausted. I knew how hard she'd been working on the event, and the drain the highs and lows of tonight must have taken on her. I found a night-shirt hanging on the side of the hamper and took a sniff to see if it was clean. It smelled like peaches and Trixie, and I had to give my cock a stern talking to as I slipped it over her head.

She blinked at me bleary-eyed, and god, she looked so tired, with little bags under her eyes and everything. "Why are you so good to me?"

"You're my girl." She always had been, and after hearing tonight about the shitty men she'd dated, I regretted not telling her how I felt a long time ago.

She closed her eyes and smiled. "Your good girl?"

"Hmm. We'll see about proving that tomorrow." And the night after, and the night after that, and for all the nights and a lot of the days after that. Was I thinking about forever with Trixie? Yeah, I was. I meant what I'd said to Lulu. "Now go to sleep."

She yawned and wiggled down into her pillow. "Come snuggle with me."

Well, hell. I was trying to be the gentleman here, but I couldn't resist that. I laid down beside her, over the covers, and pulled her into my arms. I wasn't going to risk taking my clothes off or getting in with her because one touch of her skin and I wasn't going to stop.

She gave that cute little half a snore, half a sigh sound, and in about three or four more breaths, she dropped into REM sleep. Her little eyeballs went ballistic, and I hoped she was having a sex dream, because I knew I would be.

I laid there for a moment, watching Trixie sleep. Her face was relaxed, the tension of the last few weeks dissipated, if only for a little while. I knew what I was feeling for her was more than just a high school crush that had matured over the years. It was a deep-seated, bone-deep love that terrified and exhilarated me at the same time. Marriage was a big step, a monumental one, but as I looked at her nestled in my arms, the idea didn't seem so outlandish. Was I really thinking about forever with Trixie? Hell yes, I was.

I had some soul searching to do. I gently slipped out of bed, careful not to wake her, and left her a note saying to call me when she woke up in the morning.

I needed advice. Someone who could give me perspective. Everett had been my love guru, but this was beyond winning Trixie's heart. I didn't need dating advice, I needed happily ever after advice.

I slipped through the fence from Trixie's yard and into the back yard of my childhood home. My dad was sitting there, drinking a beer, and he had a second bottle on the table next to him, unopened.

"Dad."

"Christopher, come sit with me." He popped the top of the other bottle and held it out to me, and I'd swear he was waiting for me to show up.

We sat there together in silence for a little while, just looking up at the stars.

"When did you know Mom was the one?" If he knew I was coming to get advice, he knew what I was asking him now. He was the sort of man who could smell BS a mile away. If anyone could give me an honest opinion about taking such a major life step, it was him.

He and I didn't talk about her that much, not one on one. Sure, we told stories about funny things she'd done when the family was together doing something where we wished she was there. But I never could seem to bring her up when it was just him and me. It always seemed too soon. And then it seemed too late.

"The second I saw her. She was the citiest looking city

slicker, with fake fur on her high-heeled boots that matched her flimsy ass jacket, putting all kinds of stupid shit into her basket at Tex's hardware store. And I forgot my god damned name and my manners."

I knew my parents met when my mom bought a broke down cabin near my dad's. We'd all heard the story about how he had to rescue her in a snowstorm. But I swear to god, he'd never said anything about love at first sight.

He looked over at me and chuckled. "Sometimes, when you know, you know. This about Trixie?"

"Yeah," I admitted. "I've been thinking about more with her, a life together, but..."

"You've been sweet on that girl since you were kids. I'm glad you finally pulled your head out of your ass and did something about it."

"But we just started dating." I was ten years ahead of her in the falling in love department. She'd barely had a chance to get used to the idea of being more than friends. "I don't even know if she's in love with me."

"I didn't exactly know how your mom felt when I asked her if she'd spend the rest of her life with me. I definitely fell for her first. Sure, we were hot in bed, but like you and Trixie, April was my best friend, and I became hers. Who better to spend your forever with than your best friend?"

Except he hadn't gotten forever with her.

"Even if some of that forever is just holding her in my heart." His voice had gone a little quieter and gravelly.

I had to blink up at the sky for a while and take a long slug of my beer before I could talk again.

"So you think I should ask her to marry me?" That was

the first time I allowed the thought to be real. I wanted to marry Trixie. I wanted to spend absolutely every minute with her that I could. I wanted to hear her scream my name when I made her come, and I wanted to her declare that she loved me too, and I wanted to hear her say "I do."

"We've only got one life, kid. Better to start spending it with someone who makes you ridiculously happy sooner rather than later, because we never know how long we get with them." He patted my knee and left me sitting in the yard to think about what he'd said.

His words resonated with me so deeply that a place inside that had felt hollow for a long time didn't feel so empty tonight. I left the house with more clarity than I'd had in weeks. I was going to marry Trixie. Maybe not today, maybe not tomorrow, but I would.

After we survived this damn high school reunion.

She didn't call me until late morning and said if I didn't take her to the Snoozery, a small local that everyone liked, for brunch, she would likely perish. I couldn't let that happen, so I took her to brunch.

Between bites of cinnamon streusel pancakes, she said, "Lulu made us hair and nail appointments for this afternoon. But I can cancel if you want to take me home and have your way with me."

"I very much want to do that, but Lu might have my head for that, especially after you showed up last night with your hair down and more lipstick on my lips than yours." I turned my body a bit to the side, because I'd noticed someone who thought they were being sly pretending to take a selfie, but who was actually trying to get a picture of me and Trix.

I didn't mind so much if people tried to get pictures of me, that came with the territory, but they didn't need pictures of her eating breakfast. I'd tipped the hostess a hundred bucks to get us seated fast and in the back, but we still had people around us because it was a Saturday and this place was always packed.

Trixie didn't seem to notice. She pointed her next bite on the end of her fork at me. "She does have her eye on you."

Didn't I know it. I wouldn't let Lulu or Trixie down. "Hey, Maguire wanted to know if you'd like to have coffee or something with his wife, Sara Jayne. I'm going to be flat out for the next few weeks at training camp and I thought—"

"Sara Jayne Jerry wants to have coffee with me? Umm, yes please. I love her whole platform. I wonder if I could get her to come to do a thing at the library for the teens too." She made a little face. "Ooh, is it weird to use a connection like that?"

"No, babe. It's fine." She'd learn soon enough that it was okay to rely on the connections I had as her own too. She was already in with the cowgirls, and Maguire and his wife were another extension of my team.

We didn't get out of the restaurant without a few more pictures, but whatever people posted on social media later would show me with my arm wrapped around the woman I loved and nothing more. Still, I'd warn Maguire and his PR people again.

We certainly didn't need more fodder for Rachel or the rest of Trixie's classmates to prove our relationship was real anymore. At least I was glad of that.

I dropped Trix off at home and got in a workout before I had to shower and get ready for night two of the reunion. As far as I knew, my public high school just did the one-night thing, which I hadn't gone to. But fancy-pants St. Ambrose had to make this a three-day affair. Tomorrow's picnic was the more low-key finale, and then we'd be done. I'd do my best to talk her out of going to her twenty-year reunion if I could help it.

She held my hand a bit too tightly as we walked through the doors of her high school gymnasium later that night. I think she expected Rachel to pop out from behind every corner.

We'd just gotten the name tags from the check-in and were walking through an elaborate balloon display that I think was meant to look like a beehive, but sort of resembled a really big, brown butt.

Trixie led me into the darkness of this OSHA hazard. "I just know she's planning something, and if I get pig's blood spilled on me, I swear to god, I will murder her, chop her up into tiny bits, and force feed her to my carnivorous plants."

"Okay, Seymour, but you don't have any carnivorous plants. I promise, everything is going to be fine. We'll make an appearance, let people take pictures, you can say hello to anyone you wanted to reconnect with, and we'll go." And I wouldn't let Rachel anywhere near her. "There won't be time for RayRay the cray cray to pull anything."

She squeezed my hand tighter. "What if she does something after we leave?"

We exited through the beehive butt's front hole and into what I could only describe as bee-palooza. It was tacky as hell and looked like a high school musical compared to the event Trixie had pulled off last night. "Then we won't be here and that will irk her to no end."

Trixie took one look around and literally snorted. "Oh my god. This is... this is awful. Like, are we actually supposed to be inside a hive? This is the most bizarre thing I've ever seen. It wasn't like this earlier in the week when I came to help with the decorations."

Lulu and Mina waved to us from over by the make-shift bar set up on what were probably school lunch tables, and she greeted us each with a cup of yellow punch. "It's supposed to be non-alcoholic honey mead."

"Looks to me like Jules helped with the refreshments." I took the cup from Lulu but set it down on the table.

Trixie politely took a sip but made a face and smacked her tongue against the roof of her mouth like she was trying to get scrape the flavor off her tastebuds. "Have you seen Rachel yet?"

"Yeah," Lulu said, and she did not look happy about it. "And Amanda, whose brought someone as her date that you're not going to like. I'm guessing that's Rachel's surprise."

"What? Who?" Trixie looked around the gym until she must have spotted the date in question.

The look on her face was worse than for the pee drink and it had me wanting to punch someone and then rush her out of here. "Who is it, babe?"

"Asshole Anthony. Why would Amanda bring him as her date to the reunion? Why would anyone want to bring him as a date anywhere?"

Oh yeah, let me at him. This was the creepo that had

not only proposed disgusting things to Trixie, he'd fucked up my chances with her as a consequence. If he wasn't such a slimeball, I might have been with her all these years. "Where? I'd like to have a word with him. And by word, I mean his face meeting my foot."

Trixie squeezed my hand tighter, and I needed to calm my tits and support her right now, not give into my absolute anger. "You want to go?"

"No. I want to ignore him, and Rachel, and Amanda. Like you said, not caring about what she does will probably be worse than anything I could say or do. So, let's mingle and maybe dance, and then we can go."

"You're a lot more fucking mature than I am." Lulu scowled in the direction of the asshole. "While I would enjoy watching Chris beat the snot out of that guy, I, too, would like to mingle and dance with my beautiful wife. Let's scandalize this place by not caring what anyone thinks of us and enjoy ourselves."

And that's what we did. Most everyone here had been at last night's event, so they weren't as shell shocked that I was here, and I only got asked for a few autographs. Which I obliged. The DJ did a decent job of playing a bunch of songs that were popular when we were in high school, and I put in a request for the cheesiest T-Swift slow-dance love song from back then.

When it came on, Trixie's eyes lit up. "I love this song. They played it at prom, and I almost cried because I didn't get to dance to it."

I pulled her into my arms, and we swayed to the music. "Why didn't you get to dance?"

If it was because Asshole Anthony had taken her, that

was one more mark on his already black soul. What a fucker.

"I didn't have a date." She held me a little bit closer. "Lu and I went stag, because I didn't want to miss out on the memory, even if I didn't have someone to take me."

I should have fucking asked Trixie. "I would have taken you if I'd known."

"You couldn't have." She rubbed her hand along my jaw in a way that had me longing for so much more from her. "Your prom was the same night."

"I would have skipped it for you." I barely recalled the girl I'd taken to my prom, but if I'd gone to hers, it would have been a night to remember.

"I thought you were too cool for me back then." She smiled up at me with so much love in her eyes that I wanted to pull her glasses off so I could stare into them with nothing else between us. "I never would have had the nerve to ask you to my prom."

"You really didn't know?" I'd been in love with the girl next door for a long time. "God, I had the biggest crush on you back then, Trix. I probably would have come in my pants if we'd danced this close back then." I pulled her close enough that the erection I was sporting now pressed against her belly.

"Why, Mr., Kingman," Her eyes went faux wide. "I didn't know you brought a football with you."

Such a tease. "Why don't we go home, and I'll show you my football."

"I'm a major fan of your football. So, I'd say that sounds like a great idea."

When the song ended, I kissed Trixie, long and deep,

right there in front of all her classmates, the nuns, and
God. I kissed her until there were whistles, and the DJ
started up a new song. "Ready to go?"

"Yeah. Let me just go to the bathroom first, and I'll
meet you at the beehive." She waved to Lulu and Mina,
who'd been dancing nearby, to join her, because women
had to go to bathrooms in packs, and I hit the refreshment table while I waited. No peehive punch for me, but I
grabbed a couple of bottles of water. I had a feeling I'd
need some extra hydration for the night ahead.

"So, Bea Moore, huh? I dated her back in high school."
A voice I didn't recognize spoke from behind me. But I
already knew who this was. Asshole Anthony.

"Yeah. But she goes by Trixie." Asshole. I said that part
in my head because I wasn't starting a scene two minutes
before we were leaving. But I couldn't help a little dig.
"But from what she said, you didn't really date, and she
dumped you."

"Right. She's a hell of a prude. But I'm sure you know
that."

She was far from it, but I wasn't discussing our sex life
with this jackass. "You'll excuse me if I don't stay."

I took two steps away from him to go find Trix, but he
didn't shut up. "Made for a hell of a good story for the
Sunshine Babcock fan club."

I turned and stared at Anthony, balling my up my fists.
He didn't seem to notice that I was going to smear him
across the gymnasium floor. He just kept fucking talking
shit.

"And I'm not the only one with the same story. Her
boyfriend Tate in college is in the club too, and he said he

couldn't get in her pants either. Said she'd do everything but let him fuck her." Anthony chuckled, actually fucking chuckled. "Hey man, you should join. Unless you're the one to finally pop the porn star's daughter's cherry. Bet you haven't though, have you?"

LOCKER ROOM SHENANIGANS

TRIXIE

I came out of the bathroom feeling like the night was a success. Sure Rachel had brought Anthony, or rather Amanda had under Rachel's direction. Lulu had scoped out the gossip and found out that Asshole Anthony was actually some kind of cousin of Rachel's. He'd definitely kept that fact from me in high school.

If Amanda really was dating him, I felt sorry for her. And if she wasn't, I also felt sorry for her. What an awful so-called friend Rachel was to her. But if she hadn't learned that after all these years, she probably wasn't ever going to.

Lacey, on the other hand, seemed to. I hadn't seen her by Rachel's side even once tonight. She'd come in with that same man I saw her with last night, and I think it might even be her husband. That was nice. We'd even exchanged tentatively friendly waves from across the dance floor.

"Aw, man. You guys are going to leave early so you can go home and bang, aren't you?" Lulu said as we walked back from the girl's room to the gym. It was so weird being back in these halls these past few weeks. I thought I would be a little more nostalgic, but I loved my life now so much more.

I wondered if that was why Rachel seemed to hate me even more now than she did back then. She hadn't brought a date to last night's fundraiser or tonight's dance, so either she was single, or she was with someone who couldn't be bothered to come to this with her. And honestly, I wouldn't be surprised if she was one of those people whose best days were in high school.

Mine weren't.

I looked for Chris and couldn't wait to get him home. I had a feeling my best days were just about to show up.

But then I spotted him over at the refreshment table. Talking to Rachel and Anthony. And he looked ready to take someone's head off.

I hurried toward him, but he turned his back on the two of them and crossed the gym like only an athlete in top form could, dodging couples and people who clearly wanted his attention left and right.

When he got to me, he grabbed me by the elbow and dragged me right back out the side entrance to the gym I'd just come in through. "What happened? What did they say to you?"

"We need someplace private, Beatrix."

Uh-oh. He only called me that when something was

really wrong. My gaze darted around the hallway we were in. This way there were only some bathrooms, the trophy cases, and the entrance to the locker rooms. The bathrooms were definitely not private, so I pointed toward the other door.

"They didn't do something to like... threaten your career or something did they?"

He pulled me through the swinging door and then turned on me, backing me up against the nearest bank of lockers. "No. They said a lot of bullshit, and we're going to talk about all of it. But you answer me one thing, right now, and do not evade the question. I need to know. Do you understand?"

My heart dropped all the way down into my stomach. Chris knew most of my life story. I couldn't even imagine Rachel or Anthony could have told him anything he didn't already have a clue whether it was true or not. I'd even told him about how disgusting Asshole Anthony was when I'd dated him and broke up with him. "Oh, okay. I don't intend to keep secrets from you, but you've got me a little freaked out. What did they say?"

"Are you a virgin?"

What? That was the absolute last thing I expected to come out of his mouth. I didn't even know how to begin to respond. I could feel my heart beating, but down in my intestines. What the hell had those two asshats said to provoke this question and also, he said he'd figured it out. "Why are you asking me this now?"

"I told you I need to know, Beatrix. Have you ever let any other man inside of you?" His voice went all growly, and while he already had me up against the lockers, one hand braced against the metal over my left shoulder and he grabbed my hip with the other.

"I thought you knew. You said you figured out that I didn't have any experience." I was so confused right now. Was he mad? I should have outright told him, but why was he asking this now and at my reunion? "Are you mad? What is going on?"

He grabbed at the skirt of my dress and pulled it up, then grabbed my thigh so I had to wrap my leg around his. He pressed his hips forward, and with the way he'd opened my legs, the bulge in the front of his dress pants hit me right at my core. "I'm mad, I'm so fucking angry, but not at you. I want to rip the dick off every boy you ever dated, every absolute jackass who ever thought they could treat you like a sex object, and I want to smash the eyeballs out of the ones who thought they could have you because they'd seen your mom's porn."

Oh. That's what this was about. "I saw you talking to Anthony. Whatever he said, it doesn't matter. I'm long since over it."

"I don't give two shits about him. What I do care about is that if I could go back, I'd have asked you to be my girl-friend ten god damned years ago." He narrowed his eyes and shook his head, more disgusted than mad. "We lost out on all those years because I didn't make my move. If I could lose my virginity again, it would be with you."

He lowered his face to kiss me, but I placed my hands on his cheeks and waited for him to look into my eyes. I'd never seen him like this. "Then we'll make the next ten years together so great, we'll practically forget anything that came before we were together."

He grabbed my other leg and lifted me all the way up. "Fuck, Trixie. I always thought you belonged with me. I love you so god damned much, that's all I want."

The stones of anxiety that had been weighing on my head, heart, and in my lower belly since he'd dragged me in here shattered into a thousand feathers of joy, gratitude, and love. So much love. "I do belong with you. Only you."

He dropped my legs and reached for his belt. "That's right. And you are not walking out of this locker room still a virgin, Trixie. I'm making you mine right the fuck now."

My status as a virgin didn't matter to me, but what did was that I was going to get to share my body with this man who made me so happy, made me feel so beautiful, and so loved. He was desperate for me, and I knew it wasn't just about the sex. This was affirming the bond that we both felt so deeply, and it felt so absolutely right to be so reckless that we had to have each other right this second.

He jerked the front of his pants open, and I tugged my panties off, only snagging them on my shoes like five times.

"Dammit. I don't have a condom. I didn't think I'd need one at your fucking high school reunion dance." The disappointment on his face was stinking adorable.

"In my bag." I'd dropped it on the floor when he lifted me up.

He snagged my little, tiny envelope clutch from the floor and popped it open. There was only a handful of things inside because anything more wouldn't fit. My phone, a twenty-dollar bill, my key, my ID, and strip of three condoms.

Because I'm a safety girl.

He ripped the top one open with his teeth, pulled it out and slid it down over his cock.

"Any other time, I'd yell at you for using your teeth, because you could rip the condom, but what the hell."

Chris grinned and pressed me back up against the lockers, and this time when he came in for a kiss, I didn't stop him. I pulled him to me and wrapped one arm around his neck and pushed the other into his hair. He grabbed my thighs and lifted me up again, and when I wrapped my legs around his waist again, we both moaned at the delicious contact.

"Tell me you want me to fuck you." He was getting that bossy tone that gave me the swoonies. "You want only me to be the only man who ever fucks you."

I nodded but he grabbed my chin and ran his thumb across my bottom lip, staring at it. "Tell me, Trixie. Say it."

"I want you to fuck me. I want only you."

He dropped his forehead to mine, and I could feel him trembling against me as he took a full breath. "I don't know how gentle I can be right now. Tell me you're ready for me."

I reached between us and pushed my fingers into my wet folds. "I've been turned on for a week, and a little phone sex hasn't cut it. I'm more than ready for you. There was more than condoms in that bag a few minutes ago. I didn't have to pee before we left, I was so wet after the way you held me when we danced, I went to the bathroom to change my panties."

I dragged my fingers back up and pressed them against his lips, painting them with my body's desire for him. His sparkling eyes went so dark they were almost black, and he sucked my fingers into his mouth. Then he reached between us and notched the head of his cock at my entrance.

He pushed his hips forward, slower than I wanted, but at just the right pace my body needed. "Fu-uck. You're so tight, Trixie. God, I'm not going to last long, but I promise I'll make it up to you later."

He kissed me hard, devouring my lips and tongue as he sunk in deeper, until he was buried so deep inside of me, I didn't know where I ended and he began. "Hold on, chickadee. Because I'm going to fuck you fast and hard until you want to scream my name."

We both know I couldn't, because while we might have some privacy right now, anyone could come into the locker room and catch us. And me screaming his name would definitely bring people running.

He withdrew and then he slammed his hips forward, sinking into me again, banging me up against the locker. I ran my hands all over him as he rolled his hips into mine with hard thrusts that made me moan a little louder each time.

"We're gonna get caught, babe." He covered my mouth to muffle my noises, and that in and of itself was so unreasonably hot. The thought of getting caught had me all aflutter. New kink unlocked.

Until we heard actual voices out in the hall. I froze, but my newfound kink thought this was the best thing that could have ever happened, and the walls of my pussy clenched and pulsed on the edge of orgasm.

Chris waggled his eyebrows at me and his hand stayed over my mouth while he thrust faster. He didn't relent for a second, there was no way we weren't going be discovered at any moment. Not with the rhythmic banging of my ass against the lockers. "You like this don't you, my naughty girl?"

I shook my head, but my body betrayed me, because it was all too much. I was going to come, and I didn't think I could keep it quiet. Chris lowered his face to the crook of my neck and scraped his teeth across my skin. Then he closed his lips around me and bit me, not hard enough to really hurt, but so that I could feel every beat of my heart right there, in time to the rhythm of every one of his thrusts.

"Fuck, Trix, your pussy is gripping me so god-damn tight." He withdrew, and then he slammed his hips forward, sinking into me again, making the locker clang so loud it sounded like someone punched it. "Are you going to come for me? Are you gonna be my good fucking girl and come for me right now?"

The voices drew closer and all I could do was whimper against his hand over my mouth. One final thrust threw me into an orgasm so strong that every muscle in my body clenched and then spasmed. Chris groaned or growled or both, and his body shuddered as he came buried so deep in me.

It was perfect, for the first time in my life, the love of a man was perfect.

We were both breathing hard, and Chris chuffed out a

laugh before raising his face up to mine. "Remind me to take advantage of your little exhibitionist streak again."

"Mine?" I laughed and pulled a you're-crazy face. "You're the one who was trying to get us caught. Could you bang me against the lockers any louder?"

"Yes. And I'm gonna do it again in every locker room I can. And I'm in a lot of locker rooms. Wanna come on the road with me this fall?" He lowered me gently back onto solid ground, but my knees were way wobbly. And they only got wobblier when he pinned me with his body and kissed the bejesus out of me.

I could do this all night. But I'd rather go home than get caught. Too bad the locker room door didn't lock. We'd have to come up with excuses for what anyone might have heard if they came upon this very compromising situation.

Knowing my luck, Rachel would walk in on us. Actually, it was too bad she hadn't. I wasn't ashamed that I'd had sex with my boyfriend. I was in love with him. That's what people in love did.

Oh. I was in love with him.

I was.

In love.

With Chris.

He dragged the skirt of my dress down and turned to take care of the condom. I grabbed his arm and spun him around. "I love you, Chris Kingman. I'm in love with you."

The smile on his face could light up this whole town. And it belonged to me.

SIX WAYS TO SUNDAY

CHRIS

*W*hen Trixie said those three words, the sensation that rippled through me was almost tactile, like the snap of a ball hitting my palm. My pulse didn't quicken, it deepened, as if each heartbeat was pressing further into my chest.

"I love you so fucking much, Trix. I have for so long, and I want to shout it out for the entire world to know." Saying it out loud felt like untying a knot that had been clenched in my throat for ten years. Something important released within me. It wasn't fireworks or floodlights. It was the click of the way we fit together.

The earnestness in her eyes acted like a magnet, pulling forward thoughts I'd been hesitant to form fully. Marriage, commitment, a future together. Each word built its weight in my mind and was buoyed by the fact that she loved me.

"Let's get out of here. I want to fuck you six ways to Sunday." And one of those ways was going to be pure, unadulterated lovemaking. The soul deep, there's no one else in the world but you kind of lovemaking.

She smiled up at me so beautifully that I had to remind myself how to breathe. "Good thing tomorrow is Sunday then."

Sunday already? Tomorrow was the grand finale picnic, that I was hoping I could talk her out of. I'd much rather stay home and in bed with her.

It was also the last free Sunday I'd have in a while. Training camp started next week, and I wouldn't have time for anything but football. Well, football and fucking my girl.

I heard some sort of sound coming from the door to the locker room, or just on the other side. Trixie's eyes went wide, and we broke into peals of laughter. She grabbed my hand and pulled me back out into the hall. A couple of someones were hightailing it back through the beehive butthole, but the darkness of that cavity hid whoever had gotten their little earful.

Good. I hope the rumor worked fast so that news of Trixie definitely not being a virgin spread straight to Anthony and Rachel. Those fuckers could go fuck themselves.

When we got back to Trixie's, I wanted to take her straight upstairs, but being the responsible adult that she was, we checked on the chickens first. Luke was still acting pouty, but he was a sucker for strawberries and Trixie still got in a couple of snuggles, even if her rooster did look put upon by the whole thing like one of those kids who get their cheeks pinched by their grandmother.

I wasn't going to say anything to Trix, but I think Luke was jealous like I'd stolen his girl away.

After she put them back in their pen, Trixie stared at Luke, who just copped a squat in the middle of the dirt. His girls surrounded him again, cooing and consoling him. "I don't know what's wrong with him. I might have to take him to the vet next week. I've never seen him so downright depressed before."

"I'll have a talk with him." I pulled her away from her sulky rooster and back toward the house. "Cock to cock."

"You did not just say that."

I didn't let her tease me anymore than that. I picked her up and threw her over my shoulder and carried her into the house. I was impatient to get to those six ways.

Which we did. First on her kitchen table just inside the back door. What can I say, I was hungry and impatient. And she was delicious. Especially when she was crying my name while I ate her like the snack that she was.

Then I let her ride me like the cowgirl that she was.

Halfway into the night, I finally got to make love to her.

We were so deeply together in that moment. Not just our bodies, but I was sure our very souls were intertwined and there was no separating us.

"I can feel your heart pounding," Trixie said softly, her breathy voice sending another wave of pleasure through me.

The connection between my body and hers felt unbreakable as I tasted the sweetness of her kisses,

devouring her little moans and whimpers while commit-
ting to memory every soft touch, every lush curve. I
wanted nothing more than to savor this perfect moment.
"It's beating for you, every beat, every time, is yours."

Her breath quickened again as I ravished her body
with my hands, feeling every inch of her curves and
crevices.

"Never stop, never stop loving me," she pleaded, her
voice barely audible over the sound of our breathing.

The way we made love went so far beyond anything
I'd ever experienced that I didn't want it to end. Even as
we pushed closer and closer to coming, neither of us
ever let go of the pure erotic intimacy, even during
moments when we stopped to catch our breath and
stare into each other's eyes there was a sense of...
eternity.

"Never. I love you, Trixie," I whispered against her lips.
"You're my forever."

She came apart, her orgasm dragging me with her into
a bliss that wasn't just about pleasure, but love. So much
love that I reveled in it, letting it melt everything else
away. There was only me and Trixie.

When she drifted off in my arms, it was the only way I
ever wanted to fall asleep ever again.

By the time sunlight streamed through the curtains,
the intensity of being in love and having my girl tell me
she loved me too, still tingled at the edges of my
consciousness. I reached for her, but Trixie had already
wriggled out of bed. She was naked, and unabashedly so,
flipping through her wardrobe, the look on her face
suggesting she was mentally preparing for war, or a

picnic, which, in this case, might as well be the same thing.

"Are you sure you want to go?" I watched her pause at a sundress that made my pulse quicken thinking of the ways I could push it up her thighs or stick my head underneath it. If she had to put on clothes, that one was my choice. "We could just stay here, order in, and leave Rachel and her drama in the past."

She looked over, locking eyes with me. "I've been avoiding Rachel and the Queen Bees for too long. Ignoring her last night went a long way to making every-thing she's ever done to me irrelevant. But I'm done running away. Just because she's going to be there, doesn't mean I should skip out on something I want to do."

I sat up, feeling a surge of pride and love. Here was a woman who'd taught herself to stand tall, to own who she was, and was now prepared to close a chapter of her life that had long been a source of pain. "Alright. Then we go, and we show Rachel she has no power here."

Trixie smiled, and the light that filled her eyes was so dazzling it made the morning sun look dim. "Exactly."

I caught a glimmer of our future, one where we didn't need to prove anything to anyone. We were stepping onto the field of play today, but beyond this one last game was the rest of our lives.

Rachel had no idea what she was up against.

We arrived at the picnic, the atmosphere humming with cheerful conversations and laughter. Rows of tables were covered with checkered tablecloths, an array of dishes showcasing the culinary range of Trixie's former classmates. Today was meant to be more casual, a way for classmates who'd reconnected to spend a little more time together before their goodbyes. Well, for the ones who weren't still stuck in their former glory days.

We meandered through the crowd, stopping to chat here and there. Trixie introduced me to her favorite teacher, a nun who was a vivacious woman with an infectious laugh. We moved on to greet several others, and by this time, I was feeling a whole lot more like simply Trixie's boyfriend and not the sports celebrity. Not a single one of her classmates or their families looked at me like I was a crazy god who'd come down from my throne in the sky to grace them with my presence. I was one of the guys now. It was strange and different, and I liked it.

Most of the people who'd come today had families and this felt more like something I had with the team and less like the showy affairs meant to impress from the last few days. I didn't know why they didn't do this for the whole damn reunion.

But the best part was seeing Trixie so engaged, so happy. She had genuinely moved on from the bitterness of her high school years, and it showed. I was about to suggest we grab some of the mouth-watering food when I locked eyes with Rachel, who was observing us from afar.

Unlike the relaxed smiles we'd received from everyone else, Rachel's eyes were icy, a hint of something dark lurking there. She was standing amid her group of sycophants, including Asshole Anthony, wearing a smirk that irked me from a hundred yards away, holding court amid a cluster of people who looked as if they were clinging to her every word.

She leaned into her circle, whispering something I

couldn't hear but could damn well guess the subject of. The atmosphere around her seemed to shift, the chatter of her followers falling to a murmur.

They were watching something that Anthony was showing on his phone. When he saw me looking, he quickly put it away and gave a jerk of his chin to draw Rachel's attention to us.

A ripple of tension went through Trixie. She'd picked up on Rachel's stare too. It was a stare that said, "I see you, but do you see me?" And though I wanted to steer Trixie away from that toxic cloud, her grip on my hand tightened. She was ready.

Rachel must have sensed that her silent taunt had landed because a smirk began to curl the corners of her mouth.

My body tensed, every instinct urging me to step in front of Trixie. Rachel was a storm, and I could feel the change in air pressure from here.

Rachel decided that her moment had come. Breaking away from her clique, she approached us, and the smirk that had only been budding a moment ago now blossomed into a full-blown sneer.

"Well, well, look who we have here. Bea and her... playmate."

Rachel locked eyes with Trixie and it was as if a switch flipped. Okay, so maybe she wasn't totally over Rachel's cattiness.

Trixie took a deep breath. I could see the steel forming in her eyes, could almost feel the energy she was summoning for this confrontation.

"You know, Bea, some of us overheard you and your...

boyfriend in the locker room last night. Very... spirited noises, I must say." Rachel tilted her head, her eyes glittering malevolently. "You might want to keep it in the bedroom next time. Schools are no place for that kind of inappropriate activity."

Of course it was Rachel who'd come to spy on us. Probably listening at the door like an actual high schooler.

My jaw tightened, and I narrowed my eyes to glare at this absolute bitch. I'd been raised not to call women derogatory names, but Rachel fucking deserved it. My instincts screamed at me to step in, to put her in her place. But then I felt Trixie's hand on my arm, gently restraining me. This was her battle to fight, and I was prepared to be her dragon should she need me.

TRIGGERED

TRIXIE

*L*ulu, who was never late to anything in her life, arrived late to the picnic. But it was also just in time. Just as Rachel walked up to me, so did Lu. With my two best friends at my side and a newfound peace within myself, I was ready to fucking rumble.

But so were the two of them. I felt Chris move forward, and I could see that he wanted badly to protect me. And if I let her, Lu would rip Rachel up one side and down the other, Viking blood-eagle style. Her words were more powerful than Mjolnir.

I reached out to both of them and said, "Let me fight this one on my own, you two."

They each nodded, but neither was happy about it. Lu kept clenching and unclenching her fists, and Chris looked like he was ready to murder anyone from my graduating class who even looked at me funny. Even Sister Mary Louise.

"Just knowing you're here and have my back is enough to face this particular demon for real this time." I was ready. I was. "And I promise, I'll tag you in if it gets too much."

I turned my attention to Rachel, which of course was exactly what she wanted. But I didn't protest or dispute her claim that I'd acted inappropriately with my boyfriend. I wasn't ashamed, and that more than anything took her power away. "Rachel, I ask this with all sincerity. Why do you hate me so much?"

She looked me up and down and I could see the utter disgust in her eyes. "Because you're so... uppity. You've always thought your shit doesn't stink."

Okay, the gloves were off. Good. This should be a bare knuckle, give no quarter fight. If my mother had taught me anything, it was to fight like a girl. A powerful queen of a girl.

More of our classmates drifted closer, and this wasn't quite the circle of students gathering around shouting 'fight, fight, fight,' but it wasn't far off. But more people drifted to my side than Rachel's. Including Lacey, her husband, and a very pretty little girl who must be her daughter.

I saw Rachel's complaint coming from a mile away. "Because I don't hate myself? Because I chose to be happy about who and what I am, you've gone out of your way, ten years after we went to school together, to try and make my life miserable?"

She looked me up and down and quite literally scoffed.

"Why should you be happy when you look like you do? Trust me, you shouldn't."

And there it was. This was the schtick of all the fatphobic people I'd ever had the misfortune to come across. Because I was larger than the current beauty ideal, I couldn't possibly love myself. It must be impossible for me to be a happy person. I absolutely must hate myself.

Well, I didn't. I loved myself more today than I had a day ago, a week ago, a year ago. And I was loved. By my family, by my friends, and my Chris.

"Rachel." Lacey said her old friend's name in a way that was meant to admonish. She folded her arms and took a step back, physically separating herself from the Queen Bees and the rest of the clique. I gave her a tentative nod to acknowledge I saw what she was doing, which side she was choosing.

Today was not the day I'd back down. I took a step closer to and got right into Rachel's personal space. Yeah, me, my belly, my hips, my ass, my lunch lady arms. I was taking up space. "I see you, Rachel. I've known you and people like you my whole life. You honestly think that because my body is bigger than yours, that I should be ashamed and sad and hide myself away from the world. Because I don't fit the ideal beauty standard of the day, I'm not deserving of love and happiness. But that is the stupidest thing I've ever heard."

There were murmurs from both sides of the crowd, and I saw something break in Rachel's facade. She wasn't used to people not agreeing with her. But this wasn't high school anymore, and she wasn't the god damned class president. She wasn't... anything. And that pissed her the hell off.

"Do you have any idea how hard I work to look like this?" She flung her arm and hand up and down the front of her body. She accidentally hit my stomach while doing it and physically recoiled. "I put the hard work in, Beatrix, and you're the one who gets to fuck the quarterback of the Denver Mustangs? I don't think so."

The people around us grumbled and the murmuring had a distinct disapproving tone to it.

"Rachel." Lacey stepped between us and made Rachel back up. "Shut the fuck up. That's both the dumbest and shittiest thing you've ever said."

I didn't need anyone else fighting my battle. But I think Lacey had her own horse in this race and I'd gladly ride at dawn for this fight.

Rachel jerked her head back in that way that gave everyone in the world a double chin. "You shut up, Lacey. Or should I say spacey Lacey? You haven't had a coherent thought of your own since the eighth grade."

Someone behind me whispered, "shots fired." Someone named Lulu.

"Yeah, because I listened to your bullshit." Lacey literally poked Rachel in the chest. I stepped just a little to the side. I may have a long held grudge against Rachel, but Lacey's might be... grudgier. "You're an asshole and Beatrix isn't the only person you made feel like shit in high school. I developed a fucking eating disorder because of the way you treated her and anyone else who ever deigned to wear anything bigger than a size four. A fucking size four."

Anthony raised his phone and started filming.

"Don't blame me because you wanted to eat junk food and then had to puke it up so you didn't get fat. I held your stupid limp hair for you in the bathroom every day for a year."

Lacey closed her eyes and took several deep breaths. Then she looked at her husband and her daughter. Oh god, I felt for her in this moment. And I felt for my own mother. It had to be hard to admit in front of your children that your life wasn't perfect.

I was calling my mom when this was over and thanking her for teaching me to live an authentic life by her example.

Lacey began again, her voice a little shaky. I put my hand on her arm, lending her the Queen power I had been ready to release on Rachel. She needed it more in this moment than I did. "I had to go to an eating disorder clinic my freshmen year of college so that I didn't die. Did you know that? I was so afraid of being fat that I almost. Fucking. Died."

Amanda, who'd been smirking like this was her favorite Saturday morning cartoon now looked a little shell shocked. "What? I thought you went to Europe to study abroad?"

Lacey glanced at Amanda and frowned. "I went to Europe to a clinic that had to force feed me protein mush and watch me around the clock so I didn't try to throw it up. I've spent the last ten years in weekly therapy. And do you know what my therapist told me not to do this summer? Come to this god damned reunion. Because we were both worried I would get triggered by the two of you and your fucking bullshit."

"You're a cow. Don't blame me for your weaknesses." Rachel rolled her eyes, but I saw the flash of something more in them just before that. Lacey was getting through to her in a way I wasn't sure I ever could. I wasn't sure that Rachel could ever empathize with me, and I decided right there on that field that I wasn't going to even try to get her to. She had some deep-seated issues that a quite literal showdown at a high school reunion wasn't going to change.

And it wasn't my job to change it for her.

That thought, right there, that I didn't have to defend myself, put in the emotional labor of explaining that yes, I was actually happy, or try to help someone like Rachel who may never be able to get over her own biases see how wrong she was, that set me free.

I was free to be me. Happy, healthy, in love.

I turned my back on Rachel and took Chris's hand. There was a swath of concern in his eyes, but I smiled, and he brought my hand up and kissed the inside of my wrist.

Lacey touched me on the shoulder. "Wait, Trixie. Just for a moment. Please. I decided to come to this... thing anyway because I wanted to apologize to you for the way we treated you in high school."

Holy crap. Okay. That was not something I expected.

"Lacey, you—"

She glanced over at her husband, and he gave her a soft nod. "I know you don't have to accept my apology and I'm not even sure I would if I were you, but I'd like to tell you anyway. I hated how mean we were to you. But I also hated myself so much back then, and I thought being one of the cool girls would make me, well, that doesn't matter. I'm just sorry. I wish we could have been friends instead, because you seemed to have a lot more fun in high school than I ever did."

I swallowed and didn't quite know what to say. Lacey must have taken that as all I had to give at the moment, and she turned back to Rachel and Amanda.

"Amanda, get a life." Lacey shook her head like she was completely and frustratingly confused by Rachel's second-in-command. "Stop letting Rachel dictate who you are."

Amanda looked as though someone slapped her, but in that way when you're going crazy and someone smacks you to get you to wake up and pay attention.

Rachel scoffed again and looked over at Anthony like Lacey telling Amanda off was supposed to be funny.

"And Rachel, get some therapy. I mean it." Lacey was not pulling any punches. You go, girl. "You forget, I know your parents, and so I know your trauma, and talking to someone would help. But even if you don't, stop making other people's lives miserable because you can't stand your own. It doesn't make you feel better. Trust me, I know."

Rachel took a step back and she wiped her mouth with the back of her hand. For a split second I saw the vulnerability slip through her mean girl facade. But then that mask slipped right back into place, and she opened her mouth, I'm sure to spit some more vitriol. Like the wounded animal I now recognized that she was.

So instead of letting her go on the attack again, I turned to Lacey and pulled her into a big, long hug. "I appreciate your apology, and I do accept it. I forgive you if that's what you need to hear. High school is rough no matter who you are. It's half of why I wanted to become a teen librarian, so I could help make those years just a little easier on a few kids."

Lacey was the one who was slow to answer this time, but I think it was because she was trying to hold back some tears. "Thank you, Trixie. I... I really appreciate your forgiveness. I'm not sure I deserve it, but I'll work on that in therapy."

I gave her another squeeze. "Maybe later we can get coffee or something, and you can tell me what you've been up to. It looks like part of that was creating a beautiful family."

Lacey nodded and stepped away.

I was up, and while I knew now that I didn't have to, I decided to get a few things off my chest anyway.

With a deep breath, I turned back to Rachel, who had her arms crossed and was tapping her foot. She was literally waiting for the attention to get back to her. She opened her mouth, and I could already hear the defensive tirade. I held up a hand and stepped into the boldness I had inside of me but hadn't ever really let out.

"Rachel, I've let your opinion of me matter for a long time. I don't know why I did that, but I think it has something to do with never wanting to be seen. You just reinforced the little voices in my head that said if I did take up space in the world, I would be judged in a way that hurts. But guess what? That happens to everyone."

"Umm, no." Did she have any other facial expressions besides rolling her eyes? I wasn't sure at this point. "Nobody looks at you and me the same."

"Doesn't matter whether they actually do or not. Look at us, all of us. We spent the last two and half days dressing up, probably acting like our lives are better than they are, because we want our high school classmates to think we're cool. Hell, I even asked my best friend if he would be my fake date just to show you I wasn't just a sad, nerdy chicken lady."

Everyone around us gasped. Yeah, I just admitted that out loud. Chris took a step forward and put his hand at the small of my back, showing everyone there he was with me. But he didn't say anything. He was letting me have my say, and I loved that he had that confidence in me.

"But if I hadn't, I would never have found out that I loved him." I leaned my head against his chest.

"Or that I loved her. I have for a long time. Since high school, in fact." He kissed the top of my head, and then the two of us turned our backs on Rachel and walked away. I was done with high school.

But as we left, I heard Rachel say something that I didn't like. "Anthony. Do it."

FOOTBALL IS SCANDALOUS

CHRIS

*G*od, I fucking loved training camp. It was like coming home from a long vacation and getting to sleep in your own bed again. Sure you were going to have to get back to work, but this was that perfect time in between when real life, or the actual season, began, and the laziness of summer ended.

And coach loved to make us fucking puke on the first day if he could.

Yeah, even me.

My cleats dug into the grass of the training center, and I surveyed the scene. Fresh faces, rookies who looked like they'd just gotten their learner's permits, mingled with veterans boasting beards and the weathered look of experience. And they'd all be looking to me for another killer year. I could feel it in my bones that we were standing at the cusp of a season that felt like it had destiny scribbled all over it.

The first drill was hellish, just as I'd expected. Coach had us running sprints till our lungs felt like they were trying to escape through our mouths. I heard someone heave behind me, but I pressed on. The need to set an example coursed through my veins. If the QB didn't slack, no one else could afford to either.

After we'd been adequately tortured, we moved to offensive drills. My arm felt like a well-oiled machine as I fired passes to wide receivers, fine-tuning our already killer connection. The atmosphere was electric, every completed pass or successful block amping up the energy.

At noon, we broke for lunch. As I headed towards the dining hall, I spotted my brothers congregating near the entrance. Declan, arms crossed, looked like he was already scowling at the food inside. Everett was mid-joke, a big grin lighting up his face, while Hayes, our newest recruit, looked like he was absorbing everything with a mix of awe and the ambition of a first round draft pick Kingman.

I walked over, giving each of them a slap on the back. "Well, if it isn't the family dynasty of the league. How was the morning, gentlemen?"

Everett chuckled. "You mean aside from watching you almost collapse during those sprints?"

"Hey, a QB's got to set the standard."

Declan grunted, a sound that managed to convey both agreement and criticism. He was grumpier than usual. We'd have to put him down for the meanest defense player in the league award. It was a family legacy after all.

Hayes, eyes bright, chimed in. "Man, this is intense. Nothing like college."

I looked at him and nodded. "Welcome to the big leagues, little bro. It only gets harder from here."

We walked in and grabbed our trays, loading them with lean protein and complex carbs. As we sat down, the dynamic in the whole room shifted subtly. Having three men from the same family was a rare occurrence, but four was something truly special. Some would say our father had pushed us too hard to become star athletes. But he'd molded us into the men we were today, the best way he knew how.

Declan, eyes still on his food as he shoveled it in, brought up the only other thing on my mind. "So, once again, your plans worked. Trixie's your girl now?"

A smile tugged at my lips, "Yeah, she is."

Everett laughed. "She better be your fucking good luck charm this season. We didn't work our asses off to just get you laid."

That might be the closest Ev got to admitting that being in a committed relationship was a good thing. It was for me. Not sure if it ever would be for him.

Hayes, always the sentimental one, asked, "Does it feel different? Being in love, I mean?"

I paused, not quite expecting the answer that bubbled up into my mind. "It does. It feels like I've got more to fight for now, both on and off the field."

Declan nodded, which, in his language, meant he approved. Or at least, didn't disapprove.

The conversation turned to strategy, plays for the upcoming season, but in that moment, something felt complete. As if the missing piece to my life had finally clicked into place. Trixie had done that for me, and as I looked at my brothers, I felt a wave of gratitude. For family, for love, and for the season ahead that promised to test us in every way possible.

Yeah, it was going to be a hell of a season.

Before we headed back to the afternoon practice, I made conversation with a couple of the rookies, who looked at me with a mix of awe and eager curiosity. I talked them through some of our core plays, trying to ease their first-camp jitters.

As I looked around the room, I caught sight of a photo from last season hanging on the wall, early in the year before we knew we'd win it all. There we were, a band of brothers, bound by the sport we loved. My thoughts drifted to Trixie. I'd almost give this all up to spend a few more hours in bed with her. She'd transformed my off-field life in a way that felt just as groundbreaking as any game-winning pass.

The next few weeks we wouldn't get to see as much of each other as I'd like, but I could also see us finding an easy routine once the season started. And then I'd ask her to marry me.

We wrapped up lunch with a tradition of making the rookies stand up and sing their college fight song. Their performances ranged from impressively harmonious to hilariously terrible, and we howled, clapped, and jeered in good fun. Of course, Deck, Ev, and I sang along to the DSU Dragons song with Hayes.

As I headed back to field, still laughing about our newest defensive tackle attempting high notes he had no business with, a sense of contentment washed over me. Between the love of a good woman and the camaraderie of a team that felt like it could conquer the world, this was going to be a hell of a season.

And god, I couldn't wait to get it started.

Until it came to a crashing halt of camera flashes and booing fans as I walked back out on the field. Confused, I glanced over to the stands where fans had been cheerful and encouraging earlier. Now, they were openly hostile.

"What the hell?" I muttered. "What are these, Bandits fans?

We had a long standing rivalry with the team from L.A., but fans had to buy tickets to get in here, and security generally took care of problems before they got like this. The press was going wild, their cameras flashing like fireworks, shouting questions that were almost indecipherable in their frenzy.

"Chris, any comment on the video?"

"Is it really you in that footage?"

"What's your statement, Chris?"

Everett jogged over, phone that he shouldn't have in hand, his face a mask of disbelief. "Dude, you're trending. There's some kind of video of you making rounds, and it's not a good one."

"What video?" Pro sports came with fame money, and that came temptation for a lot of guys that didn't know what to do with it. But our family and the ingrained value to be a good fucking human had thus far safeguarded me and the other guys from shit like this. "I didn't do anything that warrants this kind of shit."

Everett shook his head. "I don't know, but you need to check this out."

Deck and Hayes hurried over and the four of us looked at the screen. I grabbed Ev's phone and tried to make sense of the social media buzz. There it was, a trending hashtag with my name and the word 'scandal' next to it. But the video link was already taken down, only reactions to it left. People speculating, some condemning, a few defending. But no one fucking saying what was actually in the god damned video.

My guts twist into a tight ball, weighing me down. Hands shaking, and I was a fucking professional quarterback, my hands didn't shake for nothing, I tried calling Trixie. I had a really bad feeling about this.

Voicemail. I tried again. Still voicemail. My mind went to dark places, imagining the worst. She had to be okay. She just had to be.

"Kingman," Coach shouted. All four of us looked up. "Not you lot, the other Kingman. Quarterback Kingman. Fuck, I'm gonna start calling you KingThing One through Four. Jesus. Get your fucking social life off my god damned field. This isn't the fucking Ice Capades. This is a fucking professional football team and I expect you to be fucking professionals."

The more fucks coach said, the more sprints we were going to get later.

"Let's get back to practice," Everett said, but his tone was different now—tinged with worry.

"Right." I sent a quick message to Maguire to find out what was going on and get his ass down to the field, then I handed Everett his phone back, my eyes meeting his. "I don't like this, and whatever it is, isn't over. Not by a long shot."

Everett clapped a hand on my shoulder, the unspoken bond between brothers strong in that moment. We jogged back to the team, my physical presence there but my mind somewhere else entirely—filled with concern, rage, and a building sense of reckoning.

I took my position, my grip on the football a little too tight. But as I hurled it down the field, I knew it wasn't just a ball I was throwing, but a gauntlet.

Just as I was taking a breath, trying to center myself, Maguire rushed onto the field. Wearing his usual tailored suit, he looked wildly out of place among the jerseys and turf. Behind him was Johnston Manniway, his face set in a grim line. Shit. If he was here, this was worse than I thought. Johnston stopped to talk to Coach, and the two of them joined us. Coach's left eye was already twitching.

"Chris," Maguire said, urgently pulling me into the circle of men, "we need to talk. Now."

His intensity made it clear this wasn't a request but a demand. I looked around the field and caught the eyes of Declan, Everett, and Hayes, and gave them a quick wave to come and join us.

"Is this about the video?" I asked, not missing a beat. "What is it?"

Johnston stepped in, his voice calm but concerned. "We're gonna get you through this."

I looked from one to the other, the weight of the situation crashing down on me. My brothers joined the circle and closed it up. They didn't need to say anything, they just filled in the gaps in my armor.

Maguire pulled out his phone, showing us all screenshots of the trending topic and the comments coming in fast and furious. Those screenshots had been taken from the video, and the bitter taste of bile rose up the back of my throat. "It's bad, man. It's a sex tape, and it's very clearly you and Trixie."

This wasn't just a game anymore. My personal life had infiltrated my career, and the two were spiraling out of control.

"We need to act quickly." He closed the screen and started typing something furiously. "We'll get your statement together, see if we can do some damage control."

"What about Trixie? I can't get a hold of her. Have you tried contacting her?" My voice rose, tinged with desperation.

Maguire shook his head. "We'll get to that. But right now, you're the story. If we keep the focus on you and not her, she'll fade into the background and that will keep her safe. We need to manage this before it derails everything."

I expected Maguire to be solely focused on me and my career and how it would affect both of our financial futures. The fact that he was thinking not just about Trixie, but how to keep her out of the spotlight, was the only bit of relief I had.

Johnston placed a hand on my shoulder. "Look, kid, I've seen scandals come and go. How you handle it defines you. You're a good man. Let's not forget that."

My brothers murmured their agreement. I nodded, the gravity of their words grounding me. Was that me in the tape? Yeah. Did I think I did anything wrong? No.

Did I have an idea who the culprit was. Abso-fucking-lutely.

"Okay," I finally said. "Let's do damage control. Johnston, can you call Marie? Trixie's going to need all the friends we've got. She fucking hates the spotlight and she's going to be freaking out."

Where was she? Was she okay? A knot of worry tightened in my gut, even as I braced for the media storm ahead.

"Coach, I hate to do this on the first day of camp, but I gotta go." This afternoon was reviewing game tapes anyway, and I'd watched them all a million and a half times.

He scowled at me. "Get your shit taken care of, and don't let this get in your head. You may have a personal fiasco on your hands, but you've still got to win a fucking championship this year."

I couldn't be mad at him, he was right. I had a commitment to the team. But I'd give it all up if it hurt Trixie.

"Rachel," I muttered under my breath. "If you're behind this, you're going to regret it."

I grabbed my shit from the locker room and found my phone buzzing. When I saw Jules's name flash across the screen, a new wave of anxiety washed over me.

"Hey, kidlet," I answered, doing my best to keep my voice steady. "What's up?"

"Chris, it's insane over here. The press is everywhere, our yard, your yard, even Trixie's. They're shouting and banging on doors. Where's your security detail? Aren't they supposed to keep them out? They won't leave."

My unflappable little sister who could burn down the

world and they'd thank her for it, was freaking out. Her voice was tinged with the kind of fear you get when your personal space has been violated.

"Jesus, Jules, I'm sorry. I don't know how they got past security. Is everyone okay?" My father was going to flip his shit. He had never been a fan of the press.

"We're fine. Dad's ready to blow a gasket and pacing the house like a caged wolf. I know it's the first day of camp and all, but when are you coming back? You have to do something."

My blood boiled. I loved that neighborhood. It was more than just a place to live. It was our sanctuary, where family and loved ones should be safe and sound. And someone had violated this sacred space.

"I'll take care of it, Jules. Promise. Have you seen Trixie? Did she come home from work yet?"

"Her rooster is just standing on the fence crowing at all the reporters, and I'd like to give him a medal for it. They keep trying to shoo him away and he pecks at their faces. But she's not here. I tried calling the library, and the person who answered just said she wasn't available and I'm worried."

"So am I," I said, a lump forming in my throat. "Listen, lock the doors and stay inside. I'm dealing with this right now."

I hung up and turned to Maguire and Johnston. "I've got to get home. They've invaded my neighborhood, and I need to make sure everyone is safe."

Maguire's eyes widened. "They're at your home now? This is escalating faster than we thought."

Johnston clenched his fists. "This is crossing a line. Your family doesn't deserve to be dragged into this."

"You're damn right they don't," I said, my voice hardening. "I'm going to protect what's mine. Let's finish up here, and then I'm taking this fight where it belongs. Home."

With that, I left the field, my thoughts a whirlwind of anger, concern, and resolve. Whatever this scandal was, it had just gotten deeply personal.

I tried calling Trixie again from the car. Still no answer. If anything had happened to her, I'd be the one burning down the world.

AITA?

TRIXIE

I was in the middle of pulling titles from the shelves for the next teen book club meeting when I noticed something weird. Side glances, hushed conversations that stopped when I walked by. My colleagues seemed... uncomfortable around me, like I was suddenly an outsider. Even the regular patrons looked at me differently.

"Ms. Moore, could you please come to my office?" Karter's voice came over the intercom, icy and formal. We never used the intercom for anything other than library announcements like the fifteen and five minute warning of when the library was closing. He couldn't have just called the phone at my desk?

A sense of dread settled over me. Whatever was happening, it wasn't good. I took a deep breath and made my way to Karter's office.

"Close the door," he commanded, not bothering to look up from his desk.

My heart pounded in my chest as I complied. "Is something wrong, Karter?"

He finally looked up, his eyes colder than I'd ever seen them. "Trixie, effective immediately, your employment here is terminated for conduct unbecoming a city employee."

"What? I don't understand. What did I do?" My voice broke on the last word with a gasp, as if I'd just watched someone crack the spines on a whole row of brand new paperbacks.

"That's not up for discussion," Karter said curtly sliding an envelope across the table. "Your final paycheck."

"But I've always received excellent performance reviews." I was getting screwed here and not in the fun way. And I didn't even know why. "And don't we have a policy of warning before termination? What's changed?"

Karter sighed like this was all so beneath him. "The decision is non-negotiable. There is nothing else to say."

"Is this because Chris thought you were being an ass the other night?" I pushed, heat creeping into my voice. "Or maybe someone else heard one of the inappropriate comments you've made about me? So you're just getting rid of me before I can escalate it to HR?"

His face reddened, and I knew I was damn close to hitting the truth. But he maintained his icy demeanor. "Your personal assumptions are irrelevant. Hand over your access pass."

I looked at the hand he was holding out to me like it

was going to bite me or give me long Covid. "I have a right to know why I'm being fired."

"Colorado is an at-will state, Ms. Moore. At-will regulations stipulate that employers are not required to provide prior notice to workers being terminated, nor are they obligated to provide a reason for any firings in absence of relevant laws or contractual obligations." This sounded wrote memorized especially so he could pull it out for exactly this situation. "Your employment is not guaranteed here, and we can release you for whatever reason we see fit. Your lewd acts are reason enough."

Lewd acts?

Feeling powerless but knowing I'd been wronged, I unclipped the pass from my belt loop and tossed it onto his desk.

"Security will escort you to collect your personal belongings. You need to be off the premises in the next ten minutes." He typed something on his computer, seemingly already dismissing me from his presence.

Before I could process what was happening, Mike, the library's fit, young security guard, appeared at the door. "Let's go, Ms. Moore."

Shame and confusion swelled within me as I was led to my desk. Staff and volunteers alike watched in stunned silence as I hastily gathered my personal items into a ready and waiting box.

"Is everything okay, Trixie?" Cherie, one of the teen volunteers, asked, her eyes full of concern.

"I don't know, sweetie," I answered, fighting back tears. "I really don't know."

Mike led me out the back door of the library to where

the staff parked our cars. "Sorry about this, Ms. Moore. I don't like how any of this went down."

Even with the regret I could hear from him, he still left me in the parking lot and went back inside. The big metal door clanged shut behind me with a deafening finality. It wasn't until I reached my car that I realized I'd left my phone on my desk.

My heart sank further. No way to call Chris or Lulu, no way to call anyone. And a gnawing feeling in the pit of my stomach told me that whatever was happening was far from over. I was just going to have to go home.

When I got into the neighborhood, it was mass chaos. Why were there so many people here? They didn't live here. As I got closer to my house, I saw trucks with antennas on the sidewalk, and people with cameras on the lawn. What the hell was going on?

I slowly pulled into my driveway and was instantly inundated with people shouting at me through the windows of the car, pointing TV cameras at me, and some even got in the way, trying to make it so I couldn't get into my garage.

Barely holding it together, I navigated through the frenzy of reporters and their intrusive cameras, my pulse beating an erratic rhythm. The atmosphere was chaotic, buzzing like an angry beehive. I hurried into my garage. As the door shuttered down behind me, I took several long, shaky breaths. I'd always seen this house, my child-hood home become my adult space, as a place where I could be myself, away from judgment. Now, it felt like a fragile bubble, and the world was full of sharp edges.

I fumbled with my keys and stepped into the house,

locking the door behind me. I reached for my tablet, since I had no phone, and I wasn't going out again in that mess to try and replace it. With shaky hands, I Facetimed Lulu, hoping she could pick up even though she was still at work.

"What the hell is going on?" I blurted out as soon as she answered.

"Oh, Trix, I've been trying to reach you. You're all over social media. Some video with you and Chris doing the deed in the locker room at St. Ambrose."

My head started spinning. "Video? What?"

Someone had taken a video of me and Chris? Those bastards.

"I haven't seen it because the original has already been taken down, but it's apparently scandalous enough to set the internet on fire. It was on Anthony's stupid Am I the Asshole page."

"I got fired, Lulu." My voice was doing that cracking thing again. "Karter gave me the boot, effective immediately. For 'conduct unbecoming a city employee.' What does that even mean? He had me escorted out of the building by security."

"What? What the fuck?" I heard her tapping away on her computer. "I'll dig around and find out what's happening on the work front. Just hold tight."

She hung up, leaving me in my living room, alone and unnerved, staring at the screen that seemed to scream that everything had changed.

As if to echo the way everything else was falling apart around me I heard a horrible, distressed crowing coming from the side of the house. Oh no. Luke. If I was freaked out by the media circus, I couldn't even imagine how he felt. This was his territory just as much as it was mine.

Taking a deep breath, I unlocked the back door and stepped into my yard, trying my best to sneak around to the side. I could barely make out Luke's silhouette among the flashes of cameras and reporters who had the audacity to scale the fence to my back yard. They were scaring him and me. It was like they were everywhere, trampling on everything in my life.

"Beatrix! Beatrix Moore. Where's Chris? Who are you to him?" one reporter yelled, thrusting a microphone over the fence in my direction.

"Is your mother the infamous Sunshine Babcock?" another shouted.

At the mention of my mother, a cold, leaden feeling settled in the pit of my stomach, as if I'd swallowed every terrible thing that had happened in the last decade. The words cut through me, making everything else fade into background noise. For a split second, swallowing, breathing, even making my heart beat seemed an insurmountable task.

Ignoring them, I reached for Luke, whose feathers were all ruffled, and scooped him up, tucking him under my arm for comfort as much as for his own safety. His heart was pounding like a miniature drum against my side, mirroring my own chaotic emotions.

With Luke safely in my arms, I turned to the reporters, my eyes blazing. "If you have any decency, you'll get off my property now," I said, my voice quivering but clear. "You're trespassing, and you're scaring my animals."

I didn't wait to see if they complied, but I did hear one

of them say something about me being the indecent one. I stormed back inside, locking the door behind me, a new level of violation settling over me. My space, my sanctuary, had been invaded, and the weight of it all crashed down as I set Luke down in his indoor pen.

The tablet buzzed on the counter and this time it was Chris. My fingers trembled as I reached for it, but before answering, I cast a quick glance at Luke. For a moment, I saw a reflection of myself in his eyes—confused, scared, but also fiercely protective of the little world we had built.

"It's time to fight back," I whispered to him before taking the call.

"Trix? Are you okay? Jules called and said she saw you get home, and those assholes swamped your car." I heard honking and the sounds of traffic in his background. "I'm sending my dad over to get you and take you to our house. I'll be home in fifteen minutes."

"I got fired." That was the only thing that was even a little bit coherent in my mind right now.

"Fuck. I'm so sorry, babe. I swear we'll figure this all out. I've got Maguire trying to do damage control and Johnston is sending Marie your way." He swore and honked his horn again. "Where the fuck is my security detail?"

Out the side window, I saw Mr. Kingman step out the front door of the house, and a mob of reporters rushed toward him. He didn't even say a word but held up one hand and the group as a whole practically stopped dead in their tracks. "I see your dad. I don't think he's going to even make it to my front door."

"Look in the back yard."

Three Kingman boys, Flynn, Gryffen, and Isak, were bent over and scurrying toward the gate between our two yards like they were ninjas or Navy SEALs.

"Ah, I see. Your dad is the distraction, and the boys are the covert rescue mission. Okay, but I'm taking Luke with me."

"Whatever you need to feel safe and comfy, babe. Better pack some clothes too. I don't know how long this media blitz is going to last."

I did not like the sound of that. What had become of my life? I hurried upstairs, shoved some comfy clothes into a bag, grabbed my toothbrush and my Kindle, because lord knows I was going to need some escapist comfort if I had to be holed up at the Kingmans' avoiding reporters for the rest of my life. How long could this last?

"Trixie," one of the boys called from downstairs. "We're here to rescue you."

I hollered down to them. "Thanks. I'll be down in a minute. Raid the fridge for bunkering snacks."

I heard another of them say "Yes," declaring a victory. If I knew one thing, it was how hungry teenage and college boys could be.

I don't know how he did it, but Mr. Kingman had those reporters wrapped around his little finger. Either that or they were scared to death he was going to make them run laps or something. The boys and I snuck back over to their yard, stopping only to make sure the hens' food and water supplies were topped up. Isak volunteered to come over and check on them later if I needed him to.

When I got through the French door on the back porch, Jules met me with a big bear hug. "I'm so glad you're okay. I'd hate to lose a sister before I even officially got one."

Aww. I hugged her right back. "It's okay, I'm not going anywhere."

She and I made Luke a makeshift bed in the kitchen, but before we were even done, Chris barreled into the house. He scooped me up and kissed me so thoroughly that for a full minute I forgot about the shitshow we were embroiled in.

He pressed his forehead to mine and we both found a safe space to just breathe for a second.

"Hi," he said.

"Hi." Two minutes ago, the world was a frantic mess. But with him right here with me now, I knew we'd be okay.

Not in the next ten minutes, but we'd make it through this nightmare, together.

"Tell me what happened at work."

This man. Our asses were all over the internet, and he was checking in with my actual life. I gave him one more quick kiss just because I needed to.

"I almost don't even know." I shook my head, still not ready to believe everything that had happened so far today. It wasn't even drink o'clock yet. "Karter just called me into his office and said I was fired for conduct unbecoming a city employee. He wouldn't tell me what it was about or anything. I don't know what I'm going to do. I don't have a lot of savings, enough for a month or so at most."

"That motherfucker," Chris growled.

Yeah, my sentiments exactly. "I... I'm gonna have to move or something."

Chris nodded. He probably didn't really understand this situation, he was quite literally a millionaire. He had a jet. "The way I see it, you've got a few options here, babe. You can move in with me. I can move in with you. Or you can just stay put."

Yeah, see. While it was adorable that his first instinct was for us to move in together, I'm sure he had probably no idea what it meant to break a lease. "I can't just stay here rent free. And I don't want us to move in together because I'm mooching off you."

He nodded and seemed to be thinking about his response. "Right. Two things. I'm literally a millionaire. So you can mooch all you want. I will make you a kept woman if you want. And also, I own your house. You don't have to pay rent if you don't want to."

Exsqueeze me? "What?"

He pushed my jaw shut, and then booped me on the nose. "I own at least a third of the houses in the neighborhood, maybe more now. When they go up for sale, my company comes in and offers cash for above asking price. Then sometimes we flip it, but most of them I either keep to rent out, or you know, put one of my family members into it."

"You're a slum lord?"

Declan, Everett, and Hayes all walked into the house, looking like they came straight from practice without showering or anything. Smelled like it too. Hayes grabbed an apple off the bowl on the counter and just before he took a bite said, "Yeah, he lets us pick which one we want when we get out of school."

I looked over at Declan and Everett who confirmed. One with a shrug and the other with a scowl.

"In fact," Everett grinned and pointed at Chris, "I bet the house I live in that we'd get you to fall for him. Which was a sucker bet, because the rest of us already knew you two were head over heels for each other. Still, I won. Gimme my house."

Chris shook his head and smiled. "Worth it."

Mr. Kingman walked in, whistled to get everyone's attention, and waved his hand in the air in a circle. That must have been a signal he'd used with his family to gather around, because everyone circled up around him, me, and Chris.

"We are talking about my house, ugh, your house later," I stage whispered and poked him in the chest. "I can't believe you didn't tell me."

We all gathered in the living room where we did family game night, since it was really the only room with enough space for everyone. Before he started in, I put a hand on Mr. Kingman's arm. I needed to say thank you for helping to rescue me. What I really wanted to say was how much it meant to me that he and his whole family just instantly brought me into their fold.

"What did you say to get those crazy reporters to listen to you?" I didn't think anyone else could have done that besides this mountain of a man with the presence to match.

He raised one eyebrow with an evil grin. "I just asked them if this was the lawn they were willing to die on."

Right. That'll do it.

"All right, team. We've got a crisis on our hands, so we're circling the wagons. Let's hear ideas on what we need to do to control this situation."

Everett rubbed his hands together. "I say we all make our own sex tapes. If everyone's doing it, then it's not a big deal, right?"

Mr. Kingman rolled his eyes. "I like your family spirit kiddo, but that ain't it."

"You sure? I've got—" Everett pulled out his phone.

"Whatever you have, delete it now." Chris pointed at him.

"Who else has a suggestion?"

Hayes had the next suggestion. "Lawyer up. Sue the shit out of that asshole."

"What asshole?" Mr. Kingman asked. "We know who leaked this footage?"

Jules was the one who pulled out her phone this time. She typed in something while she was talking. "Yeah. We do. This guy has a pretty big channel. All the misguided dude bros who buy into the patriarchy watch him. Chris and Trixie are trending because of this guy. Anthony Am I the Asshole."

"How do you know Anthony?" I took her phone and looked at the screen. There was an entire playlist called 'The Sunshine Babcock Fan Club.' Oh shit. He had more than a million followers. So I guess the question was how did I not know about Anthony's channel. Probably because I mostly watched celebrity gossip, baking stuff, and funny chicken videos.

Not misogyny at its finest.

I'd let myself be free of Rachel, but her claws were dug into me deeper than I expected. And make no mistake, this was her doing. And she was probably reveling in the fallout. And I knew exactly who to call to help me and Chris figure out exactly how to deal with a hater of this depth.

My mom.

SCREW 'EM

CHRIS

*I*t took a little doing, but we finally got a hold of Trixie's mom. The pang I felt that we couldn't also call my mom was sharp, but brief. Together, these women would've been unstoppable. To me, there was nothing more powerful than a confident woman who didn't take shit from anyone.

She gave us her suggestion, and I had to admit, the press wouldn't see it coming. PR always wanted apologies and statements that sounded fake as shit about being remorseful and pledging to do better. They thought that's what the public wanted. But not Mrs. Moore. And I agreed with her.

Trixie's mom laid it out for us, no sugarcoating, no BS. "Rachel's power over you and everyone else she's always tried to control, is shame. But sex isn't shameful. People try to make it that way, but it isn't. Show her and the media that they don't have that power, and they won't know what to do with themselves."

Trixie took a deep breath and met my eyes. I gave her hand a reassuring squeeze and a nod. I was used to being in front of cameras with a barrage of flashes and questions coming at me. She bit her lip, and I could practically see the way her brain was arranging and rearranging her thoughts. She was piecing together a strategy, realigning her mindset like she was plotting out chapters in a yet-unwritten book.

"I'm going to have a tough time putting myself out there like that. You know I don't like to be in the spotlight." She looked at me, a tinge of vulnerability creeping into her voice, and then back to the screen.

Her mom sighed. "I know, darling. And I think that's my fault. I shielded you from the attention that came my way and, in doing so, maybe I taught you to keep yourself hidden. For that, I'm sorry."

Trixie shook her head. "No, you and Dad did an incredible job raising me."

"We did our best," Mrs. Moore smiled, and I could see the love she had for her daughter so clearly. "But it's hard to fight the entire world all the time. A supportive partner can make all the difference. So I'm thrilled you two finally pulled your heads out of your asses and found what was right in front of you."

My dad chuckled behind us.

"Sweetheart," she said, and somehow I felt included in that too. Mrs. Moore paused, as if giving her words the weight they deserved. Then, her voice firm and resolute, she delivered her final counsel, "Take up space, Beatrix.

Don't apologize, and don't let the world shame you for being you."

We said our goodbyes and it was my turn to make a few phone calls. The first was to Maguire to have him set up a press conference bright and early tomorrow morning. While I did that, the rest of the family called in our troops. Friends, family, and teammates. They'd all be putting themselves on the line for supporting us. And we weren't going to play by the rules.

The rules were stupid.

Which was not something I'd ever thought I would consider. I liked an ordered life, planned and then executed. Being in love with Trixie was a beautiful mess, and for the first time in my life, I didn't mind playing dirty even a little bit.

We got rid of all but the most tenacious press by telling them about the press conference in the morning and promising not to leave out any details. But we were still hunkering down until morning. I claimed my old room, and made Flynn go share with Gryffen for a night. It wasn't like they weren't used to that. The two of them only whined for, like, half an hour.

I found myself standing in the doorway of my old bedroom, arms up on the head casing, just staring at the memories. The paint had changed, the furniture had been updated, but it still held the nostalgic essence of a time when life was simpler. Right out the window was Trixie's house, and the window to her bedroom. How many times had we waved at each other? How often had I tried to catch a glimpse of something I wasn't supposed to?

A lot was the answer to that question. It was also how

often I'd wrapped my hand around my cock with her on my mind and her name on my lips in this very room.

Trixie stepped in behind me, her eyes scanning the room with delight, like she knew exactly what I was thinking. I couldn't help but watch her, the way the shifting light from the hallway lamp touched her face, illuminating her as if she was some ethereal being in a room full of everyday things.

She ducked under my arm and leaned against the trim, looking up at me like we were the only two people in the world that mattered. And in that moment, we were.

"I've been thinking," she started, her voice soft but resolute. "Tomorrow, we're going to step out there and... face whatever comes. But tonight, right now, can we just be Chris and Trixie? No media, no family, no expectations. Just us."

Her vulnerability took me by surprise, but it also made her even more extraordinary in my eyes. "Just us," I agreed, leaning down to kiss her the way I'd wanted to back in high school.

We were at the precipice of something big, something that could either crush us or free us, but for now, we chose to exist in the sanctuary of 'just us.'

"Wanna fulfill some fantasies I had about you the last time I slept in this room?"

"Yes, yes I do."

I pulled her into the room, shut the door, and made love to Trixie. Losing ourselves in each other tonight was going to give us everything we needed to make it through tomorrow.

In the morning, there were still a few reporters

camped out, and I wanted to go out there and ping them in the head with footballs until they left. I even went out on the front porch with a ball. But the universe must have heard my prayers, because I didn't have to.

Mrs. Bohacek and her Mustang-blue Olds came barreling down the street. Actually, she was maybe even going the speed limit today. But as she got closer to our house, she slowed, and I saw pure evil in those beady little eyes just poking over the steering wheel.

She pulled her Olds to the right about ten degrees and the screech that car made as it tore apart the side of the shitty news outlet's van was glorious. She rolled down her window and yelled, "I thought I told you douchepotatoes not to play in the street."

I laughed my ass off.

"Hey lady, I'll sue you and get your license revoked, you old bat." The guy who drove the van was freaking out.

"I'm a hundred and ninety-seven years old if I'm a day, you little wyrm." She flipped the guy off with her crinkly, wrinkled middle finger. "I'll likely die before it ever gets to court. Besides, I don't have a license."

That was about all those schmoes could handle, and they up and left. I waved to nice Mrs. Bo as she drove away. I think some flower deliveries from me were in her future.

After that, the ride to the stadium was a blur of phone calls, texts, and quick strategy sessions.

We decided to have the press conference at the home of the Mustangs instead of at the training facility, because the guys at training camp didn't need this kind of distraction. And if all went well, I'd be back at camp later today.

It would go well. Trix and I were solid, so really, nothing else mattered.

Maguire was already at the stadium, coordinating with the team's PR, while my brothers and the cowgirls were circling the troops. As we pulled into the parking lot, the sense of unity, of our collective strength, was a force that even the press would feel.

Today, you were either with us, or against us. And the world would know exactly who the good guys were in this situation, and who should really be ashamed.

Maguire, Johnston, Marie, my dad, and my brothers were all right outside the car, waiting for us. But Trixie took a hold of my hand and held a finger up at them to wait.

"I know what we planned to say, but I thought about this all night, and Rachel isn't ever going to stop." There was a new resolve settling into her features. She wasn't complaining or scared, she was determined. "The haters in the world aren't going to suddenly say, oh, you don't feel ashamed, well, we'll leave you alone then."

"No, probably not." That's not how being in the public eye worked. When you put yourself out there for the world to see you, there were always going to be haters. Fuck the haters.

"So, screw them." The way she mirrored my thoughts so exactly made me love her even more. Trixie had this fire in her eyes, a spark that said she was done playing it small. No apologies, no looking back. And I got to be here for it, right by her side. "Chris Kingman, do you love me?"

The world and its drama all around us disappeared. There was no press, no haters, no anything. Just me and the woman who completed me. My heart and hers, my life and hers, my love and hers. "I've loved you since we were twelve, Trix."

She smiled so brightly that I was sure we were both going to glow when we stepped out of the car. She was filled with a kind of untapped, soaring energy that was infectious.

"Okay. Then let's go make the rest of the world understand that love wins."

We exited the car, and Trixie slipped her hand into mine, her grip tight but steady. We walked hand in hand like we were walking into a fortress, walls built not of stone, but of loyalty and love.

"I've seen that look on your face, big brother. You're gonna fuck some people up, aren't you?" Declan grumbled, but his eyes were all encouragement.

"We got you, man." Everett clapped me on the back.

Johnston gave me a nod, and Marie grinned like she was in on a secret. She might be.

It was my dad's face, the one he got when he was so damn proud of one of us, that got me, and I had to clear my throat before I'd be able to answer any questions from the press.

The cameras flashed and rolled, the journalists and reporters shouted their questions, and just to give them a hint of what was to come, I smiled and waved at them like we were about to announce we'd won the championship. Again. We stepped onto the makeshift stage Maguire had set up on the steps just outside the entrance to the field and waited for the sharks to calm themselves.

"Let's do this," she whispered, her voice barely audible over the growing clamor of the crowd.

And so we stepped up to the microphones, a united front ready to reclaim our narrative, and maybe, just maybe, change a few minds along the way.

"Chris, Chris, are you going to see a therapist about your sex addiction?"

"Beatrix, what kind of example do you think you're setting for the teens at your alma mater?"

"Chris, how long have you been a chubby chaser?"

"Did you leak the tape yourselves?"

Trixie gripped my hand a little tighter and whispered, "Jesus, Mary, and Joseph, and all the saints. What the hell is wrong with all these people?"

I whispered back, "They're haters, and we're going to tell them to go fuck themselves. I think Jesus would approve, don't you?"

I stepped up to the microphone and said, "Write this down, ladies and gentlemen. I'm not apologizing for doing something that grown ass adults do. Maybe we should have saved it for when we got home, but don't blame me for being hot for my gorgeous girlfriend."

Just like we knew they would, the press exploded. But I was done listening to them or their questions. This was my game, my rules. "And don't think I don't see those of you who are writing shitty things about her. If you're the kind of garbage human being that like to try and make someone else feel worthless because of their size, shape, or what the scale says, then you can see yourself out."

That made most of them quiet down. This was definitely not the press conference they expected. And it was a hell of a lot more fun getting to tell them all off instead of kowtowing to what was expected.

One of the reporters I recognized from a reputable news outlet actually raised his hand like at a normal press conference, and so I returned the favor by calling on him. "George?"

He stood and straightened his jacket. "Yes, George Zeleny, International Sports."

"I know who you are George, ask your question."

He nodded. "Respectfully, Chris, do you and Ms. Moore not bear any of the blame? You did have relations in a public place."

"Thanks for asking, George. I already said, we aren't apologizing for being in love and showing each other that love. How about you focus the blame on the guy who filmed us without our knowledge and consent, and not only posting it for his own fifteen minutes of fame, but for selling the video for a lot of money."

Trixie pinched my thigh. Oops. I'd said too much. I was still cranky about Anthony.

Another reporter whom I didn't know didn't raise his hand and just shouted out. "Are you calling out Anthony Nergal, aka Anthony Am I The Asshole specifically?"

I looked to Trixie. I've been in the spotlight since college, and since I wasn't an asshole, I'd made a few friends and connections along the way. While I knew exactly how much that little cockroach got for that tape, we weren't going to acknowledge him.

"Are you going to sue?"

I would happily spend my entire fucking bowl

winning bonus to make sure he was exposed for the rat that he is.

Although, Trixie's mom was going to sue the shit out of him for running the so called Sunshine Babcock fan club. He'd been pirating her videos for years, and she had him dead to rights on a whole lot of copyright and trademark infringement. Mrs. Moore was a smart and savvy businesswoman at her core, and Anthony was a fly by the seat of his pants dumbass running a side gig.

But again, I stayed silent. It was Trixie's turn. She smiled at George and waited for the rest of them to quiet down again. After a full minute, she used that sexy as hell stern librarian look on them and they finally shut the fuck up.

TAKE UP SPACE

TRIXIE

*C*hris stayed silent and waited for me. The tension in the room only increased as I gave them all my patented librarian shush look. A whole gaggle of mostly male reporters finally quieted down, some of them looking a bit abashed, and awaited our next words expectantly. I felt a jittery rush of adrenaline, but also a newfound will welling up inside me.

Take up space, Beatrix. Don't apologize, and don't let the world shame you for being you.

I took a step forward and tapped the microphone, commanding everyone's attention.

"I have something to say as well," I announced. My voice was clearer than I'd expected, like the ringing of a bell that can't be unrung.

But instead of looking toward the reporters, I turned toward Chris and met his eyes. The love I found there steeled me for what I was about to do. "You see, life, society, they all have a lot of opinions about who we should be. What we should hide, and what we should apologize for."

I felt my hand tremble, not from fear, but from a pulse of audacity. I felt almost reckless, but in the best way possible.

"So, I'm asking," I glanced out at the reporters, then gestured toward Chris and myself, "will you all help us rewrite that script right here, right now? What if none of us had to declare that we won't be shamed into hiding our love or our lives?"

The room was in a stunned silence now. Even the cameras seemed to hesitate in their relentless flashing. I took a deep breath, locked my eyes onto Chris's, and while I'd just invited the world in, we were still the only two people in the world.

"Christopher Bridger Kingman," I said, "you make me want to live a big, bold life filled with friends and family and chickens and football and so much love. I want everyone in the world to know, and I'm not sorry even a little bit that people got to see the passion between us. But I want them to see the pure, unadulterated love we feel too. Will you marry me?"

The world stood still. The reporters, the cameras, the blinding lights, all of it faded away, leaving only Chris and his answer that would tip the scales of my life one way or another.

He took a step toward me, his eyes brimming with unshed tears. "Damn it, chickadee. I was gonna ask you the same thing."

He reached into his pocket and pulled out a little blue box. I didn't even look at it as he slipped it on my finger. Partly because I was blinking away my own tears and partly because I couldn't look away from his eyes.

"So, yes," he said, his voice laden with emotion but strong and clear. "Hell, yes."

He lifted me up into his arms and I squealed, wrapping my legs around his waist, and our lips met in a kiss that felt like a victorious end and an exhilarating new beginning all at once. I felt it, I felt truly seen, and not just by Chris, but by the world. And for the first time, it didn't scare me.

The room erupted into pandemonium, reporters jostling, cameras flashing, but in that moment, I didn't care. I had taken up my space. We had. And it felt like finally coming home.

The applause and cheers filled the room, and as Chris and I separated from our kiss, I looked out and saw a sea of faces. Our families, the cowgirls, our friends, they were all beaming at us, their smiles almost brighter than the flashbulbs going off around the room.

Chris turned to the crowd, holding my hand up high like we'd just won the championship game. "Ladies and gentlemen, I told you there'd be hot celebrity gossip at today's press conference. If you didn't catch the memo," he glanced at me, his eyes shining with love and mischief, "Trixie and I are now officially engaged."

The room erupted once again, and this time it was full of genuine joy rather than just professional curiosity. The cowgirls started whooping, and I spotted Jules in the back making heart fingers at me. Chris's dad was grinning from ear to ear.

"We'll leave the rest of the details for later," Chris continued. "For now, we're going to celebrate. Anyone who wants to toast to love, to breaking the norms, and to never having to say you're sorry for being truly, unapologetically yourself, you're welcome to join us. Everyone who's mad that the haters didn't take us down? Well, you can fuck off."

With Chris's last words still hanging in the air, I felt the world tilt on its axis, shifting into a reality where anything seemed possible. We left the podium to an ocean of applause and Maguire ushered us into a side door to the stadium where he had a private room where the press wasn't allowed. Chris's brothers took up standing guard at the door to ensure we weren't followed. They all understood that hell, we needed a minute to ourselves.

Once the door closed behind us, I took a deep breath, absorbing everything that just happened. Chris kissed me and his hands drifted south like he was going to try and pull up my skirt. I started giggling so hard that he actually stopped.

"What's so funny?" He pressed his forehead to mine and smiled against my lips.

"You were going to ask me? I thought I was being all spontaneous, and all along you already had a ring?"

"Yeah. All along." He grabbed my hand and kissed my finger with the ring on it. "But you're the one with the steel ovaries. I was going to wait until after the press conference. Why do you think Maguire had this room ready for us?"

"Who else knew?"

"Everyone." He shrugged and gave me that cute smile that he had when he knew he was in trouble, but that I was going to forgive him anyway. "Well, not the press. But my family, Johnston, Marie, which, since she knew, the rest of the cowgirls did too."

"Lulu?" I was going to kill her if she knew.

"I thought you'd probably want to tell her." Ooh. He was a smart, smart man.

He handed me his phone, since I hadn't had time to get a new one yet, and I called Lulu, my best friend, my confidant, and the one person who needed to know what just went down before the rest of the world did. Outside of everyone Chris had already told.

"Lulu, you're not going to believe what I just did," I blurted out as soon as she picked up. My voice was tinged with exhilaration.

"Oh my god. I'm basically scared to answer your calls right now. But you're not crying, so tell me you just won the lottery or something."

"Better." I may or may not have let out the girl gossip squeal. "I just asked Chris to marry me. In front of reporters, cameras, the whole shebang. This is going to be all over the news."

"Holy shit. No way, get out. I don't believe you, but I do. Tell me everything, immediately if not sooner." Lulu's voice crackled with excitement. "No wait, scratch that. Let me tell you something first because you're gonna wanna add this to your excitement."

What could possibly add to the happiness of this morning? "What?"

There was a brief pause, and then Lulu said, "I used my finely honed Dark Net Nancy Drew skills and found out that Creepy Karter has been sneaking onto your computer at the library when you're not there, and using it for some, let's just say, less-than-savory online activities. Tried to frame it on you too."

My jaw dropped. "Are you serious? That's just—"

"—All kinds of messed up? I know. Turns out, he's a card carrying member of the Sunshine Babcock club. He used his fucking credit card on your computer to pay for the subscription."

Oh ga-awd. What a dick. And a dumbass.

"And wanna know who tipped me off? Mike, the cutie security guard. Then his girlfriend, who works in IT, did a little digging. She's some kind of genius with computers. We sent everything to HR this morning. He's been caught red-handed, and he's probably being fired as we speak."

"Good." I wasn't normally the kind of person who reveled in someone else's misery, but that little bastard was getting what he deserved. "He shouldn't be working in the library, and he shouldn't ever be allowed to work around teens or women or people."

"You might be able to get your job back now that we've proven he set you up."

"I don't know. I love the library, you know that I do." If my life was getting flip-turned-upside-down, I might as well embrace all the changes the universe was throwing at me. "But I think I might be ready to do something... bigger."

"Ooh. Lunch tomorrow? We can strategize and plan

and I can see the ring. He did get you a big ass diamond, right?"

I glanced down at my hand, actually looking at the ring for the first time. It was pretty, but what it represented meant so much more to me. "Yeah. I think you can probably see it from outer space."

After I hung up with Lu, I snapped a selfie of me, Chris, and the ring and sent it to my mother. It was the middle of the night in Nepal, but I'm sure I'd get a call back as soon as she got up.

"So, what do we do now?" I looked up at my brand new fiancé. "We can't just hide in this room all day. Do you think the reporters are gone?"

He waggled his eyebrows at me. "Wanna go—"

The door to the room flew open, but there was no one in the doorway. A woman's voice called out from the hallway, and there was a rash of laughs and giggles behind that. "We waited as long as we could stand, so I hope you're both decent, or if you're not, I'm giving you to the count of ten before we all rush in to celebrate."

"Marie is a fricking force of nature, isn't she?" I said to Chris before I called back that they could come in.

"Just wait until the season starts and she organizes her infamous cowgirl road trips for our away games."

The cowgirls rushed in and surrounded us, and the guys sauntered in after. I got the squeals and the oohing and awwing over the ring and how romantic it was that I asked him first. The guys all did a round of pats on the back and slugs to the arm.

With everyone celebrating and congratulating us, Chris moved to stand behind me and wrapped his arms around my waist, his fingers pushing the hem of my sweater up just a tiny bit so that his thumb found the skin at my waist. He leaned down and kissed my neck and then whispered in my ear. "I love you, Beatrix. Now let's go home. I need you, with your gorgeous curves, on your knees for me. Do you want that, my good girl?"

Did I ever.

Amidst the laughter and chatter filling the room, we slipped away. Chris led me back to the car, our fingers intertwined naturally, as if they were made to fit together. The touches we shared told the story of our journey, and the love that's blossomed between us. It was more than I ever thought was possible. He was my friend, my lover, and my happy ever after.

EPILOGUE

CHRIS

Several months later~

Sundays have been my favorite day of the week for a long time.

It was game day.

And so far, this season was a real banger.

Literally. The more sex Trixie and I had, the more games the Mustangs won. Although, honestly, even if were the worst team in the league and lost every game, I'd still make love to my soon to be wife all day every day, twice on Sundays.

I'd already had her crying my name, coming on my cock, and then again, thanks to an interesting g-spot vibrator from Nepal, that also made her squirt for the first time ever.

And we weren't done for the day. We'd started our little tradition of fucking in the locker room, trying our best not to get caught, before the first game of the season.

We'd gotten caught. We'd also beat the L.A. Bandits, 42-3.

Now the boys all conveniently cleared out a secluded section of the locker room before games. Football players are a superstitious lot, and my fiancée had an exhibitionist streak a mile high. She didn't actually want anyone else to watch us, but in the safety of the locker room where we knew the assholes of the world weren't going to film us, she loved that tiny edge of danger that someone might see us with our pants down.

Who was I to deny her whatever kinky sex she wanted to have?

If I also happened to be having the best season of my life, that was just a win-win.

But this morning, I was up earlier than usual and letting Trixie sleep in. She'd been extra busy the last few weeks working to launch her Take Up Space network. She, Sara Jayne Jerry, and Marie Manniway were recruiting other plus-size movers and shakers in all sorts of industries to not only support each other, but to do outreach programs to help women from all walks of life embrace and love who they were, no matter their size, shape, or what the scale said.

I was so fucking proud of her.

She also decided that since she reads so many romances, she might try her hand at writing one. I was particularly enjoying this endeavor since she liked to use my body for "research." It's a really dirty book.

The crisp morning temperatures of Colorado's autumn were here, and I was sitting on the back porch, a steaming cup of coffee in hand, about to chat with Luke.

He'd been a bit of a bastard the last couple of months. Not his usual I'm-gonna-shit-on-your-shoes and chase me around the yard shenanigans, but more like he was trying to peck my eyes out.

I had his number though.

I walked out into the yard, my cup of coffee in hand, savoring the crisp morning air. I glanced towards the chicken coop, and there he was, sizing me up like it's his personal mission to harass me like I'm an unwelcome trespasser every time I step foot in his domain.

"Morning, Luke," I greeted, setting my coffee down on the gate post and approached the coop.

Luke ruffled his feathers and let out a half-hearted crow. Yep, still mad.

"Look, buddy, can we talk?" I crouched down to his eye level and tossed in a few chunks of strawberries, because, yeah, I'm not above a little chicken bribery. Luke fixed me with an incredulous gaze, as if to say, "You're really doing this?"

"Yeah, I am," I chuckled, taking his silence as consent. "So, listen. I know you're protective of Trixie. And I get it, she's pretty great. But you've got to stop acting like I'm here to ruin the party."

Luke shifted his weight from one leg to the other, almost like he was actually contemplating my words.

"I love her, you know. I'm not going anywhere. But that doesn't mean you're losing her. If anything, you're gaining me."

Not sure that was a selling point. But weirdly, I liked him and the way he was so protective of Trix. I wanted us to be friends.

Luke clucked, pecking at the strawberries half-heart-edly. Okay, time to go in for the kill. Not him, he was never being made into nuggets. Nope, I was going after his heart.

"I've noticed you've got a little thing going with Kylo Hen over there," I nodded toward the sleek black hen who was pecking around the other side of the coop. "She's cute. And I can tell she likes you."

Luke's eyes narrowed, and I swear he was paying attention.

"Life's too short, my man. Don't you think it's time to take that friendship to the next level? Worked out pretty well for me and Trix."

Luke looked towards Kylo Hen, who had moved a little closer, almost like she was eavesdropping on our man-to-rooster chat.

"See? She's interested." I gave a little jerk of my chin toward her. "Go for it. Love's worth the risk, believe me."

He walked right up to me, flapped his wings, and jumped up on the fence, pecked my coffee cup and sent it and the contents flying toward me. Only my finely honed football skills saved me from having the hot liquid poured right over my head.

Okay, maybe he was getting turned into chicken nuggets. He gave a shake of his long, shiny tail feathers, and then hopped down, strutting over to Kylo Hen.

She did the cutest little chicken dance, like she'd been waiting for this moment her whole life. Same, girl, same.

The two of them danced around each other for a minute, and then I got treated to very loud and feather ruffling chicken sex.

Smiling, I picked up my empty coffee mug and headed back to the house. As I opened the door, I heard Trixie's laughter floating through the kitchen, mixing with the distant crowing of a rooster in love.

"Did you just tell my rooster to go have sex? And he did?"

I rinsed out the cup and refilled it, topping it off with Trixie's favorite pumpkin spice oat creamer and set the cup down in front of her. "Yeah. I told you I was going to have a cock-to-cock talk with him."

My phone pinged with a text. I picked it up and saw the notification from Simone Stone, the young investigative journalist over at channel 9 News.

Heads up. Evening news tonight.

I typed a quick reply.

We'll be watching.

Trixie and I got to the stadium a little later than usual. And half the team, plus Coach, either gave me the evil eye, or a thumbs up as I dragged her back to our secret-not-so-secret sex spot.

"Got any new sex scenes in your book you want to try out, my dirty girl?"

"Funnily enough, I just wrote one where the hero bends his heroine over a bench in a locker room," she patted the padded bench behind her. "And takes her from behind."

"God, I love your imagination." I spun her around and

grabbed her hair, kissing her neck, and then pushing her face down to the cushion. She was wearing my favorite jersey she owned today. The one that read Kingman's Queen on the back.

"Oh, yes. Just like that. Make it fast and hard. Make me come, please."

Hearing her beg had my cock hard instantly. I flipped up her skirt, ready to rip her panties right off. And fuck me, if they weren't the god damned cock block ones.

"You wore these on purpose, didn't you?" I tugged them all the way down and off, and I shoved them into my pocket. "They're mine now, and I'm going to keep them right next to my cock, inside my cup, during the game."

I dropped to my knees behind her and kissed a path from her thick, luscious thighs up to her wet, naked pussy. I pushed her thighs apart wider, loving the way her inner thighs overflowed in my hands. "And your bare ass and cunt is going to be exposed that whole time. So you'd better be careful not to let anyone see."

I buried my face in her pussy and fucked her with my tongue in the same way I was going to take her with my cock. When she was moaning and whimpering in exactly the way that I loved, I stood up and unbuckled my pants. "Because this pussy is mine, isn't it?"

"Yes, yours. All yours." She pressed her ass closer and let out a shuddered sigh. "Christopher... please."

"That's my good girl. Now bury your fingers in your cunt and play with your clit while I fuck you. I want you to come on my cock right the fuck now."

I slipped the condom on and slid into her hot, waiting cunt. She was still so tight, and I really wasn't going to last long. The adrenaline of game day was already pumping through my blood, and making the woman I loved come was the only thing better.

And just because I loved it so much, I made her come twice.

Afterward, I cleaned her up and held her in my arms, petting her hair and letting her come down before we went back out in public. "Are you really going to keep my panties?"

"Fuck yeah, I am." I might even jack-off in them during halftime. I could never get enough of my girl.

"Good thing we're up in the box today." She laughed, crawling out of my lap. "It's cold in those sideline seats."

She went out a side entrance that would allow her to get to the elevators that led up to the suites where the cowgirls usually gathered to watch the games. While she liked the danger of getting caught, she didn't like seeing the guys in the locker room afterward. The boys all knew better than to say anything to her about our pregame ritual anyway.

I hurried back in to get suited up for the game and I did indeed slip her underwear into my pants. And then I had the best fucking game of my life.

Three touchdown passes, another touchdown I ran in myself, and Everett and I broke the previous Mustangs record for most receptions in a game. Deck had a monster game too. Four sacks. He was getting a reputation for being the meanest motherfucker in the league.

While I loved a great win, I loved coming home to Trixie even more.

The smell of buttery popcorn filled the air as we

settled into the plush cushions of the couch, ready to relax with the newest episode of the celebrity baking challenge that Johnston was on. He was doing surprisingly well for someone who could burn water.

I flicked on the TV and went first to the local news channel. "I just want to see the sports highlights real quick first, babe."

"I mean, it's not like you were there or anything." She grinned and made a face at me. "News flash, you won."

"Yeah, but I want to see if they show the Bandit's quarterback crying like a little baby after Declan smashed him into the ground for the fourth time."

The anchor and Simone were standing at the news desk. "We're starting tonight with breaking news involving a shocking revelation about St. Ambrose church and high school," the anchor said.

Trixie sat up a little straighter, locking eyes with the screen. This was the moment I'd been waiting for.

"Yes, thanks, Rosa," Simone said, taking over the report. "A local woman has been arrested for embezzling substantial funds."

The screen split to show a woman with blonde hair in handcuffs, being led into a cop car. She was having a hissy fit too. It was fucking perfect.

Trixie's jaw dropped. "Wait. Is that... Rachel?"

I smirked, taking a sip of my water. "Oh, well, lookie there. It sure is. I have no idea how that happened."

She raised an eyebrow at me, not buying it for a second. "Really? You expect me to believe that? What did you do?"

I chuckled softly. "Nothing. But I'm just saying, maybe

a PI looked into her and found some sketchy activities. When they found enough evidence, maybe someone made sure it got to the right people. You know, law enforcement, the church, and apparently, the news. I like that Simone Stone lady, she finds some really good stories, don't you think?"

She shook her head, her suppressed smile betraying her delight. "Well, thank you to whoever hired a PI."

I pulled her closer to me. "I figured it was time someone leveled the playing field. Ragnar had it coming."

Trixie nestled her head against my shoulder. Until her Facetime rang and I saw Lulu's face pop up. They gossiped right through the rest of the news, and I did indeed get to see Declan's tackle. He was getting meaner as the weeks went by.

Time to find him a woman to love too. If it worked for me and cranky Luke Skycocker, it would work for grumpy Declan Kingman.

———

Not quite ready to leave Chris and Trixie? Me either! I wrote them a bonus scene... and it's dirty. *wink

Join my Swoon Zone email newsletter and I'll send you the bonus scene right away!

———

Ready for the next Cocky Kingman to find love?

Get the next book in the series: The Wiener Across the Way

A NOTE FROM THE AUTHOR

AMY AWARD

THICK THIGHS & YUMMY GUYS

I'm gonna tell you a little story about how and why I'm writing a contemporary sports rom com book. *pats chair* *hands you glass of tasty beverage of choice*

cue Star Wars intro theme

A LONG TIME AGO, IN A GALAXY FAR, FAR AWAY~

When I was young, we moved around A LOT. By the time I was 13 we'd moved 13 times. (All in, I *think* I've moved about 35 times in my life).

And every time we moved to a new city, before I made friends, I entertained myself and escaped into books.

My mom was a voracious reader, and she had a love for medieval historical romance novels. I definitely read a few. She also had a love for all things sports, but most especially Nebraska football.

Yep, I was raised in the house of HUSKER.

On Saturday mornings in the autumn at my house we didn't watch Saturday morning cartoons, we watched college football.

We LITERALLY had a Tommy Frazier (Nebraska's QB in the 90s) Christmas ornament on our tree. (I still have it.)

I can still sing the University of Nebraska fight song and have a certain disdain for the Oklahoma Sooners. lol

I DID NOT GO TO SCHOOL AT THE UNIVERSITY OF NEBRASKA.

lol

I went to Colorado State University (who got our little Ram behinds kicked by the Cornhuskers - and yes I went to the game. ROADTRIP!).

Of course, I studied English Literature... because, what else would I get a degree in besides, you know, READING BOOKS?!

But I became a bit of a reading snob and didn't read a thing published after 1940 for like...six years. And can I just tell you, my senior seminar was on fricking Herman Melville. UGH. Moby Dick can eat a bag of dicks as far as I'm concerned. (Also, if you ever want to try a book by good ole Herman the misogynist who probably beat his wife - don't start with that old tome - try something like the *Confidence Man* or *Omoo* or *Typee* which are travel adventures instead. They're better.)

Anywhoo - After I graduated... I was... for the first time in my LIFE, tired of reading. Probs because I hadn't really read for fun in years.

I hopped right into life in corporate America, where, interestingly enough, I got to work with my mom, at the same company.

She always told me I should write a book.

Okay - time to get a tissue. #triggerwarning

And then... when I was 28 years old...

My mom died.

(Oh gosh, I'm crying right now)

And... well... my whole life changed. I loved her so very, very much. She was one of my best friends. And I was lost without her.

So... after about a year of mourning and trying to carry on, I quite literally ran away from home. I quit my job, signed up for a teacher training course in Prague, and then moved to locales far, far away to teach English.

That was a good thing. Because while I was living in Vietnam, I got bored.

I'd started reading again, but the selection of books was limited, mostly to what the backpackers brought through and left at their hostels. Or super mega best-sellers that, because Vietnam doesn't have quite the same stringent copyright laws as we do, were photocopied and sold literally off the backs of motorcycles.

In comes the advent of the e-reader! Yay!

I got one of the very first eBook readers from Sony - they don't even make them anymore. And guess what kind of books were most readily available in eBook back then?

You guessed it - ROMANCE.

I went in HARD to reading romance, now as an adult, and damn if I didn't LOVE IT.

And then a voice from not so long ago popped back into my head. *"You should write a book."*

And I thought, I'm going to write a romance!

If you've read any of my Aidy Award books, you know

that I have and always will put pieces of myself into my stories.

So what did I put into the very first romance novel I ever wrote? A curvy girl who loved to bake and who gets into an arranged marriage with a FOOTBALL player from... Nebraska. (Are there even football players from anywhere else? No? I didn't think so.)

It's called *Cookies and Cowboys* and it has NEVER been published. It's the book I learned how to write on. Someday I may pull it back out from underneath my bed and give it a TOTAL rewrite... but we'll see.

So you see, I've been trying, since the VERY BEGIN-NING to write a book that I thought my mom would read, and that she would enjoy, even if it wasn't about knights in shining armor.

And that's how we got to THIS.

The C*ck Down the Block is my love letter to my mom, to curvy girls who have to do the work to love ourselves from the inside out, and who still get told we shouldn't. This is for my fellow later in life virgins, and for everyone who had a bully in high school. This is for the girls who had a best friend who they secretly crushed on.

And this book is for my home state of Colorado. I've lived here off and on for a really long time (like... 35 years? How is that possible?), and honestly, I've never really claimed it as home.

I NEVER even imagined setting a book here.

I feel I've taken Denver for granted, and so I purpose-fully set this new series in a place that really is my home-town. So if you happen to be from Colorado, and especially if you're from the Denver metro area, I'm you'll catch a few of my inside jokes.

C'mon, S'mores Field instead of Coors Field? I think I'm hilarious.

Finally, you should know that a portion of the proceeds of this book will go to the Luvin Arms Animal Sanctuary.

Together, we're gonna save roosters!

Luvin Arms is a 501(c)3 nonprofit animal sanctuary for abused or neglected farmed animals in Erie, Colorado. Their rescued residents include cows, pigs, turkeys, chickens, horses, goats, sheep, and ducks. These beautiful residents were rescued from horrific situations including abuse and neglect cases, factory farms, religious rituals, slaughterhouse-bound trucks, bankrupt farms, and more. They were left with nowhere to turn and would have been slaughtered if they hadn't been saved.

Extra Hugs from me to you,

—Amy

ACKNOWLEDGMENTS

There were a lot of days I wasn't sure I'd ever finish this book. Special thanks goes to my Bring It On Mastermind group who kept telling me I could do it. JL Madore, Krystal Shannan, Claudia Burgoa, and Bri Blackwood. I would go crazy without you.

I so appreciate the author talks and days away from the computer at rando coffee shops around the Denver metro area with M. Guida, Holly Roberds, Parker Finch, and Nikki Hall. Y'all are my tribe.

Thanks to my Amazeballs Writers: Danielle Hart, Davina Storm, and Stephanie Harrell for writing online with me. I'd have many a day with no words if you weren't there.

All the hugs to my curvy girl author friends, Molly O'Hare, Kelsie Stelting Hoss, Mary Warren, and Kayla Grosse. We're changing the world one fat-bottomed woman at a time, and I'm so grateful you're here fighting the good fight with me.

I probably wouldn't still be writing and having a successful career without Becca Syme, who definitely, probably doesn't think I'm crazy, knows when I need to be pumped up, when I just need to cry, and when I need to question the effin' premise. Thank you from the ooey gooey fun times #7 center of my heart.

I had a little bit of imposter syndrome while writing this book and my editor Chrisandra talked me through that a couple too many times. I needed that. Thank you. Also, I'm sorry I still suck at commas.

Thank you to Ellie at Love Notes PR for taking a chance on me and my 'what's a deadline' dumb ass. I'll try really hard to get the next one too you sooner. Thanks for reading the story halfway and mini obsessing over the characters and telling me I'm funny.

Huge thanks to Leni Kaufmann for taking my half a vision for a football player and a nerdy girl with thick thighs and making them (and the chicken) into the vision of a cover. I can't wait to show you the tattoo.

So many hugs to my friend and PA Michelle Ziegler. My author life would be such a tangled mess with out. I appreciate you more than you know.

And to my Patreon Book Dragons - you are the reason I write books. I hope I continue to entertain you and make you proud. Your continual support means so incredibly much to me.

For my VIP Fans, signed books are coming your way!

- Angie K
- Barbara B
- Jeanette M
- Kerrie M
- Natasha H
- Sandra B
- Sara W
- Tracy L
- Anna Marie P

For my Biggest Fans Ever, book boxes with so much hilarious chicken stuff and signed book are on their way. Thank you so much for believing in me.

- Alida H
- Bridget M
- Cherie S
- Danielle T
- Daphine G
- Elisha B
- Jessica W
- Katherine M
- Kelli W
- Mari G
- Marilyn C
- Melissa L
- Orma M
- Rosa D
- Stephanie H
- Stephanie F
- Corinne A

ABOUT THE AUTHOR

Amy Award is a curvy girl who has a thing for football players, fuzzy-butt pets, and spicy romance novels. She believes that all bodies are beautiful and deserve their own love stories with Happy Ever Afters. Find her at AuthorAmyAward.com

Amy also write curvy girl paranormal romances with dragons, wolves, demons, and vampires, as Aidy Award. If that's your jam, check those books out at AidyAward.com

Made in United States
North Haven, CT
22 April 2024

51653791R00211